DAVID CAMERON'S ADVENTURES

David Cameron's Adventures

George Frederick Clarke

ILLUSTRATED BY
Will Nickless

EDITED BY
Mary Bernard

Chapel Street Editions
Woodstock, New Brunswick

Published by
Chapel Street Editions
150 Chapel Street
Woodstock, NB E7M 1H4

www.chapelstreeteditions.com

Library and Archives Canada Cataloguing in Publication

Clarke, George Frederick, 1883-1974, author
    David Cameron's adventures / George Frederick Clarke ; illustrated by Will Nickless ; edited by Mary Bernard.

Previously published: London: Blackie & Son, 1950.
ISBN 978-1-988299-14-3 (softcover)

    I. Nickless, Will, illustrator II. Bernard, Mary, 1941-, editor III. Title.

PS8505.L39D3 2018   jC813'.52   C2017-907897-6

Cover illustration by Will Nickless

The text is set in Adobe Caslon.

Book design by Brendan Helmuth

Dedication

To
My Sister
R. M. C.

Editor's Dedication

TO MY DEAR FRIENDS
NORA KELLY and BILL JEFFRIES

CONTENTS

EDITOR'S PREFACE

David Cameron's Adventures was first published in 1950; it is the first of George Frederick Clarke's two historical novels. David is a leading character in both of them—a boy in this book, a young man in its sequel, *David Cameron's Return*. Both books are set in the mid-eighteenth century, largely in the part of Acadia that is now the province of New Brunswick.

This new edition has an Afterword for readers who would like to learn more about the book's background.

Mary Bernard
January 2018

ILLUSTRATIONS

I have digitally restored the cover and illustrations. —M.B.

And now I will unclasp a secret book,
And to your quick-conceiving discontents
I'll read you matter deep and dangerous,
As full of peril and adventurous spirit
As to o'er-walk a current roaring loud
On the unsteadfast footing of a spear.

Henry IV.

CHAPTER 1

Childhood in Aberdeen

When I finally decided to write an account of my slavery in America, and my later life and adventures among the Indians of that country, I little knew what a difficult task I had set myself. To recall events of more than sixty years ago, and set them down in the order of their happening, to recapture from the past scenes and faces and names, the customs and material culture of remote Indian tribes, is no work for a few afternoons or evenings. Already I find myself longing for the facile pen of Mr. Job Dawkings, who wrote for me the little pamphlet printed by J. D. for Timothy Cole, following my return to my native land over half a century ago.

This, then, is an enlargement of that old book. And more accurate, I hope. For I am afraid that Mr. Dawkings allowed his imagination more freedom than the mere facts I related to him warranted. It is, moreover, a tribute to him who shared my exile, and was friend and second father to me in those stirring years, 1744 to 1748, when France and England struggled for mastery in the New World.

But first it is necessary to tell something of my childhood. I was born in the town of Aberdeen on the second of January, 1732. My mother was a Fraser of Lovat. She died shortly after my fifth birthday, so that my memories of her are few. But I do recollect that she was a sweet-faced woman and that, when she tucked me in nights, she prayed not only for my welfare, but also for that of a mysterious being across the water, whom she besought the Almighty to protect and restore to his rightful heritage. Later I learned that this personage was none other than the exiled Charles Edward of Scotland.

My father was distantly related to Cameron of Lochiel. He was an advocate, and belonged to the Society of Advocates. He had as partner a right worthy man by name of Dugald Grant. My father owned considerable property both in the Old and the New Town of Aberdeen. We lived in New Town, in a big rambling house not far from the Broad Gate, one of the old ports that from early times had guarded the town. The house had belonged to our family for more than a hundred years. During the Covenanting wars several of Cromwell's soldiers were quartered in the house, and my grandfather was forced to provide entertainment for them.

A year and a half after my dear mother's death, my father married again. His new partner was a tall, angular woman from Cockermouth. I met her some weeks before the wedding. On this occasion she made much of me, called me a dear, handsome laddie, and, I am quite sure, deeply impressed my poor father with her loving kindness and fitness to be a second mother to me. But once under his roof as wife and stepmother, her attitude towards me swiftly changed. I do not remember that in the years that followed she ever showed me the least warmth of affection. Indeed, I do verily believe she endeavoured to mould me to a mean and obstinate nature, hoping thereby to prejudice my father against me and further her own selfish ends. Also, from the very first, she made my poor father's life miserable for him. For often, when he was home from the office or the Court House, she plagued him about the changing of some paper she asserted he had promised to write shortly before he had wedded her. In fancy I yet hear her shrill, complaining voice telling him that, as an advocate, he should know that such matters ought not to be put off. And his quiet reply, "I know—I know, Hester. But it will keep." And he would bury his nose in his book, or tell the servant to bring more wine, or suddenly depart from the room with the mumbled remark that he must bolt the front door.

Not until later did I learn that she was badgering him to rewrite the will he had made immediately following my mother's death. Or that, finding out my stepmother for what she was, he on his part was determined to leave the will as it stood, thus making me principal beneficiary in case of his death.

From my sixth up to and including my ninth year, I had as tutor a Mr. Glegg. But I am quite sure he was more interested in drawing his salary, and playing chess with my stepmother, than in teaching me my simple lessons. I grew to dislike him intensely, and he returned my feelings with interest. I loved history and geography, and through Mrs. Angus, our old housekeeper, I was familiar with the wild, warlike and romantic past of the Highlands.

I was ever a thick-head at mathematics, for which Mr. Glegg held me in yet lower esteem, and declared he would cram them down my throat; yet, having set me sums to do, he would turn his back upon me and let me struggle with them by myself, much to my dismay. For I wished to do well and enter the Grammar School, the tones of whose bell summoned the few lads I knew to an intimacy I would have given much to enjoy.

I do not know why I never told my father about Mr. Glegg's shortcomings. Had I done so, I am quite sure he would have been dismissed. I suppose I accepted him as one of those necessary evils—like measles and chicken-pox, with their concomitant doses of physic—as one other item in the total that youth must endure without complaint.

At this time it was not safe for children to be alone on the streets of Aberdeen on account of the almost daily kidnappings that took place. The children thus stolen, along with others from the workhouses, were shipped to America and sold to the planters. I must confess that such a fate befalling *me*, the son of an advocate, seemed impossible to my childish mind. But my father thought otherwise, never allowed me from the house alone, and begged me never to loiter, or talk with strange men, when I occasionally went to buy sweet-cakes at the store of Mr. Rennie, only a few doors distant.

I had a playmate in Ian, the son of Dr. Malcolm, my father's dearest friend. At times he was brought on Saturdays, by their serving-man, and we played in the big garden at the back of our house. We played divers games. One of our favourite pastimes was to climb into a high fir tree, and gaze over links and bents to the sea where the great ships lay anchored in the road. These innocent vessels we peopled with alien crews, pirates from the Mediterranean, or hostile French, whose object was to await darkness and a full tide to enter the harbour and subject our town to heavy tribute of gold and merchandise.

But for the most part my childhood hours were spent alone, especially during the long winter months. A great garret occupied the whole third storey of our house. Here, among brass-bound chests, old firelocks, swords, dirks, and armour of a bygone age, as well as numerous musty books, I found companionship and outlet for my romantic nature. Especially enchanting was Raleigh's *History of the World*, which I read again and again. Or, arming myself with dirk, and the heavy broadsword used by one of my ancestors at Harlow, and a great steel morion on my head that persisted in tumbling off during exciting moments, imagined myself doing valorous deeds for Scotland, past and present. Ah, yes, in fancy I lived and fought beside Bruce and William Wallace; helped defend our town from marauding barons; strode with the clans under the Earl of Mar from Braemar into Perth, and took part in that bloody affair at Sheriffmuir. All this, and more too, little dreaming that, before many years passed, I should actually be in the midst of strife in an alien land!

On two or three occasions I spent a holiday with my father in the Grampian Hills, at the home of the old nurse of my dear mother. Here I fished for trouts in the burn to my heart's content, and drank in all the beauty and mystery of the fir-clad mountains. On these occasions my stepmother did not accompany us, much to my great joy. For at home, thanks to her desire not to allow us to be alone together, she often insisted on going with us on our walks about the town. Yet, during bad weather, which she detested, we managed to get away from her and took long and delightful rambles. Sometimes even to Gallow Hill, on the top of which was a gruesome gibbet, where murderers were hanged. Or, going between Heading Hill and Castle Hill, we walked across the Links, with its range of sandy knolls, called the Benty Hillocks, to the sands stretching between the Rivers Don and Dee. Here we had full view of the German Ocean and incoming and outgoing ships that carried my youthful fancy to distant continents and outlandish races. Or, turning by the Cross in Castle Gate, we would walk along Exchequer Row and Shiprow.

From Shiprow I could look southward to the Grampians, where the Cape of Girdleness thrust its head into the North Sea. Or we went to St. Nicholas Church, ruined and abandoned, whose churchyard and time-worn gravestones held for me a strange fascination. A few times we went to the Denburne Brook, where we angled for sea trouts that ran up from the Dee; and here, one day, I saw a bitch otter and her young being pursued by men and boys. Never shall I forget those outings. At home, in my stepmother's austere presence, my father was usually a silent man; but out in the open with me he unbent and talked freely—not only about my studies, and his hope that some day I would take up the law, but he also unfolded much of the romantic history of our town and country. On such times, too, I discovered the beauty of his mind and soul, a beauty that influenced me greatly in later years.

Well do I remember a day he took me to the clothier shop of Mr. Robert Anderson, in Huckster-Street, and bought for me enough cloth—our own Cameron tartan—for a new kilt, blue velvet for a jacket; stockings, a handsome sporran, and a small skean dhu, with a bright cairngorm set in the handle. I believe I was the happiest boy in Aberdeen that day. But little did I then dream that in a few years it would be a criminal act, punishable with fine or transportation, for anyone to wear the beautiful Highland dress, or that it would be almost two-score years after Culloden before that monstrous Act was set aside.

I have said that I was not allowed to venture into the town alone. I religiously obeyed this order until one day in my ninth year. It was a Saturday. I was feeling lonely, and this, coupled with the fact that I now felt quite grown up, decided me to go down to Huckster Row, where my father had his office, and walk home with him. He would chide me, of course, but in the end take my hand and enjoy my company.

Putting on my best clothes, I was about to open the front door when my stepmother came from her room, and in her shrill voice demanded to know whither I was going.

I told her briefly and calmly. She said, "You will do no such thing, David. You are a bad, disobedient lad! Go to your room at once and take off your fine clothes."

I gazed fearlessly up at her. "No," I said, "I am now old enough to go into the town. Father will be glad to see me." And I opened the door. At this she blazed out at me, "All right, little brat, go, and may ill befall you!"

Light-hearted and proud of my assertion of independence, I ran to the street, and skipping along, finally came to Huckster Row, with its many taverns and shops. There was quite a crowd on the Row, and, even at this late date, I can see my lithe young body worming its way between the shoppers. I remember an important and imposing red-coated beadle with his long staff; women carrying baskets on their heads; laden donkeys clattering over the cobbles; a group of sailors arm in arm coming from a tavern, singing an outlandish song; and then, as I neared my father's office, that which even now makes my blood run cold. A group of perhaps twenty children swung out of a lane. They were tied together in pairs, and accompanied by two keepers. Some of the children were older, others my own tender age. Most of them were ragged and barefoot; a few well-clad and decently shod. But each face was grimy with dust and tears, and wore a hopeless, miserable look I had never before seen on human countenance. And suddenly remembering the tales I had heard, I realized that these lads, some from the workhouse, others perhaps kidnapped from good homes, were destined to slavery in a far-off land.

Held by a force greater than my desire to flee, I stopped and watched them. As they came opposite me, one of the lads stumbled, and falling, dragged his companion with him. The nearest keeper roughly jerked him to his feet. The poor creature let out a whimper of fright that pierced my heart. I heard one of the standers-by give a cackle of mirth. Another said, "A new batch for the plantations; God help 'em, and us!"

I ran, bumped into pedestrians, dashed between others, in a perfect agony of haste, towards my father's office. He was descending the steps. He had his stick, and a book under one arm. Never in all my life had I been so glad to see him. He gave a start of surprise. My breath was coming in hoarse gasps, and I am sure my face must have shown the awful strain I had undergone. I seized his hand and clung frantically to it, and gazed up into his face, grown suddenly stern:

"Davie," he demanded, "what is the trouble? Speak, lad,"—for
I was trembling, and so out of breath that words failed me.

Finally, at his insistent "Speak, lad," I whispered hoarsely, "I saw
them, Father—the boys—the boys—"

"Ah!" He seemed to breathe a sigh of relief. "You mean the
children bound for the colonies?" He paused. I nodded miserably.
Then he said sternly,

"Davie, why, lad, did you disobey my command and come into
the town?"

"Father," I cried, "do not be angry. I but wanted to come and
walk home with you. I was lonely. I—"

At this he gave my hand a great pressure, muttered something
beneath his breath I could not catch, then said, "I—I understand,
laddie. But it was wrong of you, and you must never, never do the
like again. You hear me, Davie lad?"

"Yes, Father," I said, meekly enough. We walked on, and came
to the Broad Gate, he holding my hand comfortingly. As we went
he talked. "It is a gruesome, cruel custom, laddie; a trafficking in
human souls that, before long, I hope the right-thinking people
of Aberdeen will refuse to countenance." Then he told me that
several influential citizens were said to be concerned in the traffic.
Their agents were not only in Aberdeen, but many other seaport
towns. These agents enticed children into taverns, gave them drink,
or by other means got them into their clutches. During a pause,
I voiced a feeling I had nursed regarding my own immunity from
the kidnappers. Said I importantly, "But they surely would not *dare*
to kidnap *your* son! *You* could put them in the Tolbooth."

At this, with a tremble in his voice I never forgot, he gravely
remarked that even the son of an advocate was not immune from
the agents of the slavers, as he called the directors of the company.

His words thoroughly disillusioned me, and I told myself that
never again, until he gave me leave to do so, would I venture into the
town alone. He then changed the subject, talking of other matters
until we reached home.

He unlocked the heavy door. Inside, he told me to hasten and
wash for dinner; then he went into the sewing-room where my
stepmother sat.

I washed, and coming downstairs heard her high-pitched voice from the dining-room protesting that she had told the stubborn brat he must not go to meet his father. Then she added violently, "It might do him good to be kidnapped. At least he would learn to obey!" And my father's calm reply, "Tut—tut, Hester! He is a good boy, and you are altogether too hard on him. Why do you not love the lad?"

"Yes," she cried, still more passionately, "you always take his part. I—I am nothing to you! Aye, and you even doubt my word that he is disobedient! Well, then, ask Mr. Glegg, who well knows how he shirks his lessons."

"Mr. Glegg," returned my father, "always gives good reports on the lad's progress."

At this I entered the dining-room and gloomily took my seat. Dinner that night was a sad affair for all of us. My father spoke little, seeming absorbed in thought. My own brain was busy with the memory of the ragged and sorry herd of children I had seen being driven into slavery. My stepmother preserved a haughty and injured air, speaking only when addressed by my father, and then grudgingly. Occasionally she bent me an icy look that betrayed the hatred she kept in verbal leash only in my father's presence, for fear of antagonizing him further in the matter of the will. That she had not yet been able to cajole or browbeat him into changing it, I well knew from the many scraps of conversation I overheard between them. Indeed, hating me as she did for the innocent bar to her ambition, it is yet a marvel to me that she controlled her passion as well as she did.

I later learned that the ship that was to transport the children to America was late in making port, and that the poor creatures were taken to the Tolbooth and a piper secured to play for them that they might not unduly brood over their fate.

CHAPTER 2

I Lose my Father

When I was ten years old my father dispensed with Mr. Glegg's services, and I entered the Grammar School in School Hill. Every morning I was taken to the gate by our old gardener, who returned after school-hours to escort me home. Even yet, and for many a long day to come, it was not safe for children to be alone on the streets.

I much enjoyed my contact with other lads. I was a healthy boy, well built and perhaps a trifle tall for my years. My companions had at once nicknamed me "Red" on account of my hair, which in colour was red enough, and was later to be the cause of very great astonishment to some of the natives of North America.

I was a pupil at this old school until the latter part of March 1744, when my dear father died, and the whole course of my life changed.

Never shall I forget that Sunday. My father and I went to the Kirk for divine service. My stepmother remained home on account of a cold drizzle, half rain, half sleet, that made the pavements like glass. I remember I wore a new greatcoat of blue homespun, with small capes, and two rows of white horn buttons down the front. With my tricorn hat and its bright silver buckle, I felt quite grown up and important; and when other pedestrians bowed to my father and he acknowledged the salute, I repeated his gesture with, I hoped, quite as grand a manner. Once, an evil-looking wretch, with a patch over one eye, came from an alley, and holding out a dirty hand asked for a shilling wherewith to buy food.

He was close to us, and I caught the strong smell of spirits. My father gave him a penny piece, at which the fellow growled out a curse and slunk away. I recollect this incident well, because my father spoke seriously to me of the unwisdom of giving alms to beggars whose sole ambition was to spend it in drink.

"But," said I, "you gave him a penny; and if he gets one here and one there, he will soon have enough for his purpose."

"That is well thought out, my son," he returned, no little pleased. For I have already said he wanted me to follow in his footsteps and become an advocate. Therefore, any remark of mine showing logical reasoning was sure to win his approval.

Now, though I desired to please him, I felt sure that I would prefer the life of a soldier to taking up the law. But not wishing to give him pain, I had never voiced my ambition, and when he was laid out in his coffin, and I gazed tearfully upon his kindly placid face, I was glad I had never argued the matter with him.

There were few people in the Kirk that morning. I am afraid I heard little of the service, for my fancy was busy with the news, told my father by one of the Deacons before entering the Church, of the outbreak of war between France and England, a conflict started by Louis XVth, that was to embroil the English and French even in far-off America, and set aflame the passions of Indian tribes from the Ohio and throughout all New England and Acadia as far as Louisburg on Cape Breton Island.

But then I knew nothing of this. And during what should have been a peaceful hour for me in that holy place, I was thinking of the strife on the Continent, and wishing that I were old enough to take part in it. So that when finally my father and I emerged from the great doors, and he asked me to repeat the minister's text, I had to admit it had entirely escaped me.

It had ceased sleeting, but the rain was now coming in a downpour driven by a strong north-east wind. We spoke little as, heads bent to the storm, we hurried along the street. I had slipped my arms from my greatcoat which I now carried shawl-like over my head, more to shield my nice new hat than to protect my face. And so, being able to see only straight ahead, I did not observe that my father had lagged behind. Suddenly I realized I no longer heard the tap of his stick on the pavement beside me. I wheeled about, to see him some rods in the rear, leaning against the iron palings at the entry of Mr. Robertson's, the clothier's, house.

Even as I ran towards him, his legs crumpled beneath him. He fell to the pavement and rolled over on his side. In an agony of mind that I shall never forget, I reached him, and dropping to my knees, implored him to tell me what was wrong. His face was ashen, his eyes closed. He heard my voice, opened his eyes a moment and whispered, "I—I am ill, Davy. Tell—tell Mr. Robertson—the Doctor—" He ceased, gave a gentle sigh and closed his eyes again.

Some people were approaching. I cried to them to hurry; then in a trice had swung open Mr. Robertson's gate, dashed up the steps, and seizing the heavy knocker, banged it as hard as I could. It seemed ages before the door opened. Mr. Robertson heard my wild words, saw the little gathering behind me, and brushing me aside, hastened down to them.

Dropping my coat and hat, I ran like the wind along the slippery cobbles to Dr. Malcolm's house, a quarter mile distant. The rain and the wind beat upon my face and flying hair. Once I slipped, fell and rolled over. I picked myself up, ran on, my heart pounding like mad. Yet fast as I went, it seemed I made slow progress. Finally I reached the Doctor's house. I banged on the door. The maid came. I dashed past her, crying the doctor's name. He opened his study door. I seized his arm, implored him to come quickly. He sensed the need for haste, ran for his medicine bag, and together we reached the street. Crying out to him that they had taken Father into Mr. Robertson's house, I left him puffing after me as fast as his threescore years would allow him, and ran on ahead. But somehow I knew that no medical science would now avail my father.

I was right. Reaching the house, I was let in by the servant. They had taken my father into the big parlour. He was lying on a sofa, his face the colour of ashes. They had loosened his neckcloth, and were now chafing his hands. I ran to him, begging him to speak to me. Mr. Robertson's wife came; she patted my shoulder, and told me to come with her to another room. But I firmly told her I must stay where I was, and after more gentle coaxing, she desisted, and let me have my way.

Dr. Malcolm came, quickly made his examination, shook his head, and rising, said my father had died of heart failure. Then he turned to me, put an arm about my shoulder and said, "Come, Davy lad, I'll take you home."

He had brought me into the world, physicked me for minor ills, and had been my father's closest friend. At his words I leaned my face against him, and for the first time sobbed out my grief. He said nothing, but held me close and patted my head understandingly. After a little he said again, "Come, Davy lad." Mrs. Robertson helped me into my coat, put my hat on my head, and then I went with him, half-blinded by tears, he holding my hand.

We reached my home. He lifted the knocker. A servant opened the door, her eyes wide with curiosity at seeing me with the doctor instead of her master. We entered the great hall. Dr. Malcolm told her to bring her mistress, bade me take a chair, and drawing up one for himself, sat down beside me.

My stepmother came in. Her quick glance swept from me to the doctor, then back to my tear-stained face. Then her hand flew to her side and her pale face went paler. She began to tremble. "What—what has happened, Doctor?" she whispered.

He had risen at her entrance. Now he took her arm, forced her into a chair, and gently told her. She swayed, put out her hands blindly, and would have fallen to the floor but for his arms. She fainted dead away. And for the first time in my life I felt sorry for her.

CHAPTER 3

Kidnapped

There is no need to describe in detail all the happenings of the next three days. Many people I had never before seen came to view my father. They spoke kind words to me, offered condolence to my stepmother, who had arrayed herself in black, and continued to look pale and perturbed. I may say here and now that, other than to procure for me suitable mourning apparel, she showed no evidence of affection, nor spoke to me any least word of comfort. Had it not been for motherly Mrs. Angus, our old cook, and Mrs. Malcolm, who came to the house every day, both of whom did their best to comfort me, I do not know how I could have endured my agony of mind and soul.

The day following my father's death my former tutor, Mr. Glegg, returned and took up quarters in the house. I suppose my stepmother had sent for him. Much of the time they were closeted together, so that I saw little of them.

After the funeral service at the house, and after I had seen all that was mortal of my father laid beside my mother in the old Kirk churchyard, I was taken to my home by Dr. Malcolm. Immediately I was inside the door, I ran to my own room, and, heartbroken, flinging myself face down on the bed, cried bitterly. How long I lay there I know not, but presently a knock sounded on the door. I made no answer; then another knock, the door opened, and I heard Mr. Glegg's voice, "You here, David? Ah, there you are. Come on down to the library, boy."

I told him I wanted to remain where I was. At which he came over, touched my arm and said, in a husky voice that quite surprised me, "The lawyer is ready to read the will, David. Come quickly."

The reading of my father's will

"The will?" I faltered.

"Yes," he said. "It is necessary. Come. They want you."

I could see that he was much excited. I rose, dried my eyes, and followed him down to the library. My stepmother, Dr. Malcolm, and Mr. Grant, my father's partner, were there. Dr. Malcolm rose and led me to a chair. Mr. Glegg seated himself beside my stepmother opposite us. Then Mr. Grant took a folded paper from his pocket, opened it and announced that, following the usual custom, he would read the last Will and Testament of the late Mr. David Cameron, of New Aberdeen, Scotland.

I glanced at my stepmother. She sat bolt upright in her high-backed chair, a strained expression on her cold, thin face. But if she hoped that my father had relented before he died, and rewritten his will, Mr. Grant's first few words disillusioned her. The will was dated January 20th, 1737, about a year and a half before his second marriage. It left his whole estate, both real and personal, his money in bonds, his ready cash after all debts were paid, to his beloved son, David Malcolm Cameron. A codicil added in 1742 gave to his wife three hundred pounds a year in lieu of dower rights and stated that, in the event that I, David Malcolm Cameron, predeceased her and had not married, his executors were instructed to give her an additional £1000 and the house in the Broad Gate.

The will named the testator's dear friends, Mr. Grant and Dr. Stewart Malcolm, executors of his estate, and Dr. Malcolm my guardian until I was of age. Then followed his wish that as soon as I had graduated from the Grammar School I was to be enrolled as a student at Marischal College, where it was his fervent hope that I would prepare myself for the practice of law.

I glanced at Mr. Glegg, my former tutor. But the contents of the will had caused him any chagrin, his face did not show it. Indeed, he flashed me an amiable smile which I am afraid I did not return.

Never shall I forget the look on my stepmother's face. From crimson it went to an extreme pallor. Her long white teeth compressed her lower lip, and her steely blue eyes flashed hatred at those of us who sat opposite her. Then she snapped out at Mr. Grant.

"And the house? Am I to be robbed of it also?"

Mr. Grant took off his spectacles, slowly wiped them, then said, "The house, Madam, is David's; but until the legal formalities are settled, you may, of course, remain here. After that"—he waved a lean hand—"I am afraid you must find other quarters."

At this she rose without further words, and motioning to Mr. Glegg to follow her, swept from the room. Had she ever shown me any kindness, I assure you I had been sorry for her—she looked so baffled and defeated. Yet, considering that she had come to my father penniless, she would be very well provided for under the terms of the will.

Shortly after a call came for Dr. Malcolm. Before leaving he told me that on the morrow he would send his servant for me, and henceforth I would live in his home. Mrs. Angus and her husband would be staying on as caretakers. Then he called Mrs. Angus in and asked her to see that my clothes, books, and any other belongings I desired to take with me were carefully packed. His man would come for them at midday with the cart. Then he patted my cheek and hurried off. And that was the last I saw of him for many a long day.

Not only was I happy at the thought of living at my guardian's home, but I was heartily glad that it was to be soon. For, disliking Mr. Glegg as I did, and wholly conscious of my stepmother's hatred of me, any prolonged contact with them would have been intolerable.

Mr. Grant remained for dinner, which we ate alone, for neither my stepmother nor Mr. Glegg appeared. Mrs. Angus told us that one of the kitchen maids had been ordered to carry a heaping tray of food and a bottle of Mr. Glegg's favourite wine to my stepmother's room.

After Mr. Grant had gone, Mrs. Angus took me upstairs, and we began collecting my effects. After a while I went into my dear father's bedroom, opened his bureau drawer and took out a large locket containing a miniature of my mother, made shortly after she was married. I had but pocketed it when I heard a noise at the door. I turned and beheld my stepmother. She frowned at me, and her voice was higher pitched than usual as she cried, "What are you pilfering, David?"

I grew hot with anger that she should address me thus. I said, "My mother's portrait, Madam, if it be pilfering to take what is my own." Then I added, "I am packing my things. To-morrow I go to live with my guardian; and I shall not be sorry to see the last of you."

For a moment she gazed at me as though she had not heard aright. Her hand went to her breast, as it did when she had a pain there. Then she said, her voice trembling a little, "Ah—so, that's it! Well, good riddance to you, say I, and no regrets." With which she slammed-to the door and left me.

That night I went to bed early, for I was quite tired and sorely lacked sleep. Mrs. Angus, good old soul, came up and tucked the bedclothes about me, and before she left, bent and kissed my cheek, a token of affection no other female save she and Mrs. Malcolm had bestowed on me since my mother's death. A little comforted, I dropped off almost immediately.

How long I slept I know not, but I fancy it was midnight when I suddenly awakened with the feeling that someone had entered my room. I could hear a faint rustling beyond the drawn bed curtains. Possibly Mrs. Angus, I thought, and opened my lips to say her name. Then I felt myself seized in an overpowering grasp. I tried to yell. Something hard was thrust between my teeth, and despite my struggles I was lifted up, blankets wrapped about me, then I was carried downstairs. Who my assailant was I knew not, nor did I ever find out. I heard a door open, and shut-to behind us as we descended more steps. I tried to release my hands to pull the gag from between my teeth, and cry for help, but I was held powerless and carried along like any infant. Were Mr. Glegg and my stepmother responsible for this outrage? Was I to be murdered? A cold sweat broke out on my face and body.

We had not gone far when I heard footsteps approaching. I prayed that it might be the Watch. The steps came nearer, stopped, and he who carried me said gruffly, "Here, Jem, take the brat, and get you gone to the shore." Then the other's voice. "Aye—aye; but the balance of the siller—?"

He who carried me replied, "The money will be paid when you bring me the Captain's receipt. No bungling, now, or we'll both swing. Understand? Keep the gag in till you're well away from the shore." I felt myself transferred to the other's arms, and heard the words:

"Aye, faith, I ken weel what to do. If he's not quiet, I'll gie him a rap over the heid that'll fix him." Then the voice I recognized as belonging to him who had carried me from the house:

"Nay, Jem, easy on that. There's to be no murther in this job. Safe aboard and the Captain's receipt, is the word, or there'll be no siller. Meet me at the Lemon Tree at ten of the mornin'. Guid luck, Jem."

My first feeling of joy that I was not to be murdered was followed by the crushing suspicion that I was to be sold to the plantations. And no one but my stepmother, who would profit by my absence, would have planned this thing. The rascal who now held me seemed to be possessed of great strength. He went at a rapid walk. Once he stumbled and let out a lusty oath.

In a little while I was conscious that we had left the cobbled street, and now walked over yielding turf. I surmised I was being carried over the Links to the sandy beach beyond which I had so often watched the ships riding at anchor in the roads.

Gagged and swathed head and body as I was, I felt I must die for lack of air. Finally, there came a strange roaring in my ears, a numb feeling in my arms and legs, and I seemed to be floating away into space. I think I must have swooned, for I remembered no more until I heard, as in a dream, the rhythmic sound of oars against thole pins, the lap of water, and the sway and dip of a boat as she took the waves. The gag had been removed by my captor, and I could now breathe with greater freedom. The blanket had slipped from my shoulders, and, having nothing on but my nightshift, the cold sea air chilled me to the bone. Peering upwards, I could see stars between scudding white clouds. But I heard no sound save the creak of the oars and the wash of the waves against the bow as the rower drove the boat steadily forward. I wet my bruised, dry lips with my tongue, and spoke to him. Perchance he had not heard me, for it was not until I had repeated my question in a louder voice, that he said gruffly:

"Ye'll ken soon. In the meantime, stow your tongue in your cheek, young maister, or I'll put the gag back."

I did not want to endure that agony again, yet I would chance the punishment rather than leave unsaid what was in my mind.

"If you will take me back to my guardian, I will give you five times as much gold as the silver you are to get for this job," I told him, as best I could for my chattering teeth.

He paused a few moments in his rowing, and I thought he was favourably considering my proposal. But finally, with a grunt, he again dipped the oars, and, as the boat shot forward, he said, "One word more, young maister, and back goes the gag. Not that your shouting will help, but I'll keep my promise to ye. Oh, yes," he muttered, "I'll keep my promise."

I had no doubt he would do that. I did his bidding and made what shift I could to pull the blanket about my shivering body. But when I drew it up I uncovered my legs, so that I was in no better state than before. Fortunately there was little wind, or I had been nigh perished. So I endured the discomfort as best I could, and tried to content myself with the thought that possibly I might make a better bargain with the ship's captain.

How long he had been rowing I know not, but presently I heard the creaking of an anchor chain. Looking up, I saw the dark hull and towering masts of a vessel looming above me. Then the voice of the rascal near me cried out, "Ahoy, there, *Bon Accord*, ahoy!"

A lanthorn flashed from the deck. By its light I saw a cloaked figure bending over the rail. "Ah," it said, "that you, Jem? You're late." He paused, spoke to someone on the ship. A ladder was let down. My abductor made fast the boat's painter, picked me up bodily in his strong arms, threw me over one shoulder like a sack of meal, and clambered up the ship's side to the deck. I stood there in my nightshift, like any derelict from the slums. He with the lanthorn held it up to my face, scrutinized me a few moments, thee said, "All right, Jem, here's your receipt for the lad. You may go. We sail at once." He turned to his companion. "Call the hands, Dirck, and up with the anchor." He seized my arm in a firm grip and said, "Come on, McNab, and I'll find you trousers and a jacket."

"McNab?" I thought. "Does he then not know my real name?"

"Please, Captain," I cried, "just a moment." Then, hastily, for he was urging me forward. "My name is Cameron, David Cameron. My father was buried but yesterday. By his will, I am left wealthy, and my guardian will pay you handsomely, if you do but put me ashore. Please, please do!"

"Aye," he returned, "lots of 'em say that. Why,"—he gave a hoarse chuckle—"I've been offered castles an' knighthood afore this. Come on. You'll learn to like the *Bon Accord*, and be loth to leave her by the time you reach Virginia."

Then I knew what fate I was destined for, and remembering my dear father's words that none of the slaves had ever returned home, my heart sank within me.

I was hurried below. The Captain opened a door, pushed me into a cabin in which a lighted lamp hung from the ceiling, and then cried in a lusty voice, "Wake up, Billy! Billy, I say, round to, or I'll give you a rope's end!"

A lad not much older than myself slowly uncoiled himself from a mattress on the floor, rubbed his eyes, ran his fingers through long, unkempt hair, and stared stupidly at me several moments. Then, now more fully awake, he let out a loud guffaw and cried, "Lord lumme, is it lad, or lass?"

The Captain roared out at him, "Wake up, you! Cannot you see it's a boy? Dugald McNab's his name, and he came from the workhouse. Get him clothes at once!"

I stared dumbly at the Captain. Did he actually think my name McNab? Oh, well it did not matter. He crossed over to a table on which stood a bottle of brandy and poured himself a full glass. The boy Billy was hastily rummaging in a small sea chest. He threw a pair of trousers towards me, then stockings and coarse shoes; lastly, a soiled-looking shirt. My whole being revolted at the thought of donning those filthy-looking garments. The Captain was busy with his brandy. I glanced hurriedly at the door. Could I reach it, fling it open, dash on deck, throw myself into the sea and safely reach shore? I was a good swimmer. But it mattered not. Death was better than being shipped to America to endure lifelong slavery. My fingers went to my nightshift, undid the buttons. Then, as it fell to the floor, I made a dash for the door. Quick as I was, the boy Billy saw me. Out went his foot. It caught me above the ankle, and I crashed headlong against the door.

When I came to I was in the hold of the vessel. I felt horribly ill, and my head ached as though it must burst. The place was as dark as an unlit cellar. I could hear people snoring all about me; once a shuddering sigh, then low and heart-breaking sobs that told me I had companions—other Scots lads from workhouse and street; perhaps some like myself from good homes—to keep me company to the plantations. I laid my head on my arm and wept.

CHAPTER 4

The Privateer

The *Bon Accord* was an armed merchant vessel flying the English flag. Merchant vessel, did I say? Aye, and more than that. At will a privateer, and, when opportunity offered, a slaver. Originally she had been a French vessel, but had been captured during the previous war and sold, it was said, to Aberdeen merchants. What queer twist had caused them to rechristen her *Bon Accord*, which is the motto of the Royal Burgh of Aberdeen, I never knew.

She carried twelve guns to a side. On the forecastle and quarter-deck was a long eighteen pounder. Several smaller pieces, known as swivels, were fixed on the bulwarks, and around the masts were ranged muskets, pistols and cutlasses.

It was not until she was well down the channel that we were allowed on deck. The fresh air was like a bit of Heaven, for most of us had been seasick, and the stench of the hold had not lessened our sufferings. But the Captain was not anxious for any of his human cargo to die. We were a nondescript lot, thirty-two in number, including three girls, the latter cabined in another part of the ship. These girls were to be sold as household help to the planters.

Many of the lads seemed utterly indifferent to their destiny. Possibly they considered the Colonies much preferable to their former workhouse existence. But others—and there were several who had been kidnapped from respectable, if not luxurious, homes—woefully bewailed their fate. We were quartered in the after-part of the hold, in a small compartment that had doubtless served many other consignments of slaves. We slept on mattresses stuffed with heather.

We were now allowed on the forecastle deck almost daily, and one of the sailors, who could pipe, played for us several lively airs. One of the maids, Mary Donaldson by name, a tow-haired, freckled, and spirited lass, found the music so irresistible she stepped out from among her companions and did a dance. When she ended, the captain and several of the sailors and gunners clapped applause. After this, when the weather was fair, and no vessel in sight, we had piping and dancing, and it did indeed do us good.

We entered at least two seaports on the English coast to take on cargo which, I later learned, included several boxes of long case clocks for wealthy Virginia colonists. But we did not see these ports, being securely locked in the hold until after we had weighed anchor.

On the fifth day out we had a scrap with an enemy privateer that for some time quite satisfied my desire for conflict. I was on deck, watching the tumbling green waves against which our bow lifted and dashed, sending up showers of boiling spume. I was thinking, as I so often did, of my home, of Mr. Grant, and good Dr. Malcolm, and wondering if I should see them ever again. Suddenly I heard a "Sail ho!" from the look-out. The mate came forward, a glass under his arm, and gazed through it to starboard. I followed his gaze, but saw only what I took to be a bank of cloud against the far horizon.

But the mate knew otherwise. "Here, boy," he ordered me, "run and tell Captain Barclay to come on deck. Hurry now!"

I needed no second bidding. I ran. Clattering down the companionway, I rushed to the Captain's cabin and hammered on the door. His gruff voice bade me enter. I did so and told him my errand.

He set down the glass of brandy he had poured. "Sail, eh! Suspicious?" he grumbled. "Mr. Hervie is always sighting suspicious sails. Ah, well, no knowing—better to be safe than sorry." He lifted the glass, quickly drained it, rose, swaying on his feet, and picking up his telescope, followed me on deck.

I could now see the strange vessel quite clearly. She was a low, rakish craft, with patched sails that rose and dipped like the wings of some great bird. The Captain took one long look at her, then snapped to his glass. "French," he growled. "*Pelican*, privateer, or I'm a Dutchman. Pipe the hands up, Mr. Hervie, and clear for action."

Then he turned to me. "Go below, McNab," he ordered, "and mind you stay there."

I did not want to go below. I had read of sea fights and, now that one was imminent, I much desired to witness it. Reluctantly I turned to obey him, and saw the crew pouring on deck. I was pushed this way and that until, finding myself near the shrouds of the mainmast, I paused, ran my eye along them to the cross-trees, and then, my mind suddenly made up, I sprang into the shrouds and climbed them hand over hand.

No one saw me. I was no sooner ensconced in my dizzy perch than I heartily repented of my venture. Down below I had not been conscious that the ship was plunging and rolling more than usual; but up there, fifty feet from the deck, the perch to which I clung described a wide arc; one moment I was suspended far over the tumbling waters, the next the deck was below me. And, when we went about on a tack, and the ship heeled the opposite way, I was in like predicament. So that, if I had fallen, I had either crashed to the deck below or gone overboard. I could only cling frantically to the shrouds, as afraid to descend now as to remain where I was.

The French ship was coming up at a good clip, the water curling in white foam from her bows. She had displayed no colours, but I had our Captain's vow as to her nationality. She fired the first shot. I saw a puff of smoke from one of her forward deck guns, then a cannon-ball came skipping over the waves, passed close to our bows and plunged into the sea.

I could see the activity below me—barefooted powder-boys carrying up powder, guns being run out on their carriages, hear coarse commands from the Captain's trumpet, the thud of ram-rods as the heavy balls were forced home. And there was I, clinging desperately to the rigging, while my countrymen were preparing to come to grips with the Frenchmen. I could at least help to carry up powder from the magazines.

Summoning all my courage, I began descending the shrouds, with now the deck beneath me, now the boiling sea. I was frightfully dizzy and more than once had to stop and cling to the ropes with every ounce of strength I possessed. Suddenly I heard a tremendous discharge below me that made the whole ship quiver. A moment later a loud huzzah, and someone's voice, "We winged 'em! We winged 'em!" Evidently the shot had gone through the enemy's sail.

I was now only a few feet from the bulwark. Gingerly, for the ship was heeling over yet more to starboard, I shifted my position to the inner side of the shrouds and, as soon as she had righted herself, I dropped to the deck, where for a few moments I lay unable to rise. Finally I got to my feet. No one noticed me, everyone being busy at his appointed task.

The battle now began in earnest. The Frenchman was now no great distance away, and bearing about delivered a broadside that tore our rigging, smashed a boat and sent a shower of splinters in all directions. One struck a sailor in the face, and he let out a shriek that sickened me. Then our own guns let loose, and pandemonium reigned.

I joined a powder-boy, dashed with him below to the powder magazine. On deck again, I found that our sailors had trimmed the sails, and we were going about on a tack that would allow our gunners to discharge their larboard pieces.

"Old man's wise," my companion shouted, as we dumped our powder beside the eighteen pounder on the forecastle deck. "Makin' a runnin' fight of it," he explained as we dashed back. "Frenchie's got more men than we have, and would like to get to close quarters, hammer us well, an' then board. But they don't catch Cap'n Barclay nappin'."

I had little time to view the effects of our shots from now on. Our skipper manoeuvred the *Bon Accord* in such a manner that he kept the enemy always at a distance, and at the same time pounded him unmercifully. The cannonading was continuous. The carriages groaned as they were run out on their slides; the master gunners would aim their pieces, apply the matches, then, as the pieces were discharged, the whole ship shook from stem to stern. The acrid smoke stung my nostrils, and lay like a pall over the decks. Through it sailors pulled on ropes, or dashed here and there like mad creatures, while above the din the Captain's voice roared his commands through his trumpet. Several of our men were hit—some dead, others wounded. The latter were carried below, and the ship's doctor and his assistant were kept busy attending them.

Suddenly I heard a shout that the enemy's topmast, with all its upper hamper, yards and top-gallants, was down, and his steering gear out of order. A loud cheer went up from our decks. When it died down the look-out announced another ship coming up behind the enemy. I got a glimpse of her. She was a big vessel, with two tiers of guns, whether friend or enemy we knew not at the moment.

But our Captain was not content to depart without a final farewell. He ordered the *Bon Accord* put about. We ran in close to the enemy, gave him our forecastle eighteen pounder, then, wearing around, delivered our whole starboard broadside into his hull. With which salute we bore away down channel.

It was well, for the look-out told our Captain that the newcomer was a French frigate.

We were not followed. When last seen the frigate was close to the privateer, transferring her crew to the former vessel. Evidently our late antagonist was in a sinking condition.

Everyone unhurt now turned to and repaired the damage done. It was not serious. Some of our standing rigging had been shot away, a portion of the bulwarks and the jolly boat smashed. The sailors cut away the wreckage, spliced, knotted, ran up new yards. The guns were secured, the bloody decks washed down, and, to me a sad and unforgettable rite, the dead sewn in hammocks, a round shot at their feet. The Captain read a brief funeral service, and they were solemnly committed to the sea.

Captain and crew were jubilant over their victory. Sailors and gunners were given an extra glass of grog, and, as night fell, we reached the broad Atlantic.

If the Captain had noticed that I had disobeyed his orders, he said nothing to me. Indeed, for the following two days he remained in his cabin celebrating his victory with his favourite brandy. When finally he came on deck it was to take part in a less hazardous venture than our brush with the privateer, but possibly one equally to his liking.

CHAPTER 5

The French Brig

We had been enveloped by a dense fog all morning. By noon it suddenly lifted, and there, not half a mile distant, on our larboard side, was a small brig. Captain Barclay ordered our course shifted. The *Bon Accord* skipped over the sea like a thing alive, then swung about, broadside to the stranger. We could see her name now, *Honfleur*, and a few people on her deck.

Captain Barclay put his trumpet to his mouth. "Heave to, or I'll sink you!" he roared in French. Then to one of the gunners, "Send a shot over his bow to show we mean business."

The gunner obeyed. Barely had the round shot spumed up the water ahead of the stranger, than there was a great hurrying to and fro about her deck; presently her sails were furled and she lay gently pitching on the swell.

Now our skipper again shouted, "We will board you." Then the mate's voice, "Lower away the long boat, men!"

The long boat, manned by armed men, was quickly in the water, Mr. Hervie in command. Soon they reached the brig and clambered up her side. I could see the mate confronted by a man who I supposed was the Captain. He appeared much excited, waving his hands, shaking and nodding his head alternately. I later learned that the *Honfleur* was on her way to France from Canada, her captain quite ignorant that war had been declared.

Meanwhile, Captain Barclay kept his brig under his guns. Presently Mr. Hervie shouted to him to manoeuvre the *Bon Accord* in close, as there was considerable cargo aboard to transport.

Captain Barclay complied. Barely had our bulwarks scraped alongside the brig's than grappling irons were flung aboard her, all made fast, and the transferring of the cargo begun. While this was taking place, our Captain ordered a sharp look-out kept for the possible approach of any French man-of-war.

It took perhaps a couple of hours to remove the bales of rich furs from the hold of the brig to our own decks, furs which had been trapped by Indians and French followers of the woods on lake and stream in far-off Canada, and which, but for our interference, might perhaps have graced the pretty shoulders of the ladies of the French court.

The crew of the *Honfleur* were clustered aft, and made no demonstration at the filching of their cargo. I could not help feeling sorry for them. And yet, we were at war with their nation: one of their privateers had attacked us recently and, had she defeated us, our cargo would have fallen rightful loot to them.

Before we parted from the brig, that happened which was to have a most profound influence on my after-life in America. Through the mist of years the drama now enacted on the deck of the *Honfleur* stands out as though it all happened but yesterday, instead of sixty years ago.

I had been standing at the bulwarks, watching those on the brig, when I saw two of our brawny sailors come from below, dragging between them a tall, tawny-skinned individual. Suddenly, with a quick movement, he tripped up one of the sailors, caught the other about the middle, lifted him up bodily and flung him over his shoulder a dozen feet distant. Then, brushing aside those who endeavoured to seize him, he ran to the stern of the brig and flung himself into the sea.

There was a great clamour. The mate whipped a pistol from his belt, leaned over the rail and fired at the poor creature swimming away from us with strong, steady strokes. The mate then snatched a pistol from a sailor and was about to fire again, when our Captain stopped him. "Pick him up," he roared. Some of our sailors tumbled into the long boat alongside the brig and dashed in pursuit. As the boat approached, the fellow dived, to appear a few moments later beyond its stern. Then ensued a chase that thrilled all of us who witnessed it. Time and again the boat came up with the fugitive; repeatedly he dived like an otter and eluded the outstretched hands of those who sought to seize him. How long it would have kept up, I know not, but presently one of the sailors gave him a blow on the head with his oar. I thought the poor creature had sunk, but the second mate thrust down his hand, seized him by the shoulder and dragged him alongside. He was stunned and could make no further resistance. They lifted him into the boat and rowed back to the *Bon Accord*. A rope was thrown down, knotted under his arms, and he was hauled to the deck.

Worming my way between the surrounding sailors, I gazed awesomely down at him. He had thrown off his jacket before plunging into the sea, but was otherwise clad as any English gentleman, with ruffled shirt, plum-coloured trousers, stockings, and buckled shoes. His face was reddish-brown, his head shaved save for a long lock of raven-black hair in which was fastened what I later learned to be a hawk's feather. About his neck was a necklet of bear's teeth. His features were noble, the forehead high, the mouth and nose formed as though sculptured by a Grecian artist.

As I gazed, my heart beating with sympathy for the poor wretch, his eyelids flickered and opened, and a pair of black eyes gazed vacantly up at those clustered about him. Then his right hand went slowly to his brow as though he would brush aside the mist that befogged him. His shirt had been partly torn from his body, and I saw a nasty flesh wound where the mate's pistol ball had ploughed along his shoulder.

Now, at the Captain's command, he was bound hand and foot, and four sailors carried him below to the sick bay to have his wound dressed by the doctor. I did not see him until hours later.

Before casting off from the brig, Captain Barclay presented her skipper with a case of brandy. A welcome gift, no doubt, though it could serve no balm for the loss of his cargo.

As we separated from the brig, I saw a black-robed figure emerge from her forecastle door and make speech with the skipper. Tall he was, and powerfully built, with a rugged, pleasing countenance. And little did I imagine that ever again I should see that priest of the Society of Jesus, let alone have speech with him in the land of Acadia.

The last I saw of the brig she was tacking slowly towards the coast of France. I breathed a mental prayer that she would not be further molested.

32

CHAPTER 6

Tomah

That night a storm came up. I awoke to a terrific din. The waves pounded the ship like battering-rams, and she rolled and pitched sickeningly. A single lanthorn swung over our heads, and by its wavering light I could see my unfortunate companions huddled together for what comfort they could get. As the tempest increased, one of them, a lad from some Highland croft, who had never before seen the sea, began praying in Gaelic. From above came the creaking of gear, and the whistling of wind through the cordage sounded as though a thousand demons had been let loose. Anon came a tremendous crash as a mountain of water was hurled aboard. And, though everything was battened down, we frequently had to shift position to escape being drenched by the seepage from above. I was horribly frightened, but tried as best I could to remain outwardly calm. As the hours passed, the storm gathered in violence. One moment, as she climbed some mountainous wave, the ship seemed to be standing on her stern; the next, the stern rose so high I thought she was pitching bow first to her doom. The continued seepage of water from above finally made us most uncomfortable, for it mingled with the bilge, and the whole washed about with every roll of the ship. I felt sure she would founder, and thinking of my past life I wondered if my sins had been so great that I would be denied heaven. But I mumbled the twenty-third Psalm and felt a little comforted.

Some time later an unusually big wave bore down on the *Bon Accord*, flung tons of water on the deck, tore the long boat from its fastenings, hurled it against the main mast, and splintered it into kindling wood. I heard the crash and imagined that one of the masts had gone. The next moment the bow of the ship lifted high, and I and my poor frightened companions were hurled backwards, falling and scrambling among the bilge, one upon the other.

When finally I disengaged myself, I saw at my feet a form that I at first thought to be one of my boy companions, possibly injured in our tumble. He lay in bilge water. Seizing him by the shoulder, I tried to drag him to a dryer spot. But he was too heavy for me. Then, to my astonishment, I saw that it was the Indian we had taken from the sea the previous afternoon. I thought he was dead, for he lay there in the wash, making no effort to help himself. As best I could I made my way to the lanthorn, took it down and crawled back to where he lay. By its flickering light I could see that his eyes were open, and that he was breathing. I was horrified to note he was yet bound hand and foot.

Securing the lanthorn to a hook above us, I got down on my knees beside him, and slowly, for the rope about his wrists was firmly knotted, I undid the knots. This done, I did the same to the rope about his ankles.

His ankles free, I took his hands in both of mine and rubbed them as best I could for the rolling and pitching of the ship. All the while his glistening black eyes stared up at me as though he were wondering at my interest in his welfare. When finally I ceased, he opened his lips and said in a low, musical voice, "*Wul-e-wun.*" Then, as I gazed at him, not understanding, he added in very good English, "Tomah say thank you. Tomah not forget."

He slowly drew himself to a sitting posture, then moved his limbs this way and that to restore circulation. In a few minutes he was able to crawl to a less wet area. I sat down beside him. My companions, if they noticed him at all, were too alarmed at the possibility of disaster to think of anything but their own fate. Suddenly Tomah spoke, "What your name?" he asked.

I told him "David".

He repeated it slowly, then said, "Tomah call you *P'sazum—Kuluwazu P'sazum*. That means good star." He was interrupted by the ship careening on her side. We rolled together and were thoroughly drenched. When she righted herself, we crawled back, and sitting upright on the floor, our shoulders against the partition, we were better able to withstand the pitching and rolling.

Now he undid the thong that held the necklet of bear's teeth about his bronzed throat, and handed it to me. "You keep them, P'sazum," he said. "You keep them to remember Tomah."

At the moment I felt that if I remembered him it would be from another world. For I was quite convinced the ship would founder, and all of us die together. But I took the necklet and tied the thong about my neck. "Thank you, Tomah," I said. He looked pleased, and said they were the teeth of a very great bear. "*Moo-in*", he called him.

I asked him where his home was. He answered "*Me-dowk-tek*", which really did not enlighten me, but he went on to say that Medowktek was a big Indian village on the Wulahstukw River in Acadia. Also, that he was head chief of the Indians of this river, "which," he added, "the French call 'St. John'." For it was on St. John's day that they first discovered it.

Then I said to him, "You speak very good English, Tomah."

He nodded. "*Ah-ha*," he said, "I learn from English prisoner. Sometime prisoner stay with us long time. English, he not hard to pick up."

Then I asked him how he came to be on the French ship.

"Oh," he answered, with a dash of pride, "I thought I go to see my father, the King of France."

I wondered at this. But much later I learned that he had accompanied the Jesuit priest, Father Germain, who had been sent by the Governor of Canada to explain the necessity for more soldiers and supplies to be sent to Acadia, if it was to be held against the future military efforts of the English. Doubtless the sending of Chief Tomah had been with the intent of impressing him with the grandeur and magnitude of the French nation, and ensure his loyalty and that of his people in any future struggle for the control of the country.

I asked Tomah why he had jumped into the sea. To which he replied that he had chosen death by drowning, rather than by torture and scalping.

"But Englishmen do not torture or scalp," I assured him. He answered that he knew better. The English commanders paid their

Iroquois allies one hundred pounds for a scalp; and the houses of the English were filled with the scalps of his Maliseet brethren. "And so," he added, "your people will torture Tomah, and scalp him. But," proudly, "they will see that he can die with a smile on his face."

Say what I would, it was impossible to make him believe otherwise. And, as the storm seemed to increase rather than abate, I told him he had better say what prayers he knew, for certainly we were doomed to death by drowning. He answered calmly that he was not afraid to die. "But we not drown," he added, shaking his head slowly. "No, my grandmother she tell me long time ago, some day I go to see the King of France. And she said, 'Tomah, you not see'm. There will be a great storm, but you not born to die in water.'"

As he ended his grandmother's strange prophecy, there came a terrific crash on the deck above us. It sounded as though a giant cannonade had exploded, for the whole ship shook and rolled over with such a list to starboard that we were thrown in a heap, the bilge soaking us anew. As soon as I could I jumped to my feet, as did the miserable youngsters, my companions; we dashed to the door, tumbling against each other and fighting madly in our efforts to burst it open and reach the deck.

It was futile. The door held firmly, and though we screamed and pleaded for someone to let us out, no one appeared to hear us. Several of the poor lads broke down and wept pitifully. And one kept crying in a loud voice that the ship was going down. Another, "We shall drown." All of which, added to the pounding of the waves and the roaring of the wind, was like bedlam let loose. To add to our dismay the ship failed to right herself, and she lay heeled over at a most dangerous angle. In a momentary lull I could hear the sound of axes above, the mate's voice roaring, "Hurry—make haste, men!"

I learned later that the mizzen-mast had gone by the board, carrying away a portion of the bulwarks; and the heavy weight of mast and all the top hamper was responsible for the list of the vessel. Indeed, she was almost on her beam ends. One of the sailors was carried overboard by a big wave and never seen again. But that night the crew of the *Bon Accord* performed valorous deeds. In half an hour the wreckage was cleared and she righted herself. She sprang away like an eager runner awaiting the starting shot, speeding like a wild thing through the pounding seas and the black night and the howling wind.

Meanwhile I had gone back to Tomah. He was sitting, his back against the bulkhead, as I had left him. But now the lanthorn was on the floor, supported on either side by his feet. For a moment I wondered if he was performing some aboriginal rite to his gods. Then I saw that he held in one hand a little pipe. Putting the long stem in his mouth, he opened the door of the lanthorn, inserted the bowl, bottom up, until it touched the flame, then began sucking on the stem. Presently he was puffing out volumes of tobacco smoke. He closed the lanthorn, and looking up, saw my face. He smiled, held the pipe up to me. "Smoke," he said. "*Ta-ma-way* good."

I shook my head. My dear father had occasionally used tobacco, but I had no wish to try it. Not now, but I thanked my Indian friend and told him I was yet too young to smoke.

He nodded composedly, but made no comment. He smoked with evident enjoyment. Presently, some of the other lads came, gathered about us and watched him with tired, curious eyes—eyes in faces dirty and wretched, as doubtless was my own.

After the ship righted herself—though the storm continued with unabated fury—we breathed easier. Finally, tired out with anxiety and loss of sleep, I curled myself on my filthy, damp mattress and drifted off to sleep.

How long I slept, I know not. It must have been several hours before I awakened to my miserable surroundings. Yet not wholly the same. The storm had abated. Moreover, the doorway of our prison quarters was open, letting in some daylight, and the cook's boy had brought two buckets, one filled with steaming broth, the other with biscuits. Like a pack of famished animals my companions pressed about him, each with his pewter mug. I seized mine and joined them. As soon as I could I dipped my mug into the bucket of soup and seized a biscuit. The broth, greasy and floating with lumps of fat pork, was most palatable. I drank it off without taking the cup from my lips. Then I remembered Tomah. I glanced to where I had last seen him, and there he still sat, his dark eyes fixed on us as though we were curious creatures of another world.

I thrust in my mug again, grabbed a biscuit, and hastened back to him. "Here, Tomah," I said, "you must be hungry."

He took the mug and biscuit with a low "*Wul-e-wun*", and smiled up at me, showing teeth as white as milk. I went back to the group of lads about the cook's boy. He was telling them that the storm had smashed things pretty badly above decks. Heavy seas had washed inboard, flooded the cook's galley repeatedly and put out his fire. He spoke with pride of the ship, saying that were she not a stoutly built vessel she most certainly had foundered. Then he eulogized Captain Barclay, larding his admiration with many strange oaths quite new to me. With a bottle of brandy in each pocket of his greatcoat, the Captain and a sailor had lashed themselves to the wheel, and all night long had kept the *Bon Accord* on her course.

Suddenly the boy stopped his recital. Then, with the quickness of an adder, he grasped me by the shoulder and pulled me towards him. "I say, Dugald McNab," he cried, "what's that menagerie you got on your neck? Where'd you get 'em?" And without waiting for an answer to his questions he fingered the necklet of bear's teeth covetously, and I believe would have torn it from me had I not put up my hand and warded him off. "Where did you get 'em?" he repeated.

I told him, and he said, "Oh—the Indian—well, look here, Dugald McNab, I'll give you six pence for 'em."

I told him I would not part with it for a hundred pounds. At which he gave a low whistle of surprise and said, "I'd sell my grandmother for half *that* amount. Well, then," he added, "where is your Indian? He'll need some of this."

I led him to Tomah, who got another mug of broth and a second biscuit. The cook's boy stood by watching him drink and eat. Suddenly he turned on me and said: "He was bound when they brought him here. Did you untie him?"

I hesitated to tell that it was I who had done the service. He turned on me wrathfully. "You'll get a hiding for this, McNab, when the skipper finds out." And he blew out and sucked in his cheeks in a manner he had.

I did not care. Indeed, I was quite willing to be punished for what I had done. But it was not to be. Tomah had been regarding the cook's boy with sharp, black eyes. Now he said, "Tomah he got good teeth. Tomah bite'm rope."

"Oh, *you* did it! Well,"—the boy turned to me—"that let's you out, Dugald. Jolly good for you, too." Saying which, and with a last, longing look at my necklet, he took himself off, and proceeded on deck.

In the afternoon we were allowed up for an hour. The ship presented quite a different picture from the trim vessel I had known the day before. The foremast had been splintered off a few feet above the deck, and where the bulwark had been carried away, the ship's carpenter and helpers had erected a temporary barricade of spars and other lumber. Two of the boats were badly smashed, the oars gone, and some of the sails torn to ribbons.

Indeed, it was several days before anything like order was restored.

The sea was still running high, but the air of cheerfulness pervading the crew told me that they considered the storm had blown itself out. I did not see the Captain, and supposed he was in his cabin getting a well-earned rest.

That night I slept like a log; nor did I awake until the cook's boy again brought us food. He told us the weather was now comparatively calm, the sun shining, and the ship making good progress. Once again he admired my necklet, and this time offered me two shillings for it. When I refused, he angrily told me I was a fool, and asked me if I was a bloomin' duke. I answered I was not, but that if I had my rights I could purchase the ship and all her cargo, and still have plenty left.

He stared at me as though he thought I had taken leave of my senses. Then he said, "You're a bloody little liar, Dugald McNab; that's what you are."

If I had not thought of a plan to make use of him. I'm afraid his jaw and my fist would have cried quits, even though he was half a head taller, being a lad of fourteen or fifteen. So I forced myself to be calm and said, "You are wrong. I am not a liar," and lowering my voice, I told him who I was. "Look you," I went on, "if you will take a letter to my guardian when you return to Aberdeen, he will pay you one hundred pounds. Will you do this for me?"

He screwed up his nose and his eyes grew round in their sockets. He sucked in his breath, muttered, "A hundred pounds—a fortune!" over and over; then, "I'll be taking my life in my hands but I'll do it, if you throw in the necklet."

For a moment I wavered. Then I resolutely shook my head. "No," said I. "I will not part with the necklet, but I will ask my guardian to give you one hundred and twenty-five pounds." Again he pondered. Finally he said, "All right. I'll chance it." I told him to smuggle me down materials to write with. He promised to do this and departed.

The very next day he brought me ink, quill, and paper. He apologized for the latter, but said it was all he could find. "However," he added, "there's enough space left for our need."

And now I saw that it was a letter written by the Bailie of Aberdeen to Captain Barclay of the *Bon Accord*, and the writing took up about three-fourths of the sheet, which had been folded over as was the custom, the address on the outside.

"Oh, look here, James McArthur," I protested. "I cannot use this. It does not belong to me, or to you, but to our Captain. It is not an honourable thing to use it, and you must take it back."

He frowned and said, "It's this, or nothin'. As for takin' it back, I had too hard a time to get it. As it was, I'd just snitched it out of his despatch case, when the door opened. Oh, no, sonny, I have no wish to be triced up to the triangles and a rope's end cuttin' into my back. So swallow your conscience, Mr. McNab, or whichever your name is." And he made as though to take the letter from me. But I closed my fingers on it tightly and said quickly, "I'll have it done for you in the morning."

That night, by the aid of the lanthorn, I began my short letter to my guardian. My conscience bothered me no more. For as I spread out the sheet my own name flashed up at me. Then I read the whole thing. It told the Captain that I, David Cameron, would be brought to the *Bon Accord* at or near midnight of March 28th. If for any reason the plans miscarried, the Captain was not to sail, under pain of the writer's displeasure, until such time as he was given orders to do so. If all went as planned I was to be sold under the name of Dugald McNab. Then was appended the writer's signature—Bailie Dewar.

Perhaps you can understand the amazement, horror and anger I felt at this disclosure. And to think that the Bailie, one of the elect of our town of Aberdeen, was involved in this nefarious traffic! And only to think how several times my father had taken me with him when he went to interview the Bailie on some legal matter, and the man had patted my head and made much of me.

What hold he had on Captain Barclay I would have given much to know, but I suspected, as I knew for certain later, that the Bailie was one of the owners of the *Bon Accord.*

I had but scant room for my message to my guardian, with the added admonition to preserve the letter. Then I folded it in a small compass, and when next James McArthur came down I handed it to him. I said, "Take good care of it, James." I remember so well his answer. "Juist as if it was the Crown Jewels, friend Dugald," for he persisted in calling me Dugald throughout the voyage.

With my letter safely in James McArthur's possession I now felt happier than at any time since my abduction, for I had no doubts in my mind that if James lived to reach Aberdeen, he would see to it that my guardian got the missive that would tell him what had befallen me and under what name I had been sold.

Years afterwards I came across the yellowed receipt for one hundred and twenty-five pounds paid to James McArthur by my guardian on the account of David Cameron. But the receipt was dated almost four years after I had written my letter in the hold of the *Bon Accord!* And attached to the receipt on a separate page was the following in my guardian's angular hand-script: "To-day a strange creature came to me and gave me the best news I have had in many a long day. And though the message was written almost four years ago, I have no doubt it is actually in the handwriting of David Cameron, who disappeared from home about that time, and clears up a mystery which I have spent many hundreds of pounds trying to solve. Poor Davie—is he living or dead? If the former, I feel sure he would again have found means to communicate his whereabouts to me. I am writing Governor Clinton, at New York, to use every instrument in his power to locate the lad if living.

"The fellow who fetched me Davie's message, written from the *Bon Accord,* had had many strange adventures. As many in

Aberdeen know, on her return voyage from America the *Bon Accord* was engaged in battle by two French privateers, and though she gave a good account of herself, was so repeatedly hulled by the enemy's roundshot, that she was in a sinking condition and forced to surrender. This James McArthur was taken prisoner with those of his companions who survived the battle. The privateer in which he now found himself had lost many of her sailors, and he was forced to help sail the vessel. Several months later, in the Mediterranean, she was wrecked off the coast of Morocco. Many of the crew were drowned, but James McArthur, with some others, managed to reach shore. They were captured by Moroccan tribesmen, sold to the Bey of Tunis, and confined on one of his galleys plying between those Eastern ports. He tells me that he managed to preserve the letter, written by David Cameron, by folding it in a small compass, and sewing it in a belt which he always wore. Finally, after years of abuse and adventure, he managed to slip overboard one dark night off the coast of Spain, swim to shore, and made his way to Gibraltar. Here he found a ship ready to return to England, got a position as sail-trimmer, and landed at London six weeks ago. I gave him the sum of money David requested, also a good dinner, and he departed after many thanks.

"I am horrified and indignant at the evidence of the Bailie's inclusion in the slave traffic. Use must be made of this knowledge in good time, but at present every energy must be bent upon locating the boy."

Now I will return to my own adventures, which were to be even stranger than those I have already related as befalling my old friend, James McArthur.

The days went by without any further untoward incident. We were alone, so far as we could see, on the wide ocean, drawing nearer and nearer to the land unknown to me save through the pages of Sir Walter Raleigh's enchanting book.

Of Chief Tomah I saw much. He was allowed on deck with the rest of us, and was shown many kindnesses by the crew. When I pointed this out to him as evidence that he was not to be tortured, he said that in his country they always treated prisoners courteously before torturing them. Therefore his bearing toward the crew was proud and aloof. He talked little to anyone, save myself. He tried to teach me his language, and was most patient with my attempts to get the correct pronunciation, repeating slowly each syllable many times, until I got each word to his satisfaction. Before we had landed I was able to speak several sentences, to his delight, as well as my own.

CHAPTER 7

Chesapeake

Eight weeks after leaving Aberdeen we sighted the coast of North America. Just what part of it I know not; but coming at last to a great bay, we entered it about sundown and cast anchor.

You will never know with what mixed feelings I first viewed this new land. That I was to be sold into slavery I well knew. Of course, I wondered what my master would be like, and if I should be well treated. These thoughts were but natural. However, I had for comfort the promise of James McArthur to deliver my letter to my guardian as soon as he returned to Aberdeen. So surely, I told myself, I shall not remain long in captivity.

With my companions I was now taken down to our quarters in the hold, and the door bolted. I think all but Tomah passed a restless and more or less excited night. As for the chief, he slept well, as he told me later, and added, "Why not I sleep? Sleep good medicine."

Early in the morning the ship again got under way, but we were not allowed on deck. Later in the morning, the carpenter and his mate came down and, much to my surprise, put irons on Tomah's wrists. To this he submitted without a struggle or murmur, though I could see he expected yet further indignities.

When the carpenter and his mate had gone, I sat down beside the chief and did what I could to comfort him. I assured him he was not to be tortured. Rather did I suspect that he was to be sold with the rest of us to the planters. This seemed to hearten him, though he said that working in the fields was woman's work, not that of a warrior.

Two more days went by. Then, at nightfall, the ship was again brought to. We could feel a bumping against her side and wondered what it was all about. Another night passed.

At daybreak James McArthur came down with our breakfast and informed us that we had finally tied up to one of the wharves well up the River Susquehanah.

Barely had we finished eating when we were ordered on deck. As usual the light of day almost blinded me. However, in a few moments I was able to see clearly. There were several ships about us, some tied up, as we were, others anchored in midstream. Leading from the wharf was a long narrow street and the few hundred houses that made up the town. We were huddled together—a sorry-looking lot indeed—in the waist of the ship, dumbly awaiting our fate.

Imagine, if you can, some from workhouses, others from well-to-do homes, yet others from humble farmsteads; several leaving behind loving parents and brothers and sisters, transported across weary leagues of sea to a new world that held for most of us no smallest ray of hope in the way of freedom or happiness.

I wondered where the three maids were, but later learned that they had been sold to a wine merchant while we male children were still in the hold.

Presently the Captain came, accompanied by a burly, rough-faced man. "And here," cried Captain Barclay in a jovial voice, "here's the whole lot—thirty-three lads as hale and hearty in wind and limb as any I've brought over. Also,"—he pointed to Tomah—"the Indian I told you about. Tall, well-made—not yet middle-aged—he should bring a tidy figure."

The stranger looked us over, gave Tomah a keen glance, then said, "Good price, indeed! I'd give five times as much for another lad. Gadzooks! It's the same with Indians as with horses—you can neither make the one work, nor the other drink. However, I'll see what I can get for him." He called to a couple of men standing by. We were herded together and driven like sheep down the gangway to the wharf, thence along the dirty unpaved street, muddy from a recent rain.

As we shambled along pedestrians paused to gaze at us. And even women and children crowded to windows and doorways to see the procession. Tomah, his wrists ironed together, walked beside me. He carried himself straight and proudly, as though he were in very truth a king, rather than a captive doomed to an unknown fate. But I have found this to be a characteristic trait of these people, that all carry themselves proudly, and further indignities will but add to their proud bearing.

We passed several taverns. Finally, when we came to a large building, the door was unlocked and we were hustled in to a bare-looking room, and told to seat ourselves on benches beside a long table. We sat down, and I do not remember that any of us spoke. In a little while food was brought. A mug of ale, a small loaf of bread and a piece of cheese for each. "Now, lads," sang out the man Wilson, "fall to and eat, for you've got a long march ahead."

We needed no second bidding. The ale was very good, but to me somewhat heavy.

As soon as we had finished, we were led outside. Mr. Wilson mounted a horse, and we were told to follow him. The two helpers, armed with long whips, brought up the rear. Then we proceeded through the town. I noted that the roofs of the houses were not thatched or slated as the majority of those in Aberdeen, but shingled with wood, and some even painted. Many of the dwellings were quite large, and there was an air of prosperity on all sides that amazed me. I saw several negroes, black as coal and with white teeth between their full lips, working in the gardens next the houses. They stared at us and smiled good-naturedly.

On the outskirts of the town our guide took a road leading away from the river. It was flanked by a line of great trees utterly strange to me. The houses now were farther apart, with wide fields in which slaves were working. They were all barefooted, garbed in cotton trousers and shirts. A white overseer carrying a whip, and a pistol stuck in his belt, was in charge of each batch of slaves.

I had on the pair of shoes, much too big for my feet, given me by the cabin boy when I first boarded the *Bon Accord*. Soon my heels began to blister, and I had much ado to keep up with my companions. I lagged behind, and paused, with the intention of taking them off. But the voice of one of the helpers, "Get along there, you!" and the lash of his whip whistling about my ears, caused me to leap ahead with alacrity. And thus, for a while, I endured the pain—like a hot iron—with each step I took. But suddenly, being no longer able to endure it, I lifted up one foot, tore the shoe off and threw it from me, then I did likewise with the other.

The sun beat down mercilessly. Used to a colder climate, my face and body were soon a-sweat, and my head began to ache. But my companions suffered too with the heat, so I made no protest. Indeed, it would not have helped me. My feet were soon bruised, but I limped along as best I could.

I wondered how far we were going. In the far distance I could see an immense forest; beyond it, high mountains. Once two gaily-dressed horsemen, each with a pistol at his saddle-bow, and a sword at his side, clattered up in a cloud of dust, cried a greeting to our guide, and dashed on in the direction of the town.

How many hours we journeyed I know not. But we must have walked more than a dozen miles when we came to a big dwelling-house, with great white pillars supporting a sloping roof. On either side stretched wide fields, in which slaves worked. A couple of hundred yards to the right of the house was a large shed-like building that I learned later was used for curing and storing tobacco. Surrounding this were other large buildings, and in front more than a score of low, white-washed cabins, each capable of housing four or five workers.

We followed our guide down a wide lane and brought up in front of the pillared house. A man was seated on a chair smoking the longest-stemmed pipe I had ever seen. Seeing us, he lazily rose, spoke affably to Mr. Wilson, then came down the steps. His keen eyes swept over us, rested upon Tomah a few moments. Then he turned to Mr. Wilson. "A likely-looking lot of lads," he said; "but where did you get the redskin?"

Mr. Wilson told what he knew about Tomah.

"Ah," said the other, "an Algonkin from Acadia! Well, I'll take him, but I won't give much for him. As a rule a male Indian is too proud to do manual labour." Then, with a low laugh, "Yet I fancy my overseer will be able to get something out of him." He addressed himself to the two helpers. "Turn them over to Mr. Forsyte. Come in, Wilson, and we'll settle our account over a glass of wine. Ah, just a moment!" His keen black eyes rested on us. "Look here, lads, I've purchased you for a term of seven years. You'll have good housing, good food, and if you do your work well, good treatment. If you give trouble, my overseer will make you suffer. All right, men, take them away out of my sight."

Like a flock of sheep we were driven along a wide path to the big shed near the cabins. What emotions filled the breasts of my companions I know not. My own heart was heavy with humiliation and a great longing for my own land. Seven years of bondage was anything but a pleasing prospect. That was to be the lot of the others, at least; and mine too, should James McArthur fail in the promise to deliver my letter to Doctor Malcolm.

At the door of the shed stood a tall, very thin-faced man. His blue-grey eyes, that made me think of sharp-pointed icicles, ran quickly over us. He was Mr. Forsyte, the head overseer of the plantation.

"By my soul," he cried, "a dirty lot! Take them to the pump, Gill, and see they make themselves presentable. Then give them something to eat, and show them their cabins." He paused, glanced at Tomah, towering above us, then added, "Have the smith iron the redskin's ankle, and fasten a cannonball to it, or he'll be making for the forest the first opportunity." Then, turning on his heel, he strode off. A cold, heartless man, I thought, if ever there was one.

We were led to a pump, and a long wooden trough, filled with greasy-looking water, and told to wash.

It almost made me ill to think of the many others who had performed their ablutions in this place. Yet there was nothing to do but obey. A few cotton towels hung on a post nearby, and we were told to dry ourselves. Then we were taken to the dining-shed.

The dining-shed was a big room. We sat on benches at long tables. I think, counting our own company, fully a hundred slaves were present. There were several whites, but the majority were negroes, black as ebony, and with full lips that readily parted in laughter. Some were old and wrinkled, with white woolly hair. The speech of these negroes was soft and drawling. They ate heartily and with enjoyment. The food consisted of some kind of stewed meat, in which were boiled peas and beans. And there were big pewter platters piled high with hunks of golden coloured bread, that I later learned was made from ground corn. Our spoons and forks were of pewter, and we drank water from great pewter mugs.

After the meal, Tomah was led to the smith by Giles and another helper. The rest of us newcomers were divided among the empty cabins. They contained several rude cots. On each was a straw-filled mattress and a blanket. I laid myself down on mine and stared ruefully at the single iron-barred window, through which shone the waning light of evening. Tired I was, mentally and physically, and my poor bruised feet burned as though seared with a hot iron.

A little later the door opened. I heard the clanking of a chain, a rumbling over the floor of some heavy object. I looked. Tomah had entered. A band of iron, with a long chain attached to a cannon-ball, had been fastened about one ankle. And yet he carried himself with a dignity I cannot describe.

Giles, the keeper, watched him a moment; then, with a broad grin at us, banged the door to and left us alone.

There was a vacant cot near the window on my left. Tomah sat down on it. I reached out, touched his hand. "I'm sorry they have used you this way," I said.

He smiled, and his eyes glittered with a strange light. Then he bent, drew the cannon-ball to him by its chain, picked it up in his long fingers, then said slowly, "Maybe some day it make a good war-club, P'sazum," and he let it fall with a thud to the floor. That night he told me he would some day make his escape.

That evening, for the first time in my life, I heard the voices of negroes united in song. It came from the cabin next ours. First a single voice was raised in a low tuneful chant. Then others joined in, and the chorus swelled in volume, bass and tenor and baritone keeping time like the best-trained singers. I had heard some of the sailors on the *Bon Accord* sing their shanties, but the harmony as well as the quality of the negro voices surpassed theirs a hundred-fold. The song ended, they began another, more lively, accompanying it with a strange tapping sound that, I later learned, was made by striking the floor with the tips of their fingers.

Song after song followed. Then someone danced, was joined by others. They seemed happy. Suddenly a horn blew and a voice outside cried, "All a-bed! All quiet!" And in a short time silence reigned over the plantation cabins. I said a prayer and tried to compose myself to sleep, but the air in the cabin was so suffocatingly hot my whole body was a-sweat. I could hear some of my companions twisting and moaning in discomfort; others snored peacefully. From afar came the hoot of an owl, and there were uncanny flutterings against the small window, the sound of a mouse gnawing in a corner. For a long time I tried to sleep, then I got up and groped my way to the door, hoping to open it and get a breath of fresh air. But though I pulled at the latch with all my strength the door refused to open. I later learned that it was a customary precaution to bolt the door on the outside for a few nights until new arrivals got used to their surroundings. I went back to my hard cot. As I lay down I heard a crash of thunder, then saw a flash of lightning. It awoke one of the sleepers, who, poor lad, no doubt thinking he was still on board the *Bon Accord*, and that she was fighting an enemy, cried out to know if the broadside had hit us.

"Keep quiet, you fool!" cried another. "It's thunder you're hearing."

Then the thunder and lightning began in earnest. Clap after clap it came, rolling in mighty reverberations that shook the cabin, while bolts of lightning shot from the heavens and made the interior of the cabin one sheet of reflected flame. I remember thinking that if the cabin were struck we would be burned alive, imprisoned as we were.

Every lad was, I think, more or less terrified. But I was ashamed to show fear in the presence of Tomah's stolid indifference to the raging elements. In our wanderings during days to come—wanderings that took us over many miles of wilderness, and finally separated us, only to unite us again under the strangest circumstances that ever befell human beings—I was to see further evidences of the man's stoic disdain of danger.

Presently rain began, accompanied by a terrific wind that drove it in sheets against the cabin, so that I feared it would be hurled over. In all my life I never heard thunder nor saw lightning so appalling. I would close my eyes at each crash and flash, only to open them involuntarily the next moment. Suddenly a dazzling discharge of lightning, more terrific than any hitherto, tore out of the heavens with a crash that caused us youngsters to jump from our cots, sure that the cabin had been struck. We ran to the door, falling over each other in our haste. Those in front tried to pull it open, shrieking that we were doomed. But Francis Burns, a stout sixteen-year-old lad, roared for silence. "We're not hit. Get back to your beds, and don't act like a lot of ninnies," he told us scornfully.

Ashamed, we did his bidding. It was the end of the storm. Like a disgruntled and beaten monster, it retreated eastward. The wind ceased and the rain. The air in the cabin was cooler. We slept.

CHAPTER 8

The Tobacco Field

We were aroused at daybreak by the blowing of a horn. Then one of the overseers unbolted and opened our door. He told us to repair at once to the wash trough. Going out I saw a big tree lying across the driveway. The lightning had struck its top and riven it in twain to the very roots. We assembled at the troughs, into which we pumped fresh water, and washed ourselves. Each of us had been given a cotton towel. The overseer stood by until we had finished. "Now, boys," he said, "hurry to the dining-shed." We did his bidding readily enough.

After breakfast we were each given a hoe and taken to the tobacco fields that stretched on either side. But we were not to labour together. Each new boy was paired off with one of the old hands to learn the art of cultivating the young plants already three or four inches above ground. My companion was an old white-haired negro, whose talk in the following days interested me greatly. He was most kind to me. All the negroes worked barefooted. This old man's feet were very long, the toes splayed out, so that the extremities looked duck-like.

"Now, you boy," he said, "you watch Reuben. Yas" (he pronounced it "yer-ahs"), "Reuben Twaite's my name; same as Massa Captain's. I been his boy twenty-five years." He seemed proud of his length of service. "You see dese plants dat hab four, five, six leaves? Dey's tobacco. Now dese,"—he bent and plucked from the row a quite different plant—"dese is weeds. We throw dem away. Den we loose the earth all about de tobacco plants—dis way." With the blade of his hoe he carefully loosened up the soil. "You be careful, boy," he advised me, with a slow smile, "an' not cut de plant, or de overseer make your back hot."

I promised to do my best. I watched him a few moments with keen interest, then followed his example. An hour passed. The sun, now high in the sky, was boiling hot, and the sweat covered my face and body. Unused as I was to labour of any kind, I soon tired, and blisters raised on my palms. One of the overseers, whip in hand, came down the row, paused to watch my work, nodded and moved on. A few minutes later I heard his voice raised in fierce anger. I looked. First he addressed Francis Burns, a lad from Old Aberdeen, then the negro who worked with him, pointing his whip at one, then the other, then again at the tobacco plants. Before he left he gave Burns and the negro a cut with the lash about the legs.

My companion said to me, "Dat Mose he not care how he work. He git dat boy in trubble."

Some time later I heard a great yelping and barking in the direction of the great house. I glanced up and saw a man on horseback gallop up the lane to the high road, half a dozen big dogs strung out behind him.

"Dem's de houns," explained old Reuben. "Massa Captain he takin' 'em for exercise. Yas, dem houns is valuable dawgs. Dey can track a slave no matter where he go." He went on to explain that occasionally a slave ran away, and then the hounds were put on his trail. "Oh, yas," he added, "dey allus find him, no matter where he hide. Yas, de overseer he rings dat bell," (he pointed to a bell I had noticed above the drying-shed) "an' everyone far an' near knows dat a slave has escaped, an' is on de watch. No, Dugal, it ain't no use to run away." I shivered, and thought of Tomah's promise some day to make his escape.

Tomah was working at the lower end of the field. I could see him, hoe in hand, beside a brawny negro who had been detailed to instruct him in the work. He had discarded the clothing he wore aboard ship, and was utterly naked save for a pair of cotton trousers the overseer had given him.

On his chest had been tattooed a fish—a salmon (*bulam*, Tomah had called it). Its body was arched as in the act of leaping, as I had seen them on the upper Dee waters going over the weirs to the spawning grounds.

When he moved beyond the length of chain, he dragged the cannon ball behind him.

My companion talked as he laboured. He told me he had been born in Africa, on the Guinea coast. He had been captured by a slaver and brought to America twenty-five years before. He was treated well by his master and quite happy. "Where you come from, boy Dugal?" he asked.

I told him my name was not Dugal, but David. Then about my home in Aberdeen, and how I had been kidnapped. "If I were home," I added, "I could buy a house and plantation as big as Captain Thwaite's."

He half turned, rolled his eyes at me so that the black eyeballs looked even larger in the surrounding whites. Then he exclaimed, "Lord-a-Massy, boy! Dat some big story you tell ole Reuben!" and gave a low chuckle.

I flushed, but assured him it was all true.

He made no further comment, but shook his white head for several moments, his bent shoulders shaking with repressed mirth. Then, no doubt seeing my hurt expression, he said gently, "All right, boy. All right, Davy. You git to work now, or Massa Gill he come rampin' back an' make trouble."

I did his bidding. The sweat dropped from my brow, ran into my eyes, almost blinding me. My back ached so that I could only with difficulty straighten it after I had bent to pluck a weed. Oh, thought I, must I go on like this day after day, week after week? What if, in storm or battle, James McArthur should meet death, and my letter never reach its destination! The thought horrified me. If in a few months no one came to purchase my release, would it be possible to bribe someone going overseas to take another message? Small hope of that; little chance indeed for a slave boy to find means of carrying out such a plan.

Once, bending to pluck a weed, my hand almost touched a coiled black snake. I let out a yell and leaped back to pick up my hoe. But old Reuben reached out with his sharp hoe and cut the reptile in two.

"You watch out for dem critters, boy Davy," he said. "If dat one bite you, you good as daid."

I shuddered and thenceforth kept a sharp look-out for snakes.

It seemed ages before the horn blew for the noonday meal. But blow it finally did. Again we washed. I had a few moments' talk with Tomah, asking him if he found his work difficult. He answered by saying it was woman's work. A man's was to hunt game, trap fur-bearing animals, and go on the war-path.

Again we ate. Again we trooped back to the fields. The sun's rays grew hotter, the blisters on my hands bigger, and finally broke. I wondered if the day would ever end.

Old Reuben talked a great deal. He told me his master was very wealthy, sending every year to England many thousands of pounds of tobacco. He liked fighting too, and more than once had taken part in expeditions against troublesome Indians. The old man spoke contemptuously about Indians, though he seemed in some fear of them. He told me they scalped their enemies, put them to torture, and then ate them. The country, he said, would never be at peace until they were all killed off. I listened, but did not believe all he told me. His talk somewhat helped me to forget how weary I was.

Late that afternoon I saw a black man whipped. He was tied to a post in full view of us. His shirt was stripped from his back and one of the overseers laid on with a whip. The poor creature bore it some moments, then roared with pain. Finally, a pail of water was thrown over his back. He was untied and ordered back to the field. The only remark old Reuben made was, "Dat Gill fellah he got a mighty strong arm, so he hab."

The whole affair made me ill.

An hour later the horn blew to cease work, and I stumbled back with Reuben to the wash troughs. We washed and had our evening meal.

That night I had difficulty getting to sleep, tired though I was with my first day's toil. For a long time I lay on my hard mattress turning over in my mind the events of the day, and listening to the chants of the negroes. Some of their songs were English, others in their African tongue. And though I knew not the words of the latter, there was something about them strangely wild and primitive, recalling to my mind tales I had read of rites performed by witch doctors in dark jungles, to ward off disease or bring good luck.

Finally I slept, and it seemed only a few hours until the horn again awakened us.

CHAPTER 9

Tomah Whipped

There were several female slaves on Captain Thwaite's plantation. They were the black wives of negroes, and children, a dozen or more, from bairns in arms to lads and lasses. The latter old enough to work joined their parents in the tobacco fields.

I saw little of my master or his family. He had two daughters, now young women, and a son my own age. The latter had a tutor, and a riding master. Occasionally I saw them galloping along the highroad, or across the uncultivated fields, and longed to be in a position to join in such joyous exercise.

The days passed, and the weeks. Only occasionally did it rain during the day. On such rare times we did not work. But at night we often had heavy showers.

Sometimes there were gay parties in the great house. Ladies and gentlemen from the distant town and surrounding estates rode up, the former in gay crinolines, laces, and jewels, the men garbed in the latest London fashion. There was much feasting and drinking, and in the evening, music and dancing that often lasted until daybreak. On one occasion, two of the gentlemen quarrelled, and fought a duel with pistols by the light of the moon. One got a ball through the flesh of his right arm; the other had his cheek grazed. Each considered his honour satisfied, and they shook hands. I heard all about it later, and thought that if honour could so easily be satisfied, it were indeed a pity to jeopardize human lives by such a dangerous custom.

The tobacco plants were now more than six feet high, and near the flowering stage. Any suckers or shoots were watched for, carefully removed, each plant daily inspected for the presence of insects. If a leaf was injured, it was cut off, and everything done to ensure good healthy plants. Save for about a couple of acres that were to be allowed to grow seed for new stock, all the remainder of the plants were carefully watched. If they showed evidence of too early flowering, the buds were picked off. In September, the leaves took on a yellowish tint and began to droop. Now began the harvesting. Each plant was cut off close to the ground, the stalks spitted on long sharpened sticks and carried to the drying-shed. They were hung up, each stalk separate from its neighbour, and great care was taken that the leaves did not touch each other. We had dry weather. By mid-September, or a little later, the whole crop was in the sheds. And since none of the crop had suffered frost, Captain Thwaite and the head overseer were much pleased.

The tobacco all under cover, we slaves were put to gathering the ripe corn from the cornfield; the beans were pulled, carried to the granary and threshed by hand. Then began the fall ploughing.

All this done, we were divided into batches of ten or twelve, and taken to the wood-lot some two miles northward. Here for two or three weeks we laboured at cutting down trees and sawing them into suitable lengths to be hauled to the plantation. I enjoyed this work among the trees much more than any I had yet done. We cut hard wood and soft wood, and when it had been transported by oxen to its destination, we cut it into short pieces suitable for use in the fireplaces. Then all was neatly piled in long rows to dry until the following spring. I learned that each autumn, enough was cut to last six months, so that always the master had dry wood on hand.

I cannot describe my sensations whenever I saw a stranger ride down the driveway. Was this someone come from my guardian to buy my freedom? My heart would beat suffocatingly, and I waited in an agony of hope for one of the overseers to come and say, "Come on, David Cameron, you're wanted by the master." Then, when no one came, and the rider departed, I would actually feel ill for a spell, and tell myself that James McArthur had failed me. But, such is youth's unquenchable spirit, I soon recovered, and when the next stranger came, again lived over my golden hopes of freedom.

Winter came, with Christmas; a doleful one for me who only a year before had known a father's loving care.

The weeks and months passed. Spring again lay over the land, and, when all danger of frost was by, we went to the fields, removed the covering of straw from the old stalks, so that the sun could bestow its warmth and coax new plants from the roots. Thus we began a second season of slavery.

During the winter we had little news of the war, but now word reached us that the New Englanders were bent on capturing Louisburg, the great French fort in Cape Breton that controlled the St. Lawrence and was a constant menace to the English in Nova Scotia and the New England colonies. The New Englanders had asked for help from New York, Pennsylvania, and Virginia. But these colonies, being far removed from the French of Acadia, declared they had neither men nor treasure for such an enterprise, which they looked upon as a mad venture. What, they said, could a few thousand raw recruits do against a great fort, as strongly built as Dunkirk, and garrisoned by French regulars? So they sat by and watched with some amusement their kindred to the east prepare for one of the most romantic ventures in history.

Finally word came that they had sailed, and were joined by an English squadron under Admiral Warren. Days and weeks passed, and then, to the astonishment of the colonies, and the whole civilized world, came news that the few thousand rustics, commanded by Pepperel, had accomplished the seemingly impossible. Louisburg fell June, 1745.

I remember that Joel Venables, the carpenter, an old Yorkshireman, whose acquaintance I had lately made, declared it was the work of God, and now the French would be driven from Quebec and all of North America.

During rainy days I often visited Joel in his carpenter shed, where he was busy repairing wheelbarrows, fitting handles to hoes, and doing other jobs necessitated by a big plantation. He was a bluff, good-natured Puritan, much given to psalm singing and quoting from the scriptures. He was most kind to me; and no doubt feeling that I needed religious teaching in my rough surroundings, he tried to impress on me the necessity of constant prayer. He now loaned me a Bible to read during my spare time, and I assure you I did get much comfort from the yellowed pages. I hid it beneath the mattress of my cot. I remember well it was a very old book, and contained on one page the names of his father and mother and their children. On another page was written, "James Venables, died in ye cause of Christ ye a day of July at ye Battle of Marston Moor".

As my acquaintance with Joel ripened, and my assurance grew that for some reason James McArthur had failed me, I conceived the idea of getting Joel to write a letter for me to my guardian. But before I had mustered courage to broach the matter to him, that happened which was to send me forth on such a journey few lads of my age had ever undertaken.

It was the latter part of August; the tobacco crop daily neared the time of harvest. Ever since our coming, now almost a year and a half, Tomah had laboured, dragging about with him his cannon-ball and length of chain. Working, eating, or sleeping, it was his constant companion. Outwardly he maintained a stoical indifference, but I knew that his proud spirit chafed with resentment. One morning I was busily engaged inspecting my row of plants for insects, when I heard a commotion some distance away. I looked and saw Giles, the second overseer, plying the back of the chief with his long whip. Tomah made no outcry. This probably further enraged Giles. He laid on more heavily. Suddenly I saw Tomah leap forward, catch him about the waist, and fling him among the tall plants. There was a babble of voices, a moaning from the negroes. Giles sprang to his feet, whipped out a pistol and primed it. I fully expected he was going to shoot my friend. But he changed his mind. He called two of the other overseers—big strong men—who ran to his aid. They flung themselves on Tomah, tried to grasp him by the bare arms. But he was as sinewy as a mountain lion. And, like the mountain lion when cornered, he was fighting for his life. Evading one, he caught another about the middle and, as I had seen him do to the sailor aboard ship, lifted him bodily and sent him far over his head. Then he sprang back and bent to pick up the cannon-ball. If he had succeeded, I'm quite sure he would have brained his other assailants. But they were too quick for him. All three hurled themselves upon him. He was borne to the ground. Even yet he was not beaten. One after another he flung aside, and, had not some of the white slaves lent the overseers aid, he might again have got to his feet. But sheer weight of numbers turned the scale against him. His hands were pinioned. He was dragged to the whipping-post, tied to it, and the lash laid on his bare back by Giles.

I closed my eyes to shut out the sight. But I could hear the snap of the lash as it was drawn back, the unforgettable sound as each blow met the flesh. But no outcry fell from the lips of Tomah. Only the low voice of Old Reuben in my ear saying, "Dat injun fellah he got mighty tough hide; just like alligator." A few moments later he said, "Now Massa Forsyte see if he make him holler."

Then I looked. Already great weals showed on the chief's back. I saw Forsyte swing the lash over his shoulder and drive it forward. It fell with a sound like breaking glass. I could stand it no longer. Uncaring that I broke down tobacco plants, I ran across the rows to the whipping-post. Mr. Forsyte had already laid on with all his strength, and his arm was drawn back for yet another blow, when I sprang from behind, grasped the whip close to his hand, and held on to it with all my might. "Don't—don't beat him more, please!" I cried.

The strong arms of Giles seized me. I was dragged to one side, held firmly until Mr. Forsyte had completed his vile work. Then Tomah's hands were untied, he was pulled roughly away, and I was put in his place.

How I endured the lash I know not. I thought every bit of flesh on my back would be torn to ribbons. I gritted my teeth and endured as best I could. When finally I was released I fell in a faint. I was brought to by a pailful of water thrown over me.

That night I could not sleep for the pain. Whichever way I turned I could get no relief. On the next cot Tomah lay breathing quietly. Presently he reached out a hand and touched me, a comforting pressure that spoke volumes. Then in his own language he told me that we must try to escape. "Yes, P'sazum, I take you to my own people."

Every day since I had befriended him on the *Bon Accord*, he had been schooling me in the Maliseet tongue, and now I could speak it very well.

"All right, Tomah," I said, "I will go with you."

"*Ka-loo-ut*," he said. "Some day, P'sazum, you get a file from the old man that makes hoes—Joel, you call him. Don't let him know; hide it; bring it to Tomah. Now you go to sleep, P'sazum."

But I could not sleep, though now I was less conscious of my burning back. Of course, I knew that Tomah wanted the file to free him from the chain and cannon-ball. But even though I were able to secure one, and he had freed himself, how could we accomplish what so many had tried to do and failed? The mental picture of the great hounds on our trail caused my blood to run cold. And old Reuben's words came to me, "Oh, yas, dey sometimes gets away, but de houns allus finds dem."

When morning came I was dull-eyed and groggy, and as I ate my breakfast my brain was repeating "How can I get a file; how can I get a file?" over and over again. And I knew not any better than I had known at the start.

CHAPTER 10

We Escape

I knew there were any number of files in Joel's workshop, and, as I have already said, I frequently went there and talked with the old man. The problem that puzzled me was to steal a file and hide it on my person without his knowledge. Several times I thought of going to him and asking him for the loan of one; but I knew that he would guess for what purpose I wanted it and refuse me. Not because he would not want me to escape, but that his experience told him how futile it was, and, if I were not killed by the dogs, my life would be more miserable than now.

The very next noon hour, as we were all washing at the pump, I saw Joel outside his shop mending a wheel-barrow; and, as quick as a flash, a scheme popped into my head. Hardly waiting to dry myself I ran to our cabin, pulled out the Bible from under my mattress, and sped like the wind to Joel. He looked up, wiped the sweat from his brow with the back of his hairy hand, and said, "Eh, Dugal, lad, an' how are ye to-day?"

It was with difficulty I kept my voice from shaking as I said, "Quite well, I thank you, Mr. Venables." Then I added, "There are a few words in this chapter of Revelations I do not understand. Perhaps you will help me after you are through."

"Aye," he returned cheerily. "In a few minutes, Dugal, lad."

"Oh," I said, "don't hurry. May I—may I go in the tool-house out of the sun?"

"Aye," he answered. "Go in, lad. I'll be with you soon." And he hummed a hymn as he again bent to his task.

Although I had told him not to hurry, I hoped he would not be too long. We usually had about ten minutes before the horn sounded for dinner, and we were supposed to be at the table on time.

I entered the open door, my heart beating tumultuously. My eyes swept over his work-bench, littered with saws of different size, hammers, adzes and gouges, big and little nails, but to-day I could see no files anywhere. I glanced beneath the bench. Nothing there but a little lumber, scraps of iron, two or three augers. I could hear Joel outside say to himself, "There, that's well done."

My eyes swept back to the bench. There was a carpenter's leather apron that covered something that bulged. I thrust out my hand, drew the apron to one side, and saw a box in which were several of the coveted files. I seized one, glanced towards the door, saw old Joel's back still towards me, then thrust the file into my shirt-front and beneath my left arm. Barely was my hand withdrawn when he turned and entered the shop.

"Now, Dugal, lad, give me the good book, and I'll try to explain what bothers ye."

"The—the thirteenth chapter," I said haphazardly, as I gave him the Bible.

"Ah," he muttered, "the thirteenth? I know it well, lad. Many's the hour I've puzzled over it." He sat down on a low bench, opened the book at the desired page, and began to read:

"And I stood upon the sand of the sea, and saw a beast rise up out of the sea, having seven heads and ten horns, and upon his horns ten crowns, and upon his head the name of blasphemy." He ceased, looked up at me through his horn-rimmed glasses and shook his head solemnly. "Ah, Dugal," he said, "there be weighty matters hidden in this chapter. Coom to me on the Sabbath morning. Naay, coom in the afternoon, and we'll thresh the matter oot then."

I thanked him, feeling a hypocrite for the part I was playing. "I—I'll leave the book with you," I said. Then, the file clasped against my bare flesh, I ran back to the cabin. No one was there. I lifted the edge of my mattress, thrust the file beneath, and breathing a prayer of thanksgiving, I sped to the dining shed. All the other slaves were already seated. I found a place beside Tomah and received my helping of food.

"I have what you wanted me to get," I said to the chief in Maliseet.

His black eyes glittered with quick understanding. "*Ka-loo-ut* (good)," he answered.

That night, after dark had set in and we were all on our cots, I drew out the precious file and passed it to Tomah.

"*Wul-e-wun* (thank you), P'sazum," he said. A little later he told me to draw on my trousers, which I did as noiselessly as I could. I could hear the others snoring peacefully. Soon I heard the sound of the file against the chain that connected the cannon-ball to the iron anklet.

I could dimly see his long body sitting upright on his cot, the movement of his arm, as he filed back and forth. Once one of the lads cried out, "What's that noise?" The filing ceased. No one answered, and soon he was again asleep. The filing re-commenced; and now, to help cover the sound, I began snoring loudly.

But we were to have another interruption ere long. A lad, John Fraser by name, awakened, and said, "I say, Tomah, what are you doing?"

For a few moments Tomah made no reply. Then he whispered, "You be quiet, John. Tomah not like this iron ball. He take it off."

"Oh," mumbled the lad, "all right." Then he added in a whisper, "Are you going to run away?"

"Yes, John," came the low reply.

The lad sighed, murmured something to himself and made no further comment.

Perhaps another hour passed, maybe more. Suddenly Tomah reached out and touched my arm. "Come," he whispered.

I rose. He was on his feet. He took my arm to steady and guide me to the door.

At the door he paused to listen, then lifted the wooden latch and swung it gently open. In less time than it takes to tell we were outside, the door pulled-to behind us. A golden moon in its last quarter hung in the sky and with myriad stars made the night almost light as day. Around his waist Tomah had fastened a blanket. In his right hand he carried the cannon-ball with its length of chain about his arm.

He led me between our cabin and the next in line, then we stole along the rear of the others towards the drying-shed. Coming to it, a big form sprang up from before the door; a low growl fell on my ears. Why on this, of all nights, one of the dogs should be abroad, I never knew. I could plainly see him, the great muscles on his shoulders standing upright. Then, as he rushed us, Tomah thrust me behind him. As the beast sprang, I heard a sickening thud, as the cannon ball crashed into its skull. The next moment Tomah had me by the hand and was rushing with me across one of the harvested grain fields. He had discarded the cannonball, and we ran easily, the night air cold on our faces.

I think we had gone fully a mile before Tomah slowed to a walk. It was well that he did so then, for my breath was coming hoarsely in my throat, and I do not think I could have much longer kept up the pace he had set. We passed through a little wood, saw a house near-by, and making a detour, left it behind. We said no words. We alternately walked and ran. We were both barefoot. I had on nothing but cotton shirt and trousers; Tomah was clad only in trousers. I wondered in what direction we were going, but asked no questions. Time and again we passed dwellings, the occupants reposing in sleep. After a while the houses became fewer, and finally we saw no more. Coming to a growth of forest, we saw a brook winding among the trees and tall grass. Tomah stepped into the brook and I followed. The water was icy-cold. We splashed along its sandy bottom for several hundred yards, then Tomah climbed the bank, helped me up, and we proceeded onward through the forest. The moon sank, leaving the world dark save for the many stars shining above the tree-tops. My companion now took my hand in his; otherwise I had lost him in that dark place. My feet were bruised. I often stumbled, would have fallen but for his protecting grasp. The great trunks of trees leaped up in front of us; branches tore at our arms, our faces; and finally it seemed to me our adventure was part of an impossible and horrible dream. My knees began trembling with fatigue, yet resolutely I held on.

Finally we again came to a brook. Tomah paused, bent over, and with cupped hands lifted up cooling water and dashed it in my face. Then he said, "Drink, P'sazum." He knelt down, leaned his mouth over the brook, and sucked it in. I followed his example, and was refreshed mightily. Then Tomah stretched himself on the bank and drew me down beside him. In a few moments I was sound asleep.

I do not think that Tomah slept. At any rate, it seemed only a few minutes, as it actually was, until he roused me. Again we moved on through the dark forest. Only a few times did my friend and guide pause, glance upward at the stars, then go on again.

Some time later the stars paled; daylight filtered into the forest. As it lightened, I saw that grasses and shrubs were covered with heavy dew. It was now much easier travelling. We walked at a sharp pace. Once, to the right, I heard a twig break, then something white upflung as a big, reddish-coloured animal leaped over a fallen log and disappeared from view.

"*A-took!*" said Tomah, his eyes glistening. The creature we had seen was a Virginia deer.

Suddenly, far off to our rear, came the faint clanging of a bell. And I knew that our escape had been discovered. Soon men and hounds would be on our trail. Tomah had heard it too. He quickened his pace to a run, I after him. On we dashed, over fallen trees, moss-covered and rotting with age; through ferns and tall grasses that whipped our faces. We entered a swamp thick with vines, splashed through pools of putrid-smelling water, and suddenly, without warning, came to the bank of a small stream. For a few minutes we rested, then followed along it northward.

Possibly an hour later we came to the edge of a little clearing. In front of a bark wigwam an Indian woman squatted beside a fire. Over it hung a blackened kettle. She was stirring something in it with a long wooden spoon. We remained behind a big tree, watching her. Presently a very old man came from the wigwam and sat down beside her. She dipped a wooden bowl into the kettle, gave it to him, then helped herself. The sight of them eating was agony to me, for I was very hungry. I looked hopefully at Tomah. He understood my want, but made a wry face. In a little while both the old people rose, spoke together. The woman lifted the kettle from the coals, set it to one side, picked up a basket, and then they both walked down a path towards the river.

Tomah faces the bloodhounds

When they were out of sight, Tomah told me to remain where I was. Light-footed, swift as a cat, he stole across the open space to the fire. Picking up one of the discarded bowls, he filled it to overflowing, then turned, paused, picked up something from the ground and came back to me. As he drew nearer I saw that he carried a small iron hatchet.

His black eyes glistened as he led me a few yards back among the trees. Sitting down, he bade me eat of the mess. Tomah said it was rabbit and fish stewed together. He emptied half of the stew on to a broad leaf he plucked from a low bush, and handed me the remainder in the bowl. We used our fingers to convey it to our mouths. He seemed highly pleased with the hatchet, said it was a good *Tomahegan* of English make. It had a long thin blade, with a handle of seasoned wood, about eighteen inches long, wound with rawhide to give it a good grip. A thong was looped about the handle.

As soon as we had finished the food, Tomah left the bowl at the edge of the clearing. Then we circled back of the cabin, found a well-worn path and followed it northward. The country was flat, and covered with great trees whose names I did not know. Once we saw a big snake, its tail wound about a low-hung limb, its head a few inches from the ground. We passed it at a safe distance. Bright-plumaged birds flashed from tree to tree, or sang their sweet songs. From a pond on our left a great crane rose with a squawk of alarm and flew over the tree-tops. Two or three hours passed. Suddenly, behind us, came the bell-like baying of a hound, then another. The blood seemed to freeze in my veins and my hair to stand on end. Tomah seized my hand and we ran as fast as we could. Finally, he stopped beside a big tree, whose broad limbs spread out over the water. He dropped the blanket, then lifted me bodily high above his head. "Climb, P'sazum," he said. I seized a limb and did so without question, expecting him to follow me. Instead, he stepped into the shallow shore water, waded out until it came to his thighs, then turned, facing the shore.

Wonderingly I gazed down at him. He held the tomahawk in his right hand, the loop of rawhide about his wrist; and suddenly it came to me that he now was at greater advantage to meet the hounds than if he had remained on land. But what of the men, who could shoot him down from the bank?

Again I heard one of the creatures give loud tongue, so near I clutched in terror the limb above that which I sat upon. Then came the pattering of feet straight towards the river. A few moments later three hounds, the leader nosing the ground, came into view. In less time than it takes to tell, they were beneath my tree. Would they be followed next by the overseers? But I had little time to think. I saw the beasts, their heavy jowls flecked with slaver, pause, nose about the blanket, then go straight to the edge of the water. Then, as they saw Tomah, all set up such a chorus of yelps as I had never before heard. Then, with one accord, they jumped into the water and went with enormous leaps towards the chief. They spumed up the water ahead of them, each eager to be the first to reach that waiting figure.

Even at this late day it all comes back to me, and I find my old hand trembling as I write these words. I see the tall figure of the Chief, one foot advanced ahead of the other, the sharp-bladed tomahawk ready to strike. I see the beasts, now swimming, heads high out of the water. I see the dog in the lead come close to Tomah, then the axe descend. The blade clove the head like a rotten pumpkin. Then, as another neared him, the third swung below, and approached the Chief from the left flank. Again the blade descended, and the second hound was despatched. The third was now almost upon Tomah. I saw it hurl itself bodily out of the water, its great fangs bared, its eyes like coals of fire. The Chief swung the hatchet, missed, and, losing his footing, he fell against the beast. For a few moments they struggled together, then both disappeared from my sight beneath the water. I let out a groan of anguish. Then the head of Tomah appeared, his dark shoulders glistening with water. He found footing. Thank God he still retained his hatchet. Now the hound was again nearing him. Again it flung its muscular body half out of the water. The Chief braced himself for the onslaught. I saw his axe describe a sweeping blow, heard a muffled yelp as the blade shore through cheek and muzzle. It fell backward, struggling feebly. The water was dyed red with its blood as it went floating down stream.

In a moment Tomah was beside me. He reached up, lifted me down beside him. Then he sat on the mossy sward, breathing heavily.

I glanced backward fearfully. "The men—?" I faltered. "Will they not come?"

He shook his head, then told me that, thanks to our early start and the fact that we had travelled almost constantly, we had long since outdistanced them. That was why they had unleashed three of the dogs on our trail, hoping that they would pull us down.

"But," said I, "they have two more dogs!"

"Yes," and Tomah nodded composedly. "They keep 'em. By'm-bye they come. We be long time away." He rose to his feet. "We go now."

Some time later we forded the stream and went on.

CHAPTER 11

The Journey

For hours we travelled. We saw a rabbit, which Tomah killed with a well-aimed rock. He carried it by the hind legs, its head swinging from side to side, like something on a string. The sun sank lower, but still my guide and friend persisted onward. Dusk was settling over the world as we reached the lower slope of a quite high ridge. Taking my hand in his, the Chief helped me to the summit. Far off, through the trees on our left, we could see a large river which I now believe was the Susquehanah. North of us were more forested ridges—a vast and dark wilderness that filled me with unspeakable awe. Nowhere could we see smoke or sign of habitation of man.

We went down the north slope of this ridge. Presently, coming to a little hollow, Tomah said we would stop here for the night. First he raked aside some of the fallen leaves, then laid a circle of small boulders, and picking up several of the dried branches that littered the ground, he broke them into small pieces and placed them within the circle. Now he went to a fallen tree, and presently came back with a handful of dried punk. Then he took out of his little bag the piece of mineral stone, and holding the tomahawk in his left hand, he struck that part of it farthest from the blade a succession of quick glancing blows. After a little while, sparks began to fall, first a few, then, as his blows became more rapid, a continuous shower. All the while he kept blowing on the punk, and presently I saw a tiny circle of red that slowly grew larger, then a thin spiral of smoke. Now Tomah laid on some dried leaves, still blowing, and the whole soon burst into flame. Carefully he moved it beneath the sticks, and in a few moments they were crackling merrily.

He now took the rabbit, and in less time than it takes to tell had it skinned and disembowelled. I watched all he did with great interest. First he cut off the hind quarters, then such other flesh as he wanted to save.

Then he cut two small green limbs from a shrub, and sharpened the end of each. These pointed spits he thrust through the pieces of flesh. When I realized what he intended doing, I said, "Let me do one, please." He smiled and handed me one of the spits. It was quite some time before the meat was sufficiently browned. We had had nothing to eat since early morning, and I was almost famished. I found the flesh good, even though it lacked salt.

When we had finished, Tomah put a few more sticks on the fire and bade me lie down close to it. Which done, he laid over me the blanket he had brought. Then he took his axe, and stepping to a nearby sapling, about two inches through, he cut it down, trimmed off the branches, and cut off a five-foot length. It was now quite dark, but by the light from the fire I watched him a little while hewing at the piece he had cut. Then, unable longer to keep awake, I fell into a sound sleep.

Later I was conscious of him beside me, one arm thrown about my shoulder. I snuggled closer to him for warmth and companionship.

When I awakened, day was dawning. I was woefully cold. I glanced about me, saw Tomah seated a few feet distant, fashioning something with his little axe. Stiff in limb, I rose and went to him. He glanced up, smiled, then said, "Last night I make bow; now I make arrows." As he spoke, he laid down the hatchet, and using knife and file that had already served us so well, he deftly fashioned the arrow shaft he had roughly shaped. At his side were three others, and the bow, strung and ready for use. I asked him where he had got the string. He gave a low laugh and pointed to his leather belt. I saw it was now a third less than its original width. The bow, he told me, was of elm wood, very springy and tough. He was sorry, he said, that we had no feathers for the arrow shafts.

The fourth shaft smoothened, he notched the end of each. Then he took the leg bones of the rabbit he had killed, and breaking them into suitable lengths, made them into sharp points, and fastened one to the end of each shaft. I marvelled at his ingenuity. Now he divided with me the remainder of the rabbit flesh he had roasted while I slept. When he had eaten, he said, "Now we go, P'sazum."

We crossed the valley, climbed the opposite ridge, and saw the sun pushing its red crest about the far horizon. In the foreview lay the river, the mist rising from its surface in smoke-like spirals. We pushed on. The only sound was that of our bare feet stirring up the fallen leaves. The hours passed; the sun reached its zenith. The day was uncomfortably hot, and the sweat trickled into my eyes. My feet and ankles were scratched and bleeding. This morning Tomah picked up the remains of a grouse that some animal or hawk had killed. He smiled and feathered his arrows as deftly as any fletcher could do it.

CHAPTER 12

Tomah kills a Deer

It was well past noon-day. We had passed through swampy ground and come out of it at the base of a gently sloping upland. Suddenly Tomah paused. I was almost on his heels, and he whispered, "Don't move, P'sazum."

I stopped instantly. I could hear a rustling among the leaves ahead; though I strained my eyes, I could see nothing. Tomah was fitting an arrow to his bow. He raised it, and his tawny forearm drew the feathered shaft to his right ear. Then I heard the twang of the bow string, the whistle of the released shaft. Now, at right angles up the slope, I saw a great deer speeding like the wind, to disappear behind a thicket of evergreen trees.

I gave a muffled "oh" of dismay, for I was afraid it had not been hit. Tomah had bounded away from me and was running up the hillside. I followed as fast as I could, came to a little hollow or valley that ran to the right, and saw Tomah some fifty yards in advance, standing and beckoning me to come on.

Even as I approached, while yet some distance away, I could see the deer down, lying on its side. When I came near, I saw that the arrow shaft had gone half through the creature's neck. It was a big buck, its horns four tines to a side, and only recently in the velvet, for in places some of it still clung in shreds.

Tomah's eyes sparkled. "Plenty meat now," he said, as he drew his knife to bleed the creature.

In a short while, Tomah had removed the hide from the hind quarters forward to where the ribs met the spinal column. Then he cut off this portion of hide and laid it to one side. Now he cut off about twenty pounds of the steak. As he worked he explained that we would not carry any bone, only meat. He said we would stay for a little and let the meat cool off. In the meantime he would make some straps. I thought he intended cutting up the hide for this purpose; but, taking his hatchet, he went to a small elm tree and cut two long strips of bark from its trunk.

Coming back he laid the hide hair down on the ground, and laid the meat on it. Then he folded the sides of the hide inward and upward and made a very neat bundle. This done, he tied it firmly together with one of the strips of elm bark. Then he tied the second piece of elm bark crosswise so that it formed a sort of strap.

Now—for Tomah said it would not be wise to eat any of the deer meat until it was several hours old—we finished the last pieces of rabbit we had brought with us. Then Tomah got me to hold up the bundle of meat, and as I did so he slipped his arms through the side straps of elm bark. The pack now reposed midway between and a little high on his shoulders. With a low chuckle he moved off.

I felt more cheerful than at any time since our escape. We were now far beyond our pursuers, and thanks to my companion, we were provided with food for many days to come.

We travelled all afternoon, pausing only to rest, or drink from spring or brook. I do not think that Tomah once failed to keep a sharp look-out. His eyes roved from left to right, and when any sound reached his quick ear, he stopped and stood like a statue until he was sure it was not made by man. But we saw no one, nor any sign save in a muddy bottom the imprint of a moccasin. Tomah stooped, examined it, felt it with the tips of his fingers, broke off a bit of the soil forced up by the weight of the owner of the moccasin. Then he said, "Old, maybe two, three days, P'sazum. See,"—he held out the bit of caked soil—"sun get at'm, make'm hard." But after this he went more warily, if that were possible.

That night we camped in a hollow between two big sandstone boulders about four feet high. Tomah said it was going to rain, and after he had opened the bundle of meat, he took his little axe and cut two forked stakes, about five feet long. Then he cut a ridge pole, forced the forked pieces into the ground, and laid the third, or ridge pole, within the forks of the two uprights. In a little while he had cut several more poles, which we carried back, and laid one end of each on the ground and against the ridge pole. This done, he cut several armfuls of hemlock, or fir boughs, which we laid over the framework of the roof and against the sides, leaving the front open. Then he cut two good heaps of boughs, and using only the tips, laid them inside the camp for a bed, or mattress.

Looking at it, I thought how snug and homey it was. It had taken only about fifteen or twenty minutes to make. And now Tomah made a little fire. We cooked some of our meat, and after we had eaten Tomah took his pipe, which he always carried in a small bag hanging about his neck, filled the bowl with tobacco and lighted it with a brand from the camp-fire. Then he seated himself, his rump resting on his heels, as I was later to find was a custom among the Indians. Often my mind goes back to those days, and I find myself dwelling with tenderness on this special evening: the little *p'twigan*, Tomah and myself seated in front of the friendly camp-fire, the tongues of flame leaping into the night, the myriad forest smells, mingled with the aroma of Tomah's pipe, as the Chief sat there, his dark eyes fixed on the fire, or lifting momentarily to search the night beyond it.

We talked of our journey to his own people. He said: "I know how to go to my country, but I don't know all the country between here and the Massachusetts, where friendly Indians live. Mohawks, they sometimes go away down the Hudson River, even as far as New York. Mohawks are bad Indians. Of course," he pointed out, "the Mohawks not harm *you*, P'sazum. Mohawks and English friends. But they enemies of Tomah. They like my scalp. If we could get beyond the Massachusetts, then not hard going. Most Indians friends." He named some of the tribes: the Kennebecks, Penobscots, Passamaquoddies. "They all *Wabanaki*" (as were the Maliseets, his own tribe). "*Wabanaki*," he explained, "mean people living towards the east, or where the sun gets up."

He reminded me that the French nation was a very strong one, and that the English could never take Quebec. The English were very cruel. "They must be," he added, "when they make slaves of their own people." I understood that he was thinking of my own captivity. But I made no reply until he suggested that when I grew older I must kill a great many English to take revenge for my sufferings. Then I told him I could never do that, no matter how badly I had been treated. I was about to add that, as the English had taken Louisburg, so would they take Quebec, but thought better of it, for I did not want to say anything to hurt him. So I changed the subject, asking him to tell me about the deer and other big animals in his own country, which he did, and I was very happy. As he talked, it began to rain, a gentle rain that soon put out our little fire. We had a good sleep, one of the best since our escape.

When morning dawned, it was still raining. It was more difficult making our fire, but Tomah found plenty of dry stuff, and in a short time had it going. We cooked some of the deer steak for our breakfast.

After we had eaten, Tomah took me into the woods a short distance, and coming to a big hemlock tree that had fallen the year before, he cut off pieces of the bark. These we took back and carefully overlapped on the roof of our camp.

This morning he removed the hair from the piece of deer hide. Then he scraped off all the fat from the inside. This done, he sprinkled first one side, then the other, with ashes, and picking up a flat piece of sandstone, he rubbed it back and forth over the hide, first one side, then the other. Then more ashes, more rubbing, and finally he kneaded it with his strong hands. At length, looking up at me, gazing so intently at what he was doing, he smiled and said, "I make'm moccasins for you, P'sazum."

"Oh!" I cried, delighted. "Thank you, Tomah."

He said the hide should be treated for several days. It was best made soft by rubbing in the brains of the deer, but what he was doing wouldn't be *Mutjeg-n* (too bad), for he could see that my feet were getting sore.

I asked him if he was not going to make moccasins for himself, but he answered no. He did not need them.

That afternoon he renewed his tanning. Finally, the hide was made as soft as he could get it in the time at our disposal; he measured my foot, made a few marks on the hide with a piece of charcoal, then cut out the forms.

It was interesting watching him. For thread he used slender thongs cut from some pieces of hide. He made an awl from the small limb of a tree, cutting it down at one end to a point as sharp as a stiletto.

When finished, the moccasins looked quite crude, but when finally he laced them about my bruised and lacerated feet, I was mightily proud of them and most grateful to my friend.

That night the weather cleared, and in the morning everything was covered with frost. Tomah led me to some chestnut trees, and searching about among the leaves beneath, we found a great many nuts. They were very good to the taste, but Tomah said they would be much better and sweeter if parched in some hot ashes.

I stuffed my one pocket with as many of the nuts as it would hold, and carried a fistful with me which, when we resumed our journey, I cracked and ate along the way.

All that day we travelled, pausing only at long intervals to rest or slake our thirst from brook or spring. I found my moccasins made the going much easier. By mid-afternoon Tomah bore more eastward than northward, and presently, coming in sight of a river, we saw a canoe with two men and a dog going with the current. We hid behind trees until they had passed from view, then proceeded to the river bank. The current flowed gently and the water seemed not deep. The opposite shore was perhaps one hundred and fifty yards distant.

Tomah now hunted about and found four or five dry trees which I helped him to drag to the shore and into the water. Then he bound them together with long withes, and laid over the logs several pieces of sapling. Having cut a long pole, he suggested I take off my moccasins and tie them about my neck, which I did without question, for I knew he had always a good reason for anything he asked me to do. We now boarded the raft. It sank alarmingly with our weight, but still floated and mercifully held together while Tomah carefully poled towards the opposite shore. When we had landed I breathed a prayer of thanksgiving. We marched into the woods several hundred yards and made camp in a deep thicket.

I shall never forget that night. There was frost again, and I slept ill, for I was but thinly clad with cotton trousers and shirt, and the one blanket we had was hardly sufficient to keep out the cold. I was heartily glad when day dawned and we were again on the move. It was now six days since our escape and, save for the day it rained, we had travelled constantly.

Each ridge we climbed seemed like the preceding. Sometimes, reaching the top of some high hill, we had a view of the surrounding country—a vast realm of forest stretching as far as the eye could see. Each swamp we passed through was a dismal repetition of a hundred others we had crossed. The sun rose, pursued its course, sank below the tree-tops, and night with its strange and weird sounds cloaked the world. Owl called to owl, seeming to ask, "Who—who are you?" Forest creatures moved stealthily past our camping-place; sometimes so near I fancied I could see their dark shapes and fiery eyes. Once, camping near a small pond, I heard a splashing about in the water. Suddenly there came a crashing noise, followed by a heavy thud that caused me to grasp Tomah's arm in fright. Then he said, "That *Kwabeet*. He fall big tree." I breathed a sigh of relief, for now I understood that it was beavers at work.

Some time during the early morning hours, I missed Tomah from my side. I called his name gently, but got no response. I could hear the beavers splashing in the pond, occasionally the odd, chattering grunts of the old beavers, or the squeals of the pups. I lay listening, wondering at Tomah's absence, and no little alarmed at being alone. What if some accident had befallen him? I did not dare go to sleep again. In a little while daylight filtered into the forest, and suddenly came a series of heavy splashes from the pond, followed by a human-like groan that seemed to freeze the blood in my veins. I sprang upright, trembling in every limb. Had some prowling Indian come upon Tomah and killed him? My first thought was to climb into the branches of the tree above me; the next to run from the place. Luckily I did not do the latter, or I had been completely lost in a few minutes. Then to my great relief I saw Tomah coming towards me, carrying a beaver by its paddle-shaped tail.

He seemed mightily pleased with himself as he threw it at my feet and told me he had shot it through the heart with one of his arrows. Sitting down on his haunches, he dressed the creature, cut off the hind quarters, and splitting the tail, was soon broiling it over a little fire he had made. "*Kwabeet* tail mighty good," he said, looking up at me.

I found it practically all fat, but it was a change from the deer meat, that, save for the nuts and grapes we gathered, had been our only food for some days past. Before we left this camp Tomah cut the beaver meat into strips, roasted it over the coals, then put it in the pack with the venison. That day we walked many miles, and when night came I was glad enough to stop.

CHAPTER 13

Taken by the Delawares

It was some days later. How many I know not, for I had lost all reckoning of time. We had crossed innumerable brooks and small streams, and now came to a large river. What name it had I know not, though I have reason to believe it was one of the branches of the Delaware. For when I asked Tomah if he was going down it, he said no, that if we did we would go back to the sea, and he wanted to keep to the woods.

As a matter of fact, I think we had been travelling pretty much due north until the last few days, and were now going in a north-easterly direction. At any rate the river which we now reached was too deep to ford, so we walked upward along its bank in the hope of finding some fallen logs with which to make a raft.

Suddenly, rounding a bend of the river trail, we came in full view of a clearing and several Indian wigwams on a level knoll some two hundred feet from the bank of the river. Tomah had quickly stepped behind the trunk of a great hemlock tree, and taking my arm began retracing our steps. We had gone but a few rods, however, when I heard the crack of a branch ahead of us. Looking up, I saw two half-naked Indians armed with guns and tomahawks. They stood in our path, not fifty feet distant. I clearly saw a tortoise that had been cleverly tattooed on the chest of one of them.

I think they were more surprised than we were. Yet for us to try to escape was useless. Up went Tomah's hands above his head, the open palm towards them. "*Quay—Quay!*" he said. "*Wul-ahs-tukw Sogomo.*"

They seemed to understand, for they approached and spoke some words to Tomah in their own tongue.

I heard Tomah reply, "*Tomah Sogomo. Wul-ahstukw. Wabanaki Maliseet.*" I knew he was telling them that he was Chief Tomah, a Maliseet of the east, and his particular dwelling-place the *Wul-ahs-tukw* River.

Then both came forward, and the Indian with the tortoise on his chest pointed to me. Tomah answered, "*Kamanok.*" (He is English.)

The fellow looked me all over, then said something to his companion. He immediately stepped ahead of us, and we were motioned by the other to follow, which we did. Thus, between them, we approached the village.

Never shall I forget the sensation we created as we entered the clearing. With one accord the men, women and children sprang to their feet; the latter—half-naked lads and lasses—clustered about us, staring with wide, curious eyes. I know that even to these children of the forest I must have presented a strange appearance. My shirt and trousers in rags, hair long and unkempt; my bare ankles and my moccasins caked with mud from the swamps.

But it was my hair that most caught their fancy—my hair that had caused me to be called "Red Cameron" by my schoolmates in Aberdeen.

These people—or should I say the children, for the adults were more courteous—crowded up close to me; and one, a tall lad, gingerly reached up and touched my hair. Then he ran into one of the lodges and brought out a dressed otter skin, and coming up close to me, held it out, at the same time pointing to my hair.

At first I did not understand what he meant. Then suddenly it dawned on me that he thought my hair was some sort of head-dress that could be put on or taken off at will. I smiled at him, being hard put to keep from downright laughter, and said to him, "Take it, *ne-dup* (friend)," and reaching up with one hand, I went through the gesture of lifting it off my head. At this he boldly reached up, seized hold of my hair and gave it a good tug. I uttered a little ouch of pain, at which all the grown-ups laughed. For they now realized that my hair was a part of me.

The lad looked sheepish, but bore me no enmity, as I had cause to know later.

Following this episode, the Indian with the tortoise on his chest spoke for a minute or two. When he had ended all the men sat down. Then one of the women filled a pipe with tobacco and brought it to him who had spoken, who was the chief of the band. He gravely took it, put the stem in his mouth, drew in a mouthful of smoke, expelled it, then handed it to Tomah. Tomah did likewise and passed it to me with the words, "Smoke, P'sazum."

I obeyed, though the smoke almost choked me. Then the Indian on my left took the pipe, and slowly, with much ceremony, it passed around the circle of men.

Now one of the squaws brought a wooden bowl filled with corn mush, and handed it to Tomah, along with a wooden spoon. Another performed the same service to me.

It was the first meal of grain I had had since our escape, and I ate it as fast as I could convey it to my mouth. Now a second dish was brought, filled with some kind of fish. Lastly a gourd with water, and we drank from it in turn.

Tomah now rose, and thanking the Chief for the kindness shown us, he asked if he would have one of his men take us across the river in a canoe.

At this, the Chief looked grave; then said that it was late afternoon. We must be tired from our journey. Therefore it would be wise to have a few days' rest. He must not go back to his people in Acadia and tell them that the Lenapè were not courteous to strangers.

Of course I did not understand all he said, nor did Tomah. But since the Delawares are a branch of the Algonkin stock, enough of the words were alike for Tomah and me to get the Chief's meaning readily. Moreover, having been told that I was English, of which language the Lenapè Chief knew some words, we got along very well, and made him understand how pleased we were to accept his hospitality.

There were probably two hundred people in this village. It was enclosed with a palisade of logs set upright into the ground, the earth piled about the base and the tops lashed together with roots and withes of trees. There were two doors or openings to this enclosed space, but they were very small, and one had to stoop and squeeze oneself to get in. Within the palisade were several bark houses, as many as there were families and their relatives. Thus there were sometimes as many as twenty people in one house. Their fires were built in the middle of the floor, the smoke escaping through two holes left at each end of the ridge pole, and by each fire were pots, bowls and spoons made of wood. They had each a knife, a little basket and a gourd for drinking-water.

That night I slept in the Chief's house, or wigwam. We slept on mats or rugs made from rushes, our feet towards the fire. And even though one of the half-dozen dogs that shared the dwelling persisted in snuggling close to me for warmth, or company, I know not which, I passed a quite comfortable night. Tomah stayed the night with the sub-chief in another wigwam.

The following morning, as we were eating our breakfast of boiled eels and bread made from ground corn, I heard a great hubbub from the wigwam next the Chief's—the groaning of a man in evident pain, intermingled with the voices of women. I glanced at the faces of those about me, but no one offered to explain what was amiss, and I did not ask.

In a very short time two squaws came into our abode carrying a great copper kettle which they placed over one of the fires. When it had reached the boiling-point they carried it out, and its place was taken by another copper kettle. In the meanwhile another squaw came in with a small kettle holding no more than a quart. Into this she put a handful of herbs, and having placed it over the coals, began slowly stirring the mixture with a wooden spoon until it had begun to simmer. Then she took it off and departed from the lodge.

Later in the morning, when we were outdoors, Tomah told me that a very revered old man, who in his day had been a great warrior, was sick and they were afraid he was dying, even though they had sweated and purged him. He said they had sent for a famous Shaman or medicine man from another village.

A little later this individual came bouncing up the path from the river. The upper part of his body was garbed in furs, the horns of a buck deer were lashed to his head, his face was painted with streaks of white and red and black, and his bare legs were also painted with strange symbols. Proceeding to the wigwam of the sick man, he began roaring and stamping his feet, pausing frequently to put a big conch shell to his mouth and blow upon it lustily, making the most hideous sounds I have ever heard.

Tomah seemed much impressed with the Shaman's noise and gesticulations, and assured me that he would doubtless work a cure. But I had more faith in the ministrations of the squaws, who continued to carry in kettles of hot water which were being employed to produce a sweat on the patient. It was a very old custom among most of the tribes of North America.

But in spite of the efforts of the squaws and the diabolical howling, dancing and conch blowing of the Shaman, the old fellow died that night. The squaws lamented the passing of their relative with sobbings and wailings, alternately beating their breasts and pulling at their hair, even cutting their own flesh with knives. I watched them for some time at their strange rites, then, horrified, and much in need of sleep, I laid myself down in the Chief's wigwam and went to sleep.

I learned that the dead man was later arrayed in a new suit of dressed buckskin, then swathed in rugs or mats made from rushes, and tied about with bark splints. The day of the funeral, or burial, he was put on a wooden stretcher. Beside him were his gun, tomahawk, knife, copper kettle and two earthen bowls. The stretcher was lifted up by four stalwart bearers, and the whole village following, Tomah and myself included, he was carried through the forest some two hundred yards to a sandy terrace where a trench had been dug.

After speeches by his male relatives, the body was reverently lowered into the grave, then the personal belongings together with some powdered red ochre, and the earth was filled in. Finally stones were heaped over the place to keep away wild animals and dogs. Then wood and bark were heaped on the grave and a fire lighted. For three days and nights the fire was kept burning, and the female kindred crouched around, their faces contorted, and sometimes howling or wailing their grief.

Both Tomah and I were now anxious to continue our journey. But when the matter of our going was broached to the Chief of the band, he said it would be most unwise for us to depart for some time yet. There were Iroquois war parties in our line of travel, and we might be captured and killed. When Tomah told me of this conversation, he admitted that he was far from easy in his mind as to what these people intended doing with us, but he greatly feared they might sell us as slaves to some other tribe. He added that we must soon try to make our escape, though this, he admitted, would be difficult. Not only were we surrounded by Indians all day long, but since our coming we continued to sleep in separate wigwams.

As a matter of fact, I do not now think that these people, though detaining us, intended doing us any bodily harm. Some years previous to this, the Iroquois, or Indians of the Long House, had thoroughly defeated and reduced the Lenapè nation to vassalage, and they had been compelled to sign a humiliating treaty that described them as women. The Lenapè, with a few exceptions, were pro-French. The Indians of the Long House espoused the cause of the English. So that, for any bodily injury done any English lad, the Iroquois would have exacted a terrible penalty in Lenapè lives.

One may wonder how such an injury done an English boy could have become known to a people living many leagues distant. My only answer is that history records such cases.

But even though the Lenapè held the Iroquois in abject fear, the fact that I was with Tomah would have been very much in our favour, for Tomah was Algonkin as they were. I therefore think that Tomah's fear of being sold by these people was unjustified. At any rate, it seemed that, for some reason, these people had taken a great fancy to me, and now that was to happen which caused the Chief and his whole band to regard me with a very great affection; so great, indeed, that he adopted me as his own son. It was in this wise: the Chief had a daughter, a little lass about seven years old. One day shortly after the funeral ceremonies were over, and the women were busy at their tasks, this little girl went down with several other children to play on the sandy beach beside the river.

For some time I sat and watched one of the squaws weaving a basket, then I arose and took the path to the shore. I had gone but a few yards into the timber when I heard terrified screams and a splashing in the water. I broke into a run and met a small lad who rushed past me towards the encampment.

Reaching the shore, I saw a child struggling in the water several yards from the edge of the sand bar. In a moment I dashed in, waded as far as I could, then began swimming towards her. While yet a few yards from her she threw up her hands and sank, to reappear an instant later and renew her struggles. She was sinking a second time, when I reached out and seized her by her long hair. Then began a struggle on my part to keep both of us above water, and on hers to clutch me about my neck. It seemed ages before help arrived, and I was quite nearing exhaustion when the Chief and another Indian dashed in and relieved me of my burden.

Soon we were all back on the shore. The little girl was emptied of the water she had taken in, carried to her father's wigwam, and covered with warm blankets. Before dark had fallen she was quite herself and playing about the camp-yard with the other children.

In the meantime I was the centre of an admiring crowd of Indians who, in turn, patted my shoulder and kept up a running commentary on my exploit, some of which, from my knowledge of Maliseet, I understood. And that night, men, squaws and children in a circle about me, I was the principal in a ceremony quite new to me.

The Chief arose and drawing himself to his full height, he made a long speech to the gathering, in which he told them how dearly he loved his little daughter, who but for the brave act of the white boy would now be dead, and his heart saddened for all time. He talked for fully ten minutes. When he had finished he took from his squaw a fringed shirt of dressed buckskin, gaily ornamented with coloured wampum beads, a thing very precious to these people. Then he took me by the hand, raised me to my feet, and put the shirt on me. Then his squaw gave him a pair of buckskin trousers, and these too he put on me. Now a reed mat was brought, and when I was seated on it, he put on my feet a very fine pair of moccasins ornamented with beads and dyed porcupine quills.

And, though I had eaten not more than two hours before, I was given a bowl filled with ground meal in which fish had been cooked. Not to be thought discourteous, I began eating, but I wondered how I should ever finish the mess. Remembering how Tomah had told me that to leave any food in your bowl was a sign that it was distasteful, I knew I must consume it all. Valiantly I did my duty, though I felt disgustingly gorged. Now I was handed a pipe which the Chief had filled with tobacco and lighted. I glanced at Tomah. He nodded encouragingly, so I took a puff, smothered a cough and gave it back to the Chief. Then the pipe passed around the circle of men, each one gravely taking a puff.

When all had finished, the Chief again raised me to my feet, embraced me and said:

"Now, *Kuluwazu P'sazum*, you are *my* son, and a member of our tribe."

I was a little dazed by all that had taken place, and quite proud of the honour conferred upon me. Now, I told myself, the Chief would allow Tomah and me to depart on our journey.

That night I was given an extra blanket, and from now on no one in the village could do enough for me. I was given the choicest meat and fish and allowed everything but freedom to depart from them. And how I knew this to be so I will tell you.

We had now been with these Lenapè people about two weeks. Tomah had made himself trousers and moccasins of buckskin. Now he again told the Chief that we must leave him.

The Chief looked troubled and gravely shook his head. Not only was winter coming on, but, as he repeated, the Iroquois were on the war-path, and it would be unwise for us to risk capture by them.

But Tomah insisted that we had stayed with him long enough, and it was time he was departing for his own country. At this the Lenapè Chief frowned and said:

"Is P'sazum your son?"

Tomah said no, but that I was as dear to him as a son.

Then said the Lenapè Chief, "He is my adopted son. We will make him a chief of the Lenapè. But you, Sogomo Tomah, you go, you stay, it is all the same to Uncas."

For a few moments Tomah looked puzzled and made no reply. I could see he was greatly worried. Finally, he said, "My brother is very wise. We will stay with his people." With which he lighted his pipe and solemnly passed it to the Lenapè Chief, who took a puff and gave it back to Tomah. And Tomah smoked and thereafter spoke not to the Chief of leaving.

With the passing of each day I had learned a great deal of the habits of these Lenapè.

I was especially interested in the making of their ashwood baskets. First a tree was felled and divided lengthwise, then these pieces were dealt a succession of heavy blows with the poll of an axe, which in turn separated the layers of wood in long thin strips. These strips the women now took and cut into thinner strips with long, sharp knives. When enough strips of the desired thinness and width were ready, the baskets were woven. Some were capable of holding a half-bushel, and were not decorated. But others, small ones for holding trinkets, were artistically dyed splendid colours with the juices they extracted from alder trees, sumach, and roots they dug from the ground. They also made beautiful little work-baskets for ladies in the distant English settlements, from sweet grass they had gathered and dried earlier in the year.

These Indians grew corn on a piece of cleared land at the back of the village. The grain was stored in ground-pits lined with bark. When they desired meal for cooking, they put the grains of corn into a great mortar hollowed from a tree, and with a long stone pestle ground them into meal. This work the squaws did, as indeed the greater part of all the work required, even to dragging in wood from the forest and cutting it into suitable lengths for camp-fires. Of course, the men killed and trapped the wild animals, but the women dressed the skins. That is, they skinned the animals, after which they stretched the skins on wooden frames, took off the hair with sharp knives, then with flint scrapers removed the fat. Now the skins were rubbed on both sides with round, flattened stones, fish oil rubbed in, and they then were kneaded until soft as velvet.

When not engaged in hunting, trapping or fishing, the men-folk often played a gambling game hour after hour. It was thus: they had several flat circular objects about the size of penny pieces, made from the leg bones of a deer. On one side of these button-like objects was painted a flowered design. These were put into a wooden bowl, like a plate, and, seated in a circle, first one, then the other of the Indians brought the bowl a sharp blow on the ground. The buttons sprang into the air, some alighting flower side up, others down. Each player was provided with a bundle of tiny sticks, eighty or more in number. How they counted I never was able to determine, but with each play sticks changed hands. Tomah knew the game, and told me his tribe played it a great deal, often gambling away all their belongings. He called the game *Al-stes-tug-in-uk*.

These Lenapè were good sports, accepting their losses and the laughter of those who looked on with the utmost good nature, so that I grew to have a great respect for them. I found them stoics regarding pain. If one accidentally cut himself with tomahawk or knife, he made no outcry, but preserved a dignified deportment. One day I saw an old man working at his mouth with the blade of a knife. In a little while he had pried out a big molar tooth, which he calmly dropped into the fire.

They had many herbs and simples they used for sickness. Some of them were the sassafras, the root of the water lily, berries of the staghorn sumach, and the bark of the cherry. They also used the life everlasting, of which they made a decoction for colds and for use in the sweat bath.

The days passed. The leaves of the trees turned bronze and gold and finally carpeted the ground three or four inches deep. Several of the hunters brought in deer carcasses. Some of the meat was immediately eaten, the remainder cut into long strips, the blood expelled by pounding with stone mauls, and then the meat was laid on a scaffolding over a small fire and thoroughly smoked for winter use. I was not averse to staying with these people during the winter, but I had hopes that by the spring the war would be over and I could coax the Chief into allowing me to depart from him.

CHAPTER 14

Winter; Spring

The first snowstorm filled me with delight and surprise. I had gone to sleep, and awakened in the morning to find the ground covered with white to a depth of three or four inches. It lay like ermine capes on the evergreen boughs, blanketed the frozen river, and when the sun came up, it sparkled like emeralds and rubies and diamonds, so that to look at all the white and glitter made my eyes water until they had become used to it. It was interesting to see the tracks of animals made during the night after this and succeeding storms, and speculate what beast had made this or that track. But soon I was able to distinguish a wildcat's from that of a fox, and to note that others were made by deer, otter, mink or weasel.

The nights now were cold. In each wigwam a new circle of stones was laid, and in the circle a fire kept burning day and night. The smoke drifted up and through a hole left in the roof for that purpose. We slept on a platform raised about a foot from the clay floor. But often the place was filled with smoke, so that my eyes ran water, and I almost choked with it. Times were that, did I not know I would freeze to death, I had taken my blanket and slept outdoors.

Many an hour during this winter I lay awake in great distress, not only from smoke, but I was infested with vermin, of which, however much I tried, I could not rid myself. The river was ice-covered, as I have said, and to get water a hole had to be cut. But I did manage to bathe myself, much to the amusement of the Indian boys.

It was discomforting these winter nights lying awake listening to the snoring of my companions, and possibly the wailing of a fretful baby in a nearby lodge. Or again, there would come from the forest the scream of some night-prowling animal, or the sharp, rifle-like sound of a tree bursting open with the frost.

But though to me it seemed that it could not be colder anywhere, I was to learn that the winter weather in this part of America was mild compared to that of Acadia in Tomah's country.

The men had now donned deer-skin coats or tunics, and some of them shirts they had got in trade from the distant English settlements.

Every day now parties went on the hunt, or on trapping expeditions, to the lakes and ponds northward. Several times I accompanied the Chief. He taught me the methods of trapping the fur-bearing animals, and instructed me in the habits of the forest creatures. In a short time I had picked up enough of his language to converse quite freely with him. Though Tomah was allowed to go with us on these trips, I was not allowed to separate myself from the Delaware Chief, the reason being that he was afraid Tomah might attempt to take me away. Indeed, the fellow showed me such evidences of affection that I had not been human had I failed to feel a sense of pride.

Occasionally we had a visitor in the person of a friendly Indian who paused long enough to rest, eat, exchange the news, and then depart on his way. One such, hauling a toboggan, remained two days and gave us tidings of the war. He said the English had burned their fort at Seraghtoga, and now the French and Canada Indians were carrying the hatchet to the very outskirts of Albany, and attacking settlers in Massachusetts and Connecticut. He said that the Iroquois allied to the English had been so disgusted with the burning of Seraghtoga that they had been loth to help further in the war. But now there was a new head among the English, by name of Johnston, who was so well thought of by the Mohawks that they made him a chief. Furthermore, the English government was paying one hundred pounds for every scalp taken.

When he had gone, several of the young men were for taking up arms with the English and earning scalp money. Although the Chief, Uncas, did not have the power to stop them, he strongly advised against becoming involved in the war. Moreover, he told them that their late visitor had confided to him that the scalp money was not always promptly paid.

Then he added scornfully, "The English in Virginia, Pennsylvania, and Maryland are not sending men or money to help their brothers in New York and Massachusetts in their war."

Though I was but a lad, and had been treated so cruelly by my own people, I burned with anger and indignation at the short-sighted policy of those colonies which, far removed from actual fear of the French and their red allies, refused to realize that if the New Englanders were defeated, *their* turn would come next. But such a desirable unity of purpose in opposing the French bid for Empire was not to come for a long time.

It sickened me, too, that our people should pay one hundred pounds for each scalp taken by their Indian allies. Of course, the French did the same, but to me this fact did not warrant our side doing it.

Slowly, oh, so slowly the winter passed, and I was heartily tired of it, when the snows departed and the rivers were freed of ice. How pleasant it was when finally the trees put out new leaves and the birds again broke into song.

Now I begged the Chief, Uncas, to allow me to depart with Tomah. But he said:

"You have no father, no mother. Wabanaki country long, long journey. Too far. You stay with Uncas. He make you a chief."

I told him that I had thought of the dangers of travel to the Wabanaki country; and now, if he would let me depart, I would go instead to a seaport on the coast, and take ship to England. I added that my father had left me a great deal of money, and if I were home I could have it all. At which he said: "Uncas got plenty corn, plenty venison. Beaver meadows near. We not be hungry—"

Nor, however much I reasoned with him, could he be made to realize that going home and claiming my inheritance might be more attractive to me than remaining his adopted son and having plenty of corn and meat to eat.

You may think this attitude of the Lenapè chief singular; but it is a matter of historical record that the aborigines of North America have very deep-seated affections, and have often been very loth to give up white children they have taken a fancy to.

He had already given me a gun, and instructed me in its use, and was as proud as I when finally I shot and killed a buck deer. Now he gave me his pet dog, and a crow he had caught and tamed, and to please me further, an eagle's feather for my hair.

I could see that Tomah was very anxious to be off. One day I mournfully told him to go to his own country, for never would I have a chance to leave these people. But he stubbornly shook his head and said, "No, P'sazum, Tomah will not leave you. Some day we escape."

CHAPTER 15

The Bear Hunt

The weeks passed. Summer came. In the cornfield at the back of the village, the stalks were three feet high, and the pumpkins daily growing larger and more yellow. And then, one day, one of the Indians who had gone a day's journey northward after elm bark for his canoe, returned and reported having seen three bears on a certain ridge.

Immediately Chief Uncas took six of his best hunters, and, with me beside him, armed with my new gun, we went in search of the bears.

It was mid-morning when we set out, and, late in the afternoon, being yet far from the ridge, we made camp for the night. The following morning we were up at daybreak, had breakfast, and marched on. Two or three hours later we came in sight of the ridge. Fire had run across the centre some years before, and the burned portion was now covered with raspberry bushes.

Uncas now divided his party. He told two to go westward, keep under cover of the trees, and approach the berry patch carefully. A third he sent northward of the ridge; the fourth was to approach from the south. Then, with me beside him, he struck eastward, his intention being to approach the berry patch from that quarter.

It was a stiff climb to the top of the slope. Often we had to grasp bushes to help ourselves up, but finally we reached the timber and began cautiously to work our way along the summit westward. Several times Uncas paused to examine the ground, and once, pointing to a footmark in a wet spot beside a spring brook, said it was a bear's track.

We were yet travelling in heavy timber, and carefully approaching the burnt-over area, when I heard a musket shot from the westward. Uncas examined the priming of his gun, and I did likewise to mine, hoping I would be lucky enough to get a shot at one of the creatures.

We pushed on slowly, looking on all sides. Beyond us I could see the tall trees that had been denuded of their foliage by the fire. Now came the sound of breaking brush. We paused, guns thrust forward to shoot. Then I saw two great bears rushing towards us. For a moment they disappeared behind a clump of bushes. I thought they had seen us, but presently I saw them on our left, tossing up the dry leaves as they ran. They evidently were making for the swamp at the southern base of the ridge. They moved so swiftly it was hard to centre the sights on them. Several times Uncas seemed about to pull the trigger of his gun, but on the instant they would disappear behind tree or boulder.

My heart was thumping madly, and so excited was I, my gun barrel wobbled this way and that. There was a little open space about fifty feet distant. The bears reached this and, quick as lightning, Uncas' gun bellowed. I saw one of the beasts give a tremendous leap. It fell, and rolled over and over, biting at its side, where the bullet had entered. Its mate was making down the slope. I aimed as best I could and fired. But the only result was a blow on my shoulder from the recoil that almost knocked me backwards.

Meanwhile Uncas was recharging his gun. I reloaded mine, and rammed home the charge as I had been taught. The bear Uncas had shot now lay quite still. The chief told me to climb to the top of a big boulder and await his return. I watched him disappear between the tree trunks down the ridge. Then I clambered up the side of the boulder and sat down on the top with my gun across my knees.

CHAPTER 16

Captured

The minutes passed. A squirrel scampered over the leaves, ran up a tree trunk, then, seeing me, perched itself on a dry limb and scolded at me. A flock of crows winged slowly from the swamp, swept overhead and disappeared. I glanced at the dead bear. It was lying on its side, the lips drawn back and the long teeth covered with blood.

Presently I heard heavy footsteps from the opposite side of the ridge, coming straight towards me. Was it another bear? Suddenly I caught sight of a dark object appearing and disappearing among the tree trunks. I raised my gun, pulled back the hammer and aimed it. I was about to press the trigger when to my surprise I saw one of our men break into full view. I almost dropped the piece. He never knew how near he had been to death!

He came straight on, following the trail of the bears. When he came near I spoke, told him where Uncas had gone. He nodded, glanced at the dead bear, then ran down the southern slope of the ridge. Again I was alone.

An hour or more passed. Hungry, at length I took some of the food from my pack and slowly munched it. It was dry eating. Presently I bethought me of the little spring brook Uncas and I had passed. Getting down from my perch, I walked back. It was much farther than I had thought, but at length I found it, and kneeling, bent and drank my fill. Then I started back to find my rock.

As I went I saw a ruffed grouse on my right. It was standing on a fallen log not far distant, and as I did not want to fire my gun at it, I picked up a rock about the size of my fist, stood the gun against the tree, and stole towards the bird. But hearing me, it flew off through the woods. I watched its flight, and thought I knew the spot where it had alighted. Quickly I went in that direction. But though I looked about on all sides I could not see it, so decided to retrace my steps to where I had stood my gun. Presently I came to a tiny brook. I thought it was the one from which I had drunk, so I jumped across it and ran on. In a few moments I reached a bunch of big hemlocks I had not remembered having passed through. The sky had darkened with clouds, and the forest was now gloomy and forbidding. Suddenly it came to me that I was lost, and in terror I started running. How far I went I know not. And then, to my great delight, I saw two Indians on my left. They were going in the same direction as I. At first I thought they were of our party, and was about to shout, when I realized they were strangers. Quick as a flash I ducked behind a tree trunk. I heard them pause. Then, as they changed their course and came towards me, my heart beat excitedly. I had a wild desire to run, but had I done so I had doubtless never lived to write this. I made myself as small as possible and hoped they would pass without seeing me.

Presently I heard footsteps on my right. I glanced up fearfully and looked into glistening eyes that shone from a painted face. The head was shaved save for a scalp lock, in which was a bedraggled hawk's feather. I sprang to my feet. Then his hand reached out and grasped me by the arm.

It was useless to struggle in that vice-like grip. He was now joined by his companion. They were both armed with gun, tomahawk, knife, and carried small knapsacks.

Then he who had seized me said something I did not understand, but I sensed that he was asking who I was. And, though my tongue felt dry in my mouth, I managed to say, "I am English."

They both looked startled, spoke a few words together, and pointed to my hair and my face. Then they both at once noticed my necklet of bear's teeth, which they examined carefully, talking the while among themselves. I was sore afraid they might take it from me, but after a little more palaver, they allowed me to keep it. I was most grateful, for I had rather parted with an ear. Then one of them said to me, in quite good English, "We will take you with us." He then tied a piece of rawhide about my arm, and taking the other end in his hand, he started ahead, his companion bringing up the rear.

I thought of Uncas when he returned and found me gone. Of course he would eventually find my gun, then discover the trail of the Indians and realize what had happened. I thought of Tomah, my more than friend, who had remained with the Lenapè rather than desert me. Who these strange Indians were, where they had come from, or whither bound, I knew not. Were they Canada Indians, or allies of the English? Their language was utterly foreign to me. All I knew was that I was a prisoner who had again changed masters.

They walked at a quick pace, finally coming to a well-worn trail. If I lagged a little, I was either reminded of the fact by a push from behind, or a tug on the thong from before, sometimes both. The trail wound over hills, down valleys; we crossed brooks, splashed through muddy bottoms. Often branches of alders, birch or hazel bushes whipped my face. I murmured not. Since my escape from the plantation I was well acquainted with such hardships. Moreover, my muscles and sinews were hardened like iron.

Once I thought I heard a musket shot behind us, and wondered if Uncas and his men had killed the other bear. If my captors heard it they gave no sign. Indeed, we could have gone no faster save by running.

We had travelled about two hours when I heard the sound of running water on our right; not that of a brook, but a great body of water. Presently my captors paused in a dense thicket of evergreens, and while one remained with me, the other branched off to the left.

My companion sat down on a fallen log and motioned me beside him. He took a pipe that he carried about his neck in a small pouch made from the skin of some animal, and filled it with tobacco from the same receptacle. Then with much labour with flint and steel, he ignited a bit of dry punk and finally got his pipe going. He drew in and expelled three or four mouthfuls of smoke, then proffered the pipe to me. I realized it was a friendly act, took one pull at the stem, thanked him in English and handed it back to him.

Soon I saw the other Indian returning. He carried a light bark canoe over his head, as I had seen the Delawares do. We joined him, and in a very few minutes reached the bank of a river. The canoe launched, we got in and paddled a diagonal course upstream towards the opposite shore.

Landing, one picked up the canoe, carried it into the woods and hid it, then returned. Each now opened his knapsack and took out some dried meat. They gave me a piece and I gladly ate it. They talked among themselves. I caught the Indian name *Schenectady*, then the English names Johnston, Albany and Clinton—the last the governor of New York. Johnston, I thought, must be that brilliant young man who, sent out to manage his uncle's estate along the Mohawk River, had gained such influence over the Mohawk Indians that they had made him a chief, and the English had made him commissioner of Indian affairs. My heart began to beat more hopefully. Doubtless my captors belonged to the Five Nations, for the most part allied to the English cause, and might be induced to turn me over to my countrymen.

The Mohawks, let me say, are the most easterly nation of the great Iroquoian Confederacy, known as the Five Nations, the only great body of Indians in North America allied to the English cause. The country of these Mohawks is reached from Albany, on the Hudson, by a march of about sixteen miles to the Mohawk River, where there is a carrying-place and a small trading-post called Schenectady. Here the trail forks, one crossing the river, while the other runs along the windings of the south side of the river. The first town of the Mohawks is on Schoharie Creek. There are two other towns. Then in turn come the Oneidas, Onondagas, Cayugas, then the Senecas. These nations are the fiercest, most politic of any Indians of North America, and they are the most strategically placed of any nation. They control Lake Erie, or Oswego—the carrying-place between it and Lake Ontario. If they wanted to make war on the French of the lower St. Lawrence, they could sweep down Lake Champlain, which is known as the gate to Canada; thence by way of the Richelieu to the St. Lawrence and Quebec. Likewise, should they desire to make war on the English colonies, they could sweep down by the Hudson, the Connecticut, the Delaware, and the Susquehanah. Providential it was that they were allied to us, rather than to the French, for otherwise Canada had always remained French.

Whatever their present mission, my captors seemed in a great hurry, for as soon as we had eaten they rose, and placing me between them, though no longer tied, we again set off. It seemed to me that we travelled in a direction more northerly than hitherto.

Near nightfall we stopped and made camp—a few boughs laid over poles, the front open to a small fire.

Now I spoke to them in English, for I had found they understood enough to converse a little in my tongue. I told them that my home was in England, and that my people would pay well if I was turned over either to Mr. William Johnston at Schenectady or to Governor Clinton at New York.

They listened respectfully, nodded, then talked among themselves in their own language, nor deigned to speak to me more that night.

When finally we lay down for the night I was put between them, and the thong replaced about my wrist. Though I fell asleep almost immediately, I soon awoke shivering with cold, and very miserable. Each Indian had covered his head with the blanket. How they could sleep thus, without air, greatly puzzled me. The fellow I was tied to was a light sleeper, for if I made the slightest movement he gave the thong a tug that reminded me it was useless to try to escape. But even had I not been tied, it would have been madness to attempt to find myself alone through that wilderness.

CHAPTER 17

I change Masters

Three more days of travel followed. We had reached a river; a well-beaten trail flanked it, sometimes near, again at a considerable distance. Over ridges we went, traversed little valleys; sometimes between deep gorges flanked by mountains I later learned were the Alleghenies. We were not going with the stream, but towards its source.

One day it rained without let-up and we remained in camp until the following morning, when we again set out. The soles of my moccasins were now worn so thin that they were but little protection to my feet. My companions were no better off.

Late on the third day we came to the most westerly of the Mohawk towns, or, as they were called, castles. An immense stockade, quadrangular in shape and as much as twenty feet high, with stout bastions at the corners, surrounded many big wigwams, each capable of housing fifty or more people. What greatly amazed me was a beautifully emblazoned coat of arms over the main entrance of the stockade, as though some knight or baron were its owner. But it was not until long later that I learned that it was the arms of the Duke of York, who, as their protector, had allowed them to be affixed to all the towns or castles of the Five Nations.

We stopped here all night. I was much interested in these people, who were more advanced in the arts of carpentry and joinery than the Delawares or Lenapè I had dwelt with. These people had many European tools, plenty of muskets, pistols, and even swords.

There were at least ten families in the wigwam in which I stayed, and each family had a separate fire in the centre of the lodge, with pots of brass and copper nearby. There were woven rugs too, between sleeping quarters for greater privacy.

I saw the head chief of this town. He was a magnificent man, more than six feet tall, I should say, with such a proud, haughty bearing as I had never considered possible in a people we are wont to call savages. He had silver rings in his ears, and on his chest a great silver gorget beautifully chased with some design I was not close enough to see clearly.

The people here regarded me with considerable interest, but neither the men nor women bothered me in any way. I had a good night's sleep, and after a hearty breakfast of meat, and maize cakes, my companions rose and told me to follow them. From now on the path was wide and well beaten. When we came to brooks we crossed by means of trees that had been felled over them. At wider streams there were canoes. How many centuries these people, known variously as people of the Long House, Five Nations, or by their tribal names, had lived here, no man can say, but their occupancy must have covered many centuries.

We had now passed the third and most easterly of their towns, which is on a creek called the Schoharie, and flows into the Mohawk River. I think this part is called the Flats. At any rate, the trail follows the winding course of the Mohawk River.

Several times of late I had again heard my companions mention Schenectady, Johnston, Albany, Corlaer. The last, I later learned, was simply another name for Schenectady, and so called Corlaer by the French and Indians after a well-known Dutchman long since dead.

Finally we stopped to drink from a spring, and again I asked my two Indians to sell me to the white chief Johnston. "If you do," I said, "I will see to it that he gives you one hundred pounds within the year."

I think they understood, for they talked together some little time, then he who seemed to be the leader said, "Maybe he at Corlaer, maybe he at Albany. Don't know. We see," and we moved on.

When we came to Schenectady, as I prefer to call it, I found it to be a strongly fortified trading-post situated at a carrying-place. There were a few Dutch and English houses. The logs were loopholed for muskets. The upper stories projected over the lower, as was common in frontier dwellings in those troublous times. I saw women and children about the doors and would fain have talked with them, for I was homesick for the sound of English speech.

But after stopping for only a few minutes my companions hurried me on, after briefly informing me that the white chief had gone to Albany; often they went at a dog-trot for miles on end.

The trail had abruptly left the river of the Mohawks at Schenectady, and we travelled in a beautiful wooded valley which is a part of the Mohawk Flats. It must have been about three hours later, when that happened which was to make it impossible for my present companions to turn me over to the people of my own race.

Suddenly rounding a bend, we came almost face to face with a party of seven Indians and one white man. Not more than a hundred feet separated us. Quick as a flash my companions sprang from my side into the woods. Some of the strange Indians dashed in pursuit. I heard a musket shot, an exultant yell. In less time than it takes to tell I was surrounded by painted Indians. One flashed a knife, another a tomahawk before my face. I thought my time had come, and tried to think of a prayer to say before they despatched me. All I could repeat was, "God help me—God save me." Then one of the Indians reached out and took hold of the necklet of bear's teeth. He fingered it wonderingly. Then, his dark eyes glistening, he said: "*Tomah tup-sko-dgan pulam-wul.*" (It is Tomah's totem or mark.)

My heart leaped. He had spoken in Maliseet. In that tongue I now cried excitedly, "*Ah-ha, Sogomo Tomah, Wul-ahs-tukw.*"

They stared at me as though they could not credit their own ears. They spoke together for several moments, and I gathered that someone, whom they called Father Germain, had returned to Acadia from France and reported Tomah's capture by an English ship. My news that their Chief still lived pleased these warriors exceedingly.

The chief of these Maliseets was called Moxus, a tall, fine-looking Indian despite the hideous war paint upon his brow and cheeks. Another, Arodowish, though half a head shorter, was one of the most powerfully built men I have ever seen. In the days that followed I was to witness numerous evidences of his great strength.

The French officer now joined them. They told him I was English, but could talk their tongue. Then he addressed me in Maliseet, which he spoke very well, asking me how I came to be with the Mohawks. As briefly as possible I told him of my meeting with Chief Tomah, our slavery in Virginia, our escape, our stay with the Lenapè, and finally my capture by strange Indians. "I think," I added, "they were taking me to Albany."

He had stared at me with growing amazement as I talked. Now he gave voice to a French oath, and declared in Maliseet that, though it was a strange story, he believed me. Then he added, "Well, young man, one of your Mohawk friends will never reach Albany," and he pointed to one of his red warriors. I looked, and saw a dripping scalp at his belt. He did not tell me, though I learned later, that they had found important papers in the poor fellow's knapsack from the Governor of Virginia to General William Johnston.

They now hurried along the trail in the direction I and my Mohawk companions had been going when we met these people. However, they only went a short distance when they took a smaller path that branched off to the left. In less than an hour we reached the Hudson River, where a good trail led northward; but presently, coming to where they had secreted two small canoes, we embarked and crossed the river. Landing, they carefully hid the canoes, and we proceeded along the bank of the river until nightfall, when they made camp, but did not light a fire. The Frenchman, whose name was LaForce, stationed a couple of sentries, and the rest of the party lay down to sleep.

In the morning, after a light meal, the march was resumed. About noon we reached the Hoosac River, and still travelling, finally came in contact with a great body of men camped in a clearing that had once been cultivated. There were more than six hundred French soldiers and about three hundred Indians, the whole commanded by Rigaud de Vaudreuil, younger brother of the Marquis de Vaudreuil, later Governor of French Canada. Before I was taken to the commandant, I noticed two French priests, one with the French troops, the other with the Indians.

Rigaud looked me over from head to foot. Doubtless my bedraggled appearance amused him, for he smiled, then in broken English asked me if I had seen any bodies of English troops of late.

I told him I had not. Then I was asked how I came to be with the Mohawks. I answered as I had told when previously questioned by LaForce. When I had ended, he said my account of my travels was either a very great falsehood, or one of the most remarkable experiences that had ever come to his notice.

I replied that it was all quite true, and asked him how it was that, if I had not met Tomah, I could speak the Maliseet tongue fairly well. At which he nodded and said to LaForce:

"Take him away and keep a good watch on him."

LaForce bowed, but reminded him that since he had lately promised his savages that they might keep any prisoners, it would be poor policy to put them out of humour by taking me from Moxus, whose captive I was.

Rigaud looked puzzled. I could see he did not want to give me up, nor did he want to antagonize his red allies. Finally he called Moxus and spoke to him through an interpreter. Evidently the Indian agreed to his proposal that I be well taken care of, for Rigaud told me to go with Moxus, and if I did not attempt to escape I would not be harmed.

That night, within their camp-fire circle, I was asked many questions by the Maliseets. There were three of this tribe, the remainder of the Indians attached to Rigaud's army being Christian Iroquois from Caughnawaga, the Ottawa Penobscots, Kennebecks, Wabanaki, and a large body of western Indians.

I repeated to the Maliseets in their own tongue all I had formerly told Moxus, and much more. They listened attentively, with grave faces, until I had finished. Then each one in turn inspected the necklet Tomah had given me, and declared that the *bulam* (salmon) incised on each tooth was indeed the Chief's totem mark.

I was given a blanket and slept that night between Moxus and Arodowish. Needless to say I slept well, for I felt that these Indians were friendly to me.

CHAPTER 18

Fort Massachusetts

By daybreak all the camp was astir. We had breakfast, then the force was divided. One half took a road flanking the left bank of the Hoosac (or Kaskekouke, as our Indians called it), the other the right-hand road. Indian scouts ranged well in front and on both flanks. I was on the right with Moxus, who cautioned me to keep close to him.

The reason for the presence of this large force of French and Indians so far from the fortress of Quebec was this:

Following the successful attack on Louisburg, in Acadia, the governor of Massachusetts had planned to capture Fort St. Frederic, a strong stone fort the French had built on Lake Champlain. Learning of the English plan, the governor of Canada sent a large body of men under Rigaud de Vaudreuil to assist its commander in defending it. When Rigaud arrived at the fort he learned that the plan was abandoned; and an ensign, who had just returned from a scouting expedition down the Hudson, reported the country clear of English troops. Feeling that some use must be made of his forces, Rigaud decided to attack Schenectady. At first his Indian allies agreed to this, but when about ready to depart, the Caughnawaga Indians told him that since many of their kindred were with the English force, they would not go against it. Rigaud tried to reason with them, but they were firm in their resolve not to attack Schenectady. Finally a Wabanaki chief informed Rigaud they would go against Fort Massachusetts. This place the English had built far up the Hoosac River to guard the western frontier of Massachusetts. I later learned from Moxus that a Wabanaki chief had been killed there the year before, and his people were anxious to avenge him and destroy the English settlements. Rigaud agreed to this, and was advancing up the valley of the Hoosac when I joined them.

We walked eight or ten miles that day, and owing to a drizzling rain, and attacks from myriad mosquitoes and black-flies, I was most uncomfortable. In fancy I can yet see the polyglot force of French regulars, Canadian militia, and Indians. The latter were half-naked, their faces bedaubed with paint—blue, white, and red. All were armed with musket, tomahawk, and the dreaded scalping-knife. We passed many farmsteads, but the people had fled, having learned of our coming, so that other than killing some fowl and pigs for food, no damage was now done.

We made camp about four in the afternoon, and Moxus told me that we were now only a short distance from the fort. After eating, Rigaud ordered scaling ladders to be made. I watched these preparations for attack on my countrymen with interest and no little dismay. Many times in my Aberdeen home I had read of assaults on forts, and imagined myself taking part in them; but I had never dreamed I would be an unwilling witness of an affair like this in a New World wilderness.

It ceased raining during the night, but daylight showed louring clouds in the sky. The priests said mass, and I noticed the Indians were very attentive. When breakfast was over, Rigaud spoke to them through Doty, his interpreter. He said, "My children, the time is near when we must eat other meat than fresh pork, and we will all eat it together." By this they knew he meant prisoners.

The Indians looked grave, and one of the chiefs said to Rigaud, "We thought our Father had earlier promised us that any prisoners were to be meat for the Indians, and *not* for the French."

Rigaud again spoke through Doty. "My children, you alone will have the prisoners to turn in for ransom at Quebec. Prisoners are worth more to you than scalps, as they are to us, for we can exchange them for some of our French now in English hands. In this way we shall *both* have meat, which is what I meant."

The Indians expressed their understanding and pleasure at this assurance. Camp was broken and we again pushed forward. In the distance I could see a high mountain.

After about an hour's walk we came to a ridge, climbed it, and there, below us, was the fort in a low meadow near the Hoosac.

I had expected to see a great stone structure with bastions and many cannon, but here before us were merely a few log houses and other buildings, surrounded by a high wall of logs; not stuck in the ground, but laid one on top of the other, lengthwise. At one side was a block-house, with a watch-tower or look-out. I could see what looked like a well, with a long sweep, within the enclosure.

The garrison of the fort usually was fifty, but a month previously, several of the men had accompanied the commander to the rendezvous for the contemplated invasion of Canada, and were still absent. I later learned that the day before our arrival a dozen or more of those left had gone to Deerfield for powder and shot, of which there was a serious shortage in the fort. The garrison now totalled only twenty-four men, and several of these were sick. There were also a few women and children. Thus the place that some eight hundred French and Indians had come to subdue numbered only ten or a dozen defenders fit for combat.

As soon as the Indians saw the fort, they set up a mighty howling and yelling, and dashed forward like hounds let loose, firing their guns as they went. This upset Rigaud's plan, which had been to make an assault after dark.

Immediately we had come in sight of the fort, Moxus took a deerskin thong and was about to tie me both hand and foot. But I begged him not to tie me, telling him that the mosquitoes and black-flies would devour me were I not able to fight them off. I also assured him I would not try to escape. "What will it profit me?" I asked bitterly. "I am but a lad, and would soon get lost in the woods. Do but let me remain unbound, and I promise you, Moxus, I will not try to escape."

He gazed at me a few moments in silence, then said, "All right, P'sazum, I will trust you to keep your word." Then he shouldered his musket and joined his kinsmen.

Left to myself, I joined a party of French soldiers, and lying down behind the trunk of a big tree, watched what went on in the valley below.

At the first musketry fire of the Indians, the garrison in the fort returned it. I saw the Indians dart behind stumps and trees, but not before a bullet had struck a Wabanaki chief and stretched him lifeless. The French soldiers now entered the fray, firing on the fort from behind trees, while the Indians kept up a frightful din, yelling wildly and discharging their pieces as fast as they could load them.

On my right were French regulars, among whom I recognized Rigaud de Vaudreuil. Presently I saw him clap a hand to his left arm and stagger backward. It was only a flesh wound, but it bled so freely he was taken to the rear to be dressed by the surgeon. I saw several slain, both French and Indians. The sight of them dropping made me feel ill. But my sympathies were wholly with the brave defenders of the fort. I did not then know how few they were, nor how little powder and ball they had. They fired only when they saw an enemy rush from stump to stump. But though these moving targets were difficult to hit, the marksmen were good border shots, and did kill and wound several of the attackers.

All day the musketry fire was kept up, intermingled with yells and taunts from the Indians. At nightfall they united in a terrifying war-whoop that I shall never forget, then withdrew behind the ridge, but not before a cordon of French and Indians was thrown around the fort to intercept any of the garrison who might attempt to escape and get help.

I went and joined the Maliseet warriors. Moxus nodded to me and gave me a portion of the food that had been prepared. I was very hungry and ate heartily.

Before dark set in French and Indians gathered faggots, and cut fir and spruce boughs, which they piled in heaps near the crest of the ridge. I asked Moxus why they did this. He answered that trenches were to be dug before daylight in front of the fort, and then the walls fired with the collected brush.

I got little sleep that night for thinking of the terrible thing that was going to happen, and I wished I was anywhere but in that place. But providentially it began raining during the night and drenched everything. Young as I was, I realized that the brush would be too wet to burn, and I thanked God that it was so.

After mass and a hasty meal, the Indians and troops moved forward, and, taking up positions behind trees and stumps, renewed their musketry fire, which was answered from the fort. As on the previous day, I now crouched behind my tree and watched the proceedings. Several French and Indians were hit, some mortally; but how the defenders fared I knew not at that time. Later I learned the garrison was reduced to eight.

About noon I heard the French bugler sound the cease fire. Then I saw three officers walk down the ridge, one holding aloft a white flag. They marched up to the gate of the fort and two of the garrison came out. In a few minutes one of the officers returned to the ridge and conferred with Rigaud, who presently went down the slope and joined those at the gate. Later I understood that he promised that if the English surrendered, they would be treated with the greatest humanity, would not be given to the Indians, and exchanged as soon as possible for French prisoners in English hands in Boston.

The commander of the fort asked for time to consider this proposal. It was granted, and meanwhile a truce was called on both sides. At the end of a couple of hours he signalled to Rigaud, who again went to the fort accompanied by his officers. They entered. A little later I saw the tricolour raised on the flagstaff. Then more French regulars entered. Presently they came out with the prisoners, and, as Indians were crowding about with fiendish howls, the troops quickly formed a cordon about the poor people and escorted them towards the ridge. As they approached nearer I could see two women and four or five children. It was heart-rending to watch the faces of the latter, and the drawn, haggard looks of the women, as they slowly struggled up the slope, helped by their menfolk—sick, wounded, and well. They were led to the French camp and placed under heavy guard, for it was feared the Indians might kill and scalp all of them in revenge for the death and wounding of their own kindred.

The Indians had not been allowed to enter the fort with the French regulars, but as soon as the prisoners were evacuated they forced their way in, and I could hear them whooping and yelling wildly. Soon they rushed out carrying all the movables, then the fort was set on fire. Sadly I stood and watched the flames eating up the place, while smoke billowed in clouds down the valley.

Now the Indians came to Rigaud and demanded that the prisoners be given up to them. He refused, saying some were ill and wounded, but he assured his red allies that, as he had previously promised, they alone would get the ransom money.

At this they were very angry, and an Abenaki chief pushed forward in front of Rigaud and cried in a loud voice, "Our Father has given us double words! Father, listen, we will go home, and allow you to find your way back to the lake as best you can, unless the prisoners are given up to us. Father, listen, open your ears to your children. We are of one mind."

Then other Indian chiefs joined in threats and denunciations. Doty tried to pacify them, but it was no use. Rigaud now called their priest, who spoke to them in their own tongue. They listened respectfully, but still insisted Rigaud's promise must be kept. Finally, after he had given them presents as a peace-offering, and exacted a promise not to harm any prisoner, Rigaud allowed them all the men but two. These, with the women and children, were kept in the French camp all that night.

Of course Rigaud had solemnly given his word to the garrison that none of them would be turned over to the Indians; but he had formerly assured his red allies they should be allowed to keep any prisoners taken. Some may blame him for breaking his word with the English, but his was a most difficult position. It was war, and to keep his Indians loyal he must do what he considered best for his master, the King.

The French commander's arm was now much swollen, giving him a great deal of pain, and he was anxious to get back to civilization as soon as possible. After breakfast the next morning, camp was broken and the whole force began the return journey.

As before, I walked beside Moxus, who told me that when we reached Fort St. Frederic he would take me with him to his own country on the Wulahstukw River. "You like that, P'sazum?" he asked. I told him I preferred to be given to the English at Albany, if it could be arranged, for then it would be possible for me to get back to my own country. At this he shook his head. "Moxus not go to Albany," he said. "English kill him and take his scalp."

"Oh, well," said I, as cheerfully as I could, "there is then nothing for it but to go to Acadia; but I do hope your people will treat me kindly."

He nodded. "*Ah-ha*, P'sazum," he said. And we walked along the rough, muddy road, slippery with the late rain. It was slow going, owing to the sick, wounded, and the women and children.

The Indians carried the children and two men who were unable to walk. One had been wounded in the foot; the other was very ill. And they, like the children, were carried pick-a-back. Indeed, the Indians were in much better humour to-day. One took a great fancy to a lad of five or six years, and one evening made him a bow and arrows, which greatly pleased the little fellow. As a matter of fact, I have observed most Indians to be very fond of young folk. The poor man who was sick died the second day of our journey. That evening one of the women gave birth to a girl child; thereafter, she was carried on a litter made by French soldiers. Thus we went, a strange cavalcade indeed—children on the backs of Indians, the mother on her litter carried by two Frenchmen, her newborn child in her arms; weary, wounded and sick soldiers, wounded Indians, and Rigaud himself, his face drawn with pain from his wounded arm, stumbling along.

On the third day it rained, which wet us all and added to our misery. Four of the wounded Indians died that day. One was a Maliseet. Moxus and Arodowish fell behind, I with them. They dug a trench on a sandy knoll, stripped bark from a great birch tree, and tied it about the body with withes, then laid it in the grave, with the dead warrior's gun, knife, and tomahawk by his side. Then they wrapped a little red ochre in bark and placed this by the head. The chaplain said a prayer in the Wabanaki language. The body was covered with earth, and stones heaped on the grave to keep wild beasts from digging it up. Then we went back and soon rejoined the rear.

I was now to witness border ruthlessness such as I had never imagined possible. Indians and French-Canadians alike sacked and burned houses, barns and outbuildings on both sides of the river. Sheep, cattle, hogs and horses were killed, and the crops destroyed, so that what had been a peaceful and prosperous country-side was now desolate. Moxus and Arodowish had joined the raiders, and I now walked beside the prisoners. For a time I carried one of the children—the little lad for whom the Indian had made the bow and arrows. We talked together as we bounced along, and he sadly told me a toy gun one of the soldiers of the garrison had whittled for him out of a piece of wood had been left in the fort and burned.

Passing the clearing where I had first joined the army, we soon came to a trail that branched off to the north. We took this and travelled through dense woods for four days. Finally we reached the Seraghtoga River, crossed it and some small brooks, and at length reached the dead-water where the guard had been left with the canoes.

At this place Rigaud gave permission to more than half of the Indians to continue their ravages against the Dutch and English settlements along the Hudson and as far as Boston. These departed in four groups with French officers in charge. The Indians left with us were Caughnawagas, Wabanaki of St. Francis, some of the western Indians, and the two Maliseets from Acadia.

CHAPTER 19

I Dance

There must have been at least one hundred canoes in the flotilla. Some were of birch, others of elm bark. Several were thirty-five pieds (French measurement), thirty-six English feet; yet others twenty-five, others eighteen feet long. The great canoes were manned by eight paddlers. The canoe I embarked in with Moxus, Arodowish, and two Wabanaki was of birch bark, eighteen-feet in length, and belonged to Moxus, having been brought all the way from Acadia by river, lake, and portage.

The whole of the force now left proceeded towards Lake Champlain. For many miles the stream was a mere thread winding through boggy ground covered with stunted white spruce, wild grass, Labrador shrubs, sheep laurel and reeds. Hundreds of wild fowl flew up at our approach, and I saw two great animals as big as a horse, called moose. One was a female and had no horns, but the male bore enormous antlers with a spread of at least six feet, and as wide as the top of a small table. The Indians shot off their muskets at them and killed the bull, and when we later ate of it, I found it like to beef. One of the Abenaki Indians with us said it was not usual now to find these animals in this place, and that they had evidently come from some pond or lake much farther east.

We passed numerous beaver-houses, heaps of alders and white birch piled several feet above the surface of the stream. But of the inmates we saw no sign. I was keenly interested in everything. In fancy I can yet see that long cavalcade of canoes, winding through these "drowned lands" as I heard them called by some of the whites. I can see the painted faces and scalp locks, the continuous lifting and falling of white and tawny arms, hear the rhythmic dip of the paddles, and the purling of the water, and feel the lift of our own canoe as Moxus and Arodowish drove it resistlessly forward. And I can hear the chansons the French Canadians sang to the time of the paddles. And I remember my feeling of sadness that men who had treated our wounded with such kindness, and could sing with such tenderness, could, on the other hand, be so ruthless and barbarous.

At sundown we reached Lake Champlain, a long, beautiful sheet of water, its placid bosom reflecting the crimson afterglow. Here and there along the shore, a maple, its leaves touched by an early frost, flaunted its loveliness beside the sombre and cathedral-like evergreens of pine and spruce.

In all my life, neither before nor since, have I seen anything so beautiful and peaceful as was this wilderness lake as we entered it.

Paddling northward along the westward shore, we finally came to a point jutting out into the lake, and saw the great stone ramparts of Fort St. Frederic. They were about twenty feet high and mounted with many cannon. A high tower overlooked the ramparts, and this, too, was mounted with cannon and swivel guns. From the flagstaff proudly floated the lilies of France.

We drew in to shore. Soldiers, Indians, prisoners, loot, disembarked. The commandant of the fort came down, spoke to Rigaud, then took him to the fort to have his wound dressed. Tents and wigwams were set up nearby, food cooked and eaten.

That night a huge fire was built, and around it in a great circle over one hundred Indians, and five hundred French, sang and danced half the night. One of the French soldiers had a kettledrum, and he beat lustily at this as the others performed.

I sat beside Moxus and Arodowish, and during the evening some of the Caughnawaga Indians came to Moxus and told him that it was time that his prisoner danced. One of the foremost seized hold of my arm and cried in English, "Dance, English; time for dance."

Moxus tried to buy me off, but they would not have it, and some of the Wabanaki of St. Francis came too, and said to Moxus, "Let him dance."

So Moxus said to me, "They will not hurt you; dance, P'sazum," for both he and Arodowish now called me by this name.

Reluctantly I rose. What to do, I at first knew not. The dance the Indians did was a monotonous series of raising the feet and stamping on the ground to the rolling of the little drum. And suddenly it came to me that if these Indians thought to make game of me, I would show them something they had never seen before.

I turned to Moxus and said to him, "I will dance, but this dance calls for two swords; it matters not if they be little swords, or big, but I must have them, for it's a part of the dance."

Moxus looked grave, for he knew not what my intention was; but finally he told the chief of the Caughnawagas what I wanted. For a little while there was a great palaver among Indians and French Canadians, but at length two swords were given me, and they spread out to see what I would do. And I tell it as it happened, surrounded by all those Indians and French, and the great fire casting its light over the circle left about it, making all as bright as day.

I walked over about five paces from the fire, and I placed the swords cross-wise on the ground. Then I began my dance between the crossed blades, just as I had done it so many times in the garret at home, winter afternoons, with old Angus playing the pipes—the glorious pipes!

And to-night I could feel the presence of our old servant among the myriad faces surrounding me, and as the kettledrum kept time to my steps, I heard it not as a kettledrum, but as the pibroch of my native land, and I danced as I had never danced before.

And there was not a sound from that assemblage. I was conscious of their eyes, the eyes of Caughnawagas, Ottawas, Wabanaki, Penobscots, Kennebecks, the eyes of French soldiers from beyond the seas; and those of Canadian French whose ancestors perhaps had come with Champlain to the cliffs of Quebec over a century before, and they were fastened on my moccasined feet as I did the Highland sword dance.

And the drummer did well. He fell in with the mood of the dance, and when I quickened or slowed, he seemed to sense beforehand what I was about to do, so that I could have hugged him for the part he played.

And at last it was all over, and I picked up the swords and stood there bewildered by what was taking place. For such a shout went up from more than six hundred throats as I never heard before. And when it ended, seeing the Indian who had given me the swords, I walked over and presented them to him, handles first.

Gravely he took them, and as I walked back to Moxus, I caught sight of the commandant of the fort with Rigaud and his interpreter, Doty, standing just on the outskirts of the circle.

Doty said to me in Maliseet, "That was well done. Even the Indians liked it, as well as our French."

"*Ah-ha*," I answered, "maybe both were Scots before they became French and Indians."

He laughed, and I heard him repeat my retort to Rigaud and Monsieur the commandant.

For two days we remained at Fort St. Frederic. Moxus and Arodowish made themselves and me a pair of moccasins. Then Moxus announced his intention of proceeding at once to Quebec. Rigaud, who had been most kind to me, offered to buy me from Moxus, but Moxus resolutely shook his head. I was his prisoner and his prisoner I must remain.

"You will not turn him over to the commandant at Quebec and get your bounty?" asked Rigaud anxiously.

"I not say now," was Moxus' evasive reply. "Anyway," he added, "I not scalp him."

A little later, as I was standing on the beach idly watching the wavelets lapping the shingle, Doty, Rigaud's interpreter, came and said to me in a low voice that if I desired, I could hide in the fort until all the Indians had gone; then I could later be sent to Quebec and exchanged for some French lad in English hands.

I thanked him heartily, and added, "No, M'sieu, I have given my word to Moxus, and I must abide by it, come what may."

"Very well," he said in a disappointed voice, "I have done what I was told to do," and he said goodbye, shaking my hand. I felt quite sure that General Rigaud had sent him to me with the above proposal.

A little later we set off. Moxus took the stern paddle. Arodowish got in the bow, and I slightly ahead of Moxus. Some of the Wabanaki of St. Francis accompanied us. The majority remained at Fort St. Frederic until the sick and injured were able to travel.

It would only be tiresome to tell in detail about our canoe journey down the lake and the Richelieu River to the St. Lawrence. When we got hungry we landed and made a little fire and ate beside it. At night, before dark set in, we drew in to shore, found a suitable spot on the bank, and used our canoe for shelter. It was in this wise: we turned it bottom up, with two forked sticks stuck into the ground and the forks resting over the upper gunwale. Then we laid ourselves on the ground beneath it. Thus the canoe served us for carriage by day and a roof by night.

Several times we had to portage around bad rapids, and at one of these places the St. Francis Indians left us. We were now alone on the great river, and save for one day when it rained and there was a strong upriver wind, we proceeded with little pause save to eat and make camp at night. I think it was five days after leaving Fort St. Frederic (though at this time I cannot be sure) that we came in sight of the ramparts of Quebec.

This Rock—this gateway to New France—had now become a legend in my mind. Here had come Cartier and Champlain. From this place soldiers, fur traders and Jesuit priests had pushed southward, northward and westward, building forts and missions; the latter to Christianize the pagan inhabitants of the country; the former to control and protect the great peltry trade of the west, and divert it from Albany to Montreal and Quebec.

From this mighty bastion Frontenac had hurled defiance at the English invader, and sent his French troops and militia and his Indian allies to ravage and destroy the farmsteads and villages of the English colonies.

Here, in season, came the six-fathom bark canoes of the fur brigades, laden with furs that found a ready market in far-off France; and here, too, repaired Christian Iroquois, Hurons, Montagnais, Ottawas, Micmacs and Maliseets, Penobscots and Kennebecks, to turn in prisoners or scalps and receive their bounty in the form of powder, lead, muskets, blankets and brandy.

Rounding the Rock, we came to a wharf at the foot of the lower town. We landed. The Indians lifted the canoe out of the water and turned it bottom up on the wharf. First we went into the lower town. It was a very curious place, some of the streets, especially the little *Rue de Notre-Dame*, so narrow that the roofs of the houses that flanked them almost touched. There was a smell of tar and cordage and fish that reminded me of Fish Row in Aberdeen, and filled me with a great homesickness.

I revisited the place many years later, and tried to follow the route I took with Moxus and Arodowish fourteen years before, along the narrow, lane-like streets that wound up high hills to the battlements with the cannon commanding the broad river. There had been ships at anchor then, and boats and canoes plying between the city and the Lévis shore—even as on this second occasion—but instead of the Union Jack the Fleur de Lys of France had floated from the staff above the citadel.

But this second time another was with me of whom I have to tell later. My fair companion was familiar with the place, and so we saw all that there was to see of interest.

It was mid-afternoon when Moxus, Arodowish and I again reached the wharf. They had each purchased some provisions, blanket cloth, powder and ball, some few trinkets like glass beads, two small hand-mirrors, and finally, a big bottle of brandy.

We embarked, paddled across to the Lévis shore and made camp for the night. They each drank of the brandy, offering me some, which I refused; then we had supper, after which they built a fire. Before midnight they had emptied the flagon and were quite intoxicated. They sang strange chants and kept me awake most of the night. And because of this, and the knowledge that I was to be taken into the heart of Acadia, I was very miserable. There was only one bright spot in an otherwise hopeless picture, and this was that mayhap I should again meet with Tomah. For I was well assured in my mind that following my disappearance he would do everything in his power to reach his own country again.

CHAPTER 20

Acadia

We were paddling a very rapid and shallow stream flowing southward through a wild, hilly country. It was one of those rivers used from time immemorial by the Indians of Acadia and the St. Lawrence, and it was called the Rivière du Loup. Shortly after leaving Lévis, Arodowish had shot a calf moose, so we had plenty of fresh meat for our needs. We travelled this river for two days, going at a leisurely speed, because the water was low and our bottom was frequently cut by rocks and had to be mended with balsam and ashes.

Finally the canoe was taken from the stream, and Moxus said, "Now we make long carry. *Ah-ha*. Eighteen leagues."[1]

Now the paddles were lashed lengthwise across the two centre cross-bars, which done, Moxus seized the gunwales of the eighty-pound craft, lifted it above his head, turning it bottom up as he did so, then let it sink downward until the paddles rested on either shoulder. Then he started off along a well-worn trail. Arodowish and I followed, carrying the guns and baggage, and it was all we could do to keep up with Moxus, so fast he went.

On and on we walked. When Moxus grew tired carrying the canoe, Arodowish relieved him. Thus we went, league after weary league, the trail winding between great leaves of pine and spruce and birch and maple, the leaves of the latter forming a symphony of colour I had not imagined possible. Gold were the leaves, and scarlet and purple, and, fatigued though I was, for my

---

1 GFC gives some distances in leagues. A league is 3 miles, or
  4.8 kilometres.

load was heavy, the beauty often made me forget my tired and aching limbs.

The Indians had said, "By'm-bye we come to big lake," but so long we had travelled since I had been told this, that I often found myself wondering if they had mistaken the route.

But in two days we reached it. They called it *Temisquoata*. It was a long lake, about six leagues in length, and two thirds of a league wide. As the waves were very high by reason of a head wind, we made camp and rested until it subsided, which was not until some time the following morning, when we embarked.

Shortly after midday we entered a river. In this stream, which was narrow, and the water very clear, I saw many big trouts on the bottom. My companions caught three, each about two pounds in weight, with a bone hook attached to a line of rawhide, and baited with moose meat. That night we cooked two of the trouts. They were very good and a welcome change from our diet of meat.

The following evening brought us to the confluence of this river with the Wulahstukw, a much bigger body of water. Here was a small Indian village called St. Francis. We landed and made our way to it. Some men, women and children sat about the wigwams, which were made of hemlock bark.

When they saw us all jumped to their feet, the men seizing their weapons. But Moxus raised his hand above his head and called, "*Quay! Quay!*" Evidently they recognized him, for they put down their arms and awaited our coming. When we were a few feet distant, one of the squaws rushed towards us, and giving me a filthy grin, she cried, "English—English!" and seizing me by one arm she tried to drag me towards the wigwam. But I braced myself and, for I was a strong lad, she could do little with me. Then Moxus interfered. He told her I was his prisoner, and she must not harm me. Then he advised me to keep close to him, which I did, for I liked not such rough greeting.

We stayed in the Maliseet village that night. During the evening several of the squaws came to Moxus and pleaded with him to allow me to dance for them. I knew, from my talks with Tomah during our plantation days, what this meant. As I danced they would beat at me with hazel switches to make me go faster, and I must keep on until

I dropped from exhaustion. But Moxus said no to their pleadings. When they persisted, he finally laid down a present for the squaw who had first assaulted me, and was now the most insistent that I be given to them. It was a silver brooch he had taken from one of the Dutch houses on the Hoosac. Thus was I bought off from fiendish torture by a bauble once worn by some poor housewife a thousand miles away.

Beside a big camp-fire that night Moxus and Arodowish told the assembled Indians of the campaign to the westward. They listened attentively and then asked how many prisoners, how many scalps had been taken. Moxus answered he had taken one, Arodowish one. Then they were asked what price had been paid for the scalps at Quebec.

It was like a merchant being asked the price he had received for a piece of merchandise. And I felt that our civilization was very barbarous indeed that human scalps should be bartered for gold. Nor did I greatly blame these Indians, but rather the two countries, England and France alike, that traded in such gruesome emblems of victory.

Then, while Moxus and Arodowish remained silent, one of these St. Francis Indians gave them the news of the campaign in Acadia. I heard Louisburg mentioned, then Minas and Gaspereau, other posts in what is now Nova Scotia; Boishebert, the name of the French commander on the lower Wulahstukw or St. John River; also LaCorne, Coulan and Marin, leaders of French troops in Acadia.

Though far from the actual scene of conflict—the distance being over two hundred miles—these Indians were well supplied with information concerning the war. For hardly a week went by that runners did not pass along this river with despatches to or from Quebec,

I slept between Moxus and Arodowish that night, And it was well, for several of the women had lost husband or relative at the hands of the English, and very possibly might have done me injury. I was glad when morning came and we again embarked.

Late that afternoon I heard a great roaring noise ahead, and asked Moxus what it was. He said, "That is *Chik-seen-i-beeg*," which in their language means a destroying giant. Seeing I looked puzzled, he said we were nearing the Great Falls and must portage around it. A little later I saw a great wall of mist high in the air, and the thunder of the falls was so loud I could hardly hear the dip of the paddle blades.

Now my canoemen turned the canoe to shore. Landing, they took it from the water and carried it overland and down a steep bank to the basin below the Falls. Embarking again, we went about a mile downstream, landed and made camp.

That night they told me an old, old legend about their people. It seems that a party of Mohawks in the old days came down the river and stopped at Madawaska. There was only one young girl in the village at the time. They captured her and asked her where her people were. She said they were downriver a day's journey, camping in the woods, where they had gone to cut up a moose. Then they promised her her life if she would lead them to the spot. She said she would, and setting her course led the way downriver. Night came on, and they were still some miles from the Great Falls. They wanted to go ashore and camp, but she said no, it was now but a short distance to her people. So they paddled on. At last they heard the thunder of the Falls. Then the Chief of the Mohawks asked her what the noise was. She told him it was *Chik-seen-i-beeg.* "But," said she, "we will soon land and go around it." Then she paddled on. The thunder grew louder, the water swifter. And again the Mohawk Chief asked if it was not time to land. But she said, "No, a little farther, O *Sogomo.*" And she paddled on. A little later they were being swept forward at a terrific speed. The moon suddenly pushed its head above the horizon, and they saw the wall of mist, only a few hundred yards distant. Now they knew that they had been led to their doom. They plied their paddles desperately, but only one canoe with two men in it was able to reach shore. The rest went over the falls.

Later they told the tale to men in their own country. They said they saw the Maliseet maid on the edge of the pitch, standing upright in her canoe, and it seemed that she was surrounded by a bright flame from head to foot. Just as she entered the mist she lifted high her paddle, and cried in an exultant voice that rose like a bell over the sound of the falls, "I have saved my people."

When Moxus had ended his tale, I was shivering with excitement. It had seemed so real. And I have wondered since what essence of fact and what of fancy there was in its origin.

I went to sleep with the sound of the distant falls rumbling in my ears, and the boil of the swirling waters a few yards away, lit by a golden moon and reflecting myriad stars.

After a breakfast of moose steak, and a little pounded corn rolled into a paste and baked on a hot stone, we embarked again. The river now began to widen; but as it was the season of the year when it is lowest, the channel was not always clear to my eyes. Sometimes it seemed that the submerged rocks would split the frail birchbark shell; but my companions were familiar with every foot of the way. Often they must needs paddle rapidly across the river to reach the main channel. Then we would dash through leaping rapids, the waves striking the bow and throwing aside diamonds of spray. I enjoyed this very much. The river was as clear as crystal, the flats and uplands covered with birch, maple, pine, spruce and hemlock, some of which I had seen in New York and Pennsylvania.

Here and there we saw a wigwam and the smoke of a fire where a family of Indians had made camp. But save a wave of the paddles in greeting from my canoe-men, we had no words with anyone until about noon, when we reached a village by a good-sized river that entered the Wulahstukw on the left. Moxus and Arodowish paddled to shore and spoke with the Chief a few minutes. He made us a present of a big salmon he had speared the previous night, and we moved on.

The following day I saw another large encampment near a stream called the Sikstahaw. But we did not stop. Moxus told me that the name Sikstahaw signified in English "where he killed him". It seems in the long ago a Mohawk and a Maliseet chief fought a terrific duel. Each was armed with stone tomahawk and knife, and after they had fought from midday until near sundown, the Maliseet killed his enemy. And from that day to this the place has been called Sikstahaw. Two more hours' paddling brought us opposite a stream my Indians called *Et-la-guim-ik*. They told me we were now only a little more than six leagues from their village of Medowktek. Since leaving Quebec, we had come more than a hundred leagues. Many times on the long journey I had thought of Tomah and wondered if he had safely arrived at his own village. I had questioned Moxus as to the route he would likely take did he manage to escape capture by roving bands of Iroquois. They told me it would be much shorter than the way we had come—a route known to the Maliseets from time immemorial.

I thought what a mutual surprise and joy would be ours did I find him at Medowktek, and now that we were only a few hours' paddle from it, I was filled with excitement. Yet what would be my fate should the Chief have met death at the hands of his enemies? Must I stay with these Maliseet Indians year in and year out, perhaps be made to slave for them, be beaten, tortured? True, both Moxus and Arodowish had treated me with every kindness since I had joined them, had bought me off with a present to those who would have ill-treated me at Madachoeka. But would he be as easily able to pacify his people at Medowktek, many of whose kindred had suffered at the hands of the English and their Iroquois allies? I could only hope and pray that they would have pity on my youth.

Such were the thoughts that filled me as we swept nearer and nearer the chief village of the Maliseets. And, finally, seeing afar off the smoke from many camp-fires, Moxus touched me on the shoulder and said:

"Keep close to me when we land, P'sazum."

CHAPTER 21

At Medowktek

Barely had the canoe touched the beach when, from the bank above, half a hundred women and children and as many men rushed down to the shore, crying greetings to Moxus and Arodowish. My eyes swept over the gathering, hoping to see the well-known face of Tomah. But I saw him not, and my heart sank.

I was helped out of the canoe by Moxus, and a fierce-looking squaw pressed close to me, gazed at my face, and said, "White boy!"

I returned her gaze with all the calmness I could muster, "*Ah-ha Wulligiskik*," I said, nodding at her.

"*Pl-etch-emin?*" she queried, which meant was I French.

I evaded her question. "*Ba-kwe-nox-e-wun?* (How do you do?)" I returned.

Naturally she was puzzled at my use of her own tongue. She turned to Moxus. "Who is he? Where did you get him?" she asked.

Moxus took me by the arm. Then he told her I was English, and his prisoner.

At this she let out a yell that was taken up by the other squaws. Two or three laid hold of me and tried to drag me away from Moxus. But he held me close, and sternly ordered them away. Yet, though they fell back a little, they screamed, "English—let us beat the English!"

Moxus held up his hand for silence. When the din had ceased, he told them I was the friend of their Chief Tomah. "Has Tomah returned?" he asked of another squaw who stood nearby.

"*Kadama* (no)," she sadly replied. "Tomah is dead, or he is still a prisoner among the English. What does this English boy know about the great *sachem* of the Maliseets?"

"He knows much, squaw of Tomah," answered Moxus. "He was with the Chief during the ripening of berries." Then he touched the necklet of bear's teeth about my neck, and added, "That I have spoken truth, you will see by this necklet of Moo-ins' teeth, which Tomah gave to the English boy. See, here is his *tup-sko-dgan*."

She came forward, a tall, rather good-looking woman, and gravely inspected the necklet. "It is his," she said finally. "Where is Tomah now?" she asked. "I know not," answered Moxus. "No one knows. Come. There is a time for all things. After we have eaten, I will tell you all I know. But this English boy is my prisoner. He is Tomah's *ne-dup* (friend)." He ceased, and led me up the incline to the intervale on which stood the fort and wigwams of his people.

The Fort, I noted hastily, was a palisade of logs about fourteen feet high, seventy paces long, and fifty in width. The logs were set into the ground and were sharpened at the top. The earth had been thrown up about the base, leaving a quite steep embankment. Beyond it was a small chapel, with a belfry, and the bell which Tomah had told me had been sent all the way from France by the King for his Maliseet children.

This Fort was the most important of its kind in all Acadia. Not only did it guard the famous portage that led into New England, it was also the rendezvous in times of war for all the Indians on the river, as well as for their Micmac allies as far distant as Cape Sable in Nova Scotia.

South of the Fort, and flanking the river, were about thirty conical-shape wigwams, big and small. Fires were burning before many of them, and I could see pots and kettles lying about on the ground. These camps were now in use, for the Indians preferred the open flat during summer and autumn, rather than the confined area within the Fort.

The flat was perhaps a mile in length, and a quarter of that in width from the river to the forested upland to the westward.

I was led to one of the wigwams. It was simply constructed: the frame of small saplings set into the ground in a circle, bent together at the top, and sheets of birchbark laid over them. A tanned moose skin was suspended over an opening that served as door.

We sat on the ground in front of it. A big kettle was brought us containing boiled salmon and corn mush. I was given a wooden bowl filled with this mess, and a wooden spoon. I ate this with relish, and some corn bread, and drank water out of a birchbark bowl.

When we had finished, pipes were lit. Everyone smoked in silence until the pipes were empty. The men sat on one side, the squaws opposite, the children squatting beside the latter. They gazed at me with wide, curious eyes. Both boys and girls had long black hair which fell about their faces and gave them an elfish look.

The men were garbed in loose-fitting trousers of buckskin. A few had shirts, but the majority were naked from the waist up. The women had cotton dresses, doubtless purchased from some French trader. Practically all were barefooted; but some wore moccasins gaily ornamented with dyed porcupine quills.

Fifty years before my coming, a New England boy had been brought to this place a captive, and remained for six long years. Not only Gyles, but many another English captive had been made to endure all the abuse and torture of which their masters were capable of inflicting.

It was dark now. More brush and logs were laid on the coals, and the flames soared into the night, lighting up the circle, and fell upon the impassive faces of men, women and children. The moon, that for ages had looked down on many a savage dog-feast, pushed its crimson disk above the opposite hills and threw a path of gold upon the river. Back of us an owl whoo-hooed. But other than this, and the river rippling over the bar, no sound broke the profound and solemn stillness.

Now Moxus rose to his feet, and gazing down at his kindred, began speaking. He told them of the expedition against the English of Massachusetts, the number of men and canoes, the routes taken; how he, with other scouts, had come upon me with two Mohawks, going in the direction of Albany; the killing of one of the Mohawks and the taking of his scalp.

At this a howl of satisfaction went up from the gathering. When it had ended, Moxus resumed his oration. He repeated almost word for word the account I had given him of my meeting with Tomah, our life among the Lenapè, my final separation from the Chief.

He told it well, with a dramatic rising and falling of his voice that produced a profound effect upon his hearers. Finally he said: "Whether our Chief lives, or is dead, I know not. But if he is dead, we know that he fought well." He paused a moment, then added solemnly, "We must treat this friend of our Chief with kindness." Then he sat down.

I glanced at Tomah's squaw. She was sitting opposite me. I saw her pull the cedarbark robe, that was about her shoulders, over her face and hide it. But neither sigh nor sob came from her. She sat there as motionless as a statue.

Now one of the old men got to his feet and said, "Moxus, you have told us what this English boy told you. How do we know he spoke the truth? The English are all liars. He says Tomah gave him the necklet of Moo-ins' teeth. Maybe this English struck our brother on the head with a tomahawk, while he was asleep." He sat down. A howl went up from the assembly, and one jumped to his feet, a youth not more than fifteen or sixteen years. He whipped a knife from his belt, and cried in a loud voice:

"It is a long time since we have seen the colour of English blood. Let us cut a finger from this English captive!" Leaping into the circle, he made for me where I sat between Moxus and Arodowish.

My blood ran chill with terror, and I seized Moxus by the arm. But before the young man could touch me, Moxus sprang to his feet, dragging me with him. Confronting the fellow, he roughly pushed him backward. Then he said, "Go, Gwaksis, and see what the blood of a man is like, before you try your knife on a boy!"

A laugh went up from some of the older Indians. Gwaksis, which means the fox, slunk back to his place. His rebuke was well earned; for I later learned that he had not yet been on the war-path.

Moxus now said sternly, "This English boy is my prisoner. No one must harm him. I have said it!" Then he took me with him to an unoccupied wigwam, gave me a bear-rug to lie down on, and a blanket to cover me. I thanked him heartily for his kindness to me.

He told me that he might not always be able to protect me from the squaws, but he would do what he could. The squaws, he went on, were most bitter against the English, and tried by every means to have their will.

I asked him where the priest in charge of the chapel was. He answered that he had gone downriver two months since with thirty warriors to fight the English in Nova Scotia.

I soon fell asleep, to be awakened some time later by the barking of dogs. Moxus got up and went out of the wigwam. Presently he returned, and picking up his musket and other weapons, told me to follow him to the Fort. He explained that Bonus St. Castin, of Penobscot, with Sactowino, a Kennebeck Indian, had arrived from Quebec, and brought word that two English officers, with a war party of fifty or sixty Mohawks, were encamped twelve miles up the river, on an island.

His words sent a thrill through my body. Englishmen but a few leagues distant! If they attacked and subdued the Fort, I at last might have a chance to go back to my own country.

"Perhaps there be a big fight," added Moxus. "You bring bearskin and blanket, P'sazum; we sleep in Fort."

Quickly I did his bidding. As we stepped out into the night I saw all the inhabitants of the village astir and hurrying to the Fort with their belongings.

Entering the stockade gate, Moxus led me to a small cabin near the east end of the Fort, opened the door, and led me inside. There I saw a man of about forty-five years seated at a table. The light from two pine knots stuck in the wall fell upon his dark, handsome face and coal-black eyes. His cap lay beside him on the table, with a long musket and a pair of pistols. His hair was glossy-black, tied at the nape of his neck with a bit of scarlet ribbon. He was talking to some of the Maliseet warriors, and used their tongue as well as they did.

Later I learned that he was the younger son of the Baron St. Castin, by his Indian wife, a daughter of a great Penobscot Sachem. And this gave him vast influence over all the tribes from The Kennebeck to Cape Sable in Nova Scotia.

I heard him tell Arodowish and another Indian to go up to the north end of the Flat and remain on sentinel duty. They took their guns and departed without a word. Then St. Castin's eyes fell upon me.

"Who is this boy?" he asked of Moxus.

Briefly Moxus told him. When he had ended, St. Castin turned to me. "So you speak Maliseet, boy?" he said.

"*Ah-ha*, Monsieur. *Ka-ma-ju-dah* (I speak it quite well)," I answered.

He smiled slightly. Then to Moxus, "Let him lie down there, in the corner. And, boy," to me, "if you want to keep your scalp, do not leave the Fort unless I give you leave."

I bowed to him, laid the bearskin rug on the floor, and stretched myself upon it. But I could not sleep. I heard him say to the assembled warriors:

"If we had enough men," he cried, "I would suggest going upriver and attacking them while they sleep. But with so many of our warriors with Marin, we must wait here, and if they attack us, give a good account of ourselves!"

I noticed that several of the Indians looked very grave. One or two suggested that they take the women and children and flee downriver. But St. Castin silenced them with a few words.

"What!" he demanded scornfully, "would you run away from a few Mohawks, led by a couple of beggarly English? Does the mere mention of the Mohawks turn your blood to water?" And he brought his fist down on the table with a bang that made the pewter vessels clatter. And, though he was an enemy of my race, I could not help but admire his spirit.

Finally I fell asleep, but I awakened several times to see some of the warriors melting lead in the little stone fireplace, and pouring it into bullet moulds. Others sharpened knives and tomahawks. Once I heard a quavering whoop nearby, and thinking it was the warning shout of one of the sentinels, my blood raced through my veins. But a few moments later it was repeated, and I recognized the cry of the great horned owl.

CHAPTER 22

The Attack

At daybreak I was awakened by Moxus. He told me it was time to eat. I found that most of the Indian warriors had gone back to their wigwams. St. Castin was seated at the table eating some food a squaw had brought in. He nodded to me, then said, "Go out and wash, boy. You look dirty."

I felt my face burn to the roots of my hair. Then I said quietly, "I was not always so, I assure you." And, being stung to the quick by his manner and words, I went out and took the path to the river. Kneeling down on the sandy beach, I saw by my reflection in the water how unkempt I really was. I washed my hands, then my face, and brushed back my long hair as best I could with my fingers.

So intent was I on my job that I heard no one approach. Suddenly I was pushed from behind with such force that I shot forward and splashed into about two feet of water. I came up choking, got to my feet and turned, expecting to see one of the dreaded Mohawks. But it was one of the Maliseet boys, perhaps two years older than myself, who stood grinning and making faces at me.

Quicker than it takes to tell, I was beside him, my fists clenched. And, as my father had taught me, I gave him a right with all the strength I could put into it. It struck him over the left eye, and he went down like a ninepin. But in a moment he was on his feet again. Seizing a beach rock as big as a coconut, he flung it straight for my head. I ducked, gave him my left to his nose, and followed it with my right to his chin.

He fell to his knees, and stared up at me stupidly, the blood streaming from his nose. Then I saw several squaws running down the bank, and, having no desire to be thrown into the river, or beaten unmercifully, I ran as fast as I could up the shore away from them, then wheeled, scrambled up the bank, ran into the Fort, lifted the latch of the French cabin, and sprang in, all dripping as I was, and quite out of breath.

Those within, including St. Castin, who was smoking his pipe, stared at me in amazement. I heeded them not. I glanced about hoping to see Moxus; but he was not now in the cabin.

I can hear St. Castin's voice now: "Well, English, so you decided to have a swim!" I made no reply. I could hear footsteps outside, a chatter of many voices. Springing over to the table, where lay St. Castin's pistols, I grabbed one and backed into a corner. It was foolhardy, I realized later; but I had endured so much misery since I had been kidnapped, I was quite desperate. Yea, verily do I believe I would have killed the first squaw that entered the door. No doubt St. Castin realized this, for he glided to it and shot the bolt. Then, unheeding the screams of those outside, he turned to me. "What have you done, English?" he demanded.

My heart was hammering so that I could not speak for several moments. At last, "An Indian boy pushed me into the river," I said. "And, sir, I did what you would do. I knocked him down with my fist."

His mouth twisted in a smile. Then he looked grave, as did the assembled warriors. "I'm afraid," he said, "I'll have to give you up to them. Look here," he added commandingly, "put down that pistol!" For I held it in front of me, my finger on the trigger.

"I am a prisoner," I said boldly, "and I demand to be treated as courteously as you would treat any Englishman."

At this he gave a wry smile, and said, "Ask any Indian here how Captain Pote was treated at Medowktek a year ago."

Who Captain Pote was I did not know; but from his words I gathered that he had been ill-used. "I am not Captain Pote," I answered. "I am an English boy, who never did any of these people harm until to-day; and then only because I was first assaulted. If I have any master, it is Moxus. But, sir, if the great Sachem Tomah were here, he would not see me suffer any indignity."

Whether because I still had the pistol, or that he saw reason in my words, I know not. He said, "I promise you I will not turn you over to the squaws today. As a matter of fact, we may have more serious business to attend to. In the meantime, put my pistol back there on the table. Quick!" And he glowered at me.

"All right, sir," I said. And walking over, I restored the weapon beside its mate.

He now turned to the door, pulled aside a square of board that hid a small opening, and spoke to the squaws on the other side. "What!" he demanded, "would you take time to torture the boy, and the Mohawks only a few miles distant? I tell you, no! Take the canoes, food, and blankets, go to the opposite shore, and stay in the woods back on the hill until all danger is past."

When they had departed, he told me to eat my breakfast. "After you have eaten," he added, "you can melt lead and pour bullets for us."

"I'm sorry, sir," I replied, "but I cannot do *that*."

"Why not?" he demanded. "What is the matter with you?"

I returned his gaze as calmly as I could. "I cannot make bullets to kill my own countrymen," I explained.

He sprang towards me with the quickness of a panther. His black eyes blazed with fury, all his hot French-Indian blood at fever heat. I think he would have struck me; but I slipped behind the table out of his reach, picked up the pistol again and pointed it at him.

He ground out oaths in two languages. But he stepped back quickly, for all that. Then, as I gazed at him, two of the Indians rushed me, the pistol was wrenched from my hand, and my arms pinioned securely.

"Ha!" he cried. "You will not cast bullets to kill your own people!—Your own people?—Two miserable scouts, and a party of Mohawks out after scalps and plunder! Bring him here, Sactowino."

What punishment he would have meted out to me I know not. But at the moment a musket shot reached our ears, followed by a distant war-whoop. There came a pounding at the door. He turned, flung it open. Moxus and Arodowish entered. Arodowish was breathing heavily. He reported that the enemy had arrived, were now on the hill north-west of the village. They had left their canoes farther up the river, and were filing along the ridge-side when he saw them. He had barely made his escape. His companion had been killed.

Now other warriors entered. St. Castin asked if the squaws had got safely across the river. He was told yes. I was heartily glad, for I feared them more than I can say.

I was now to witness further examples of St. Castin's authority over his red kindred. He flashed orders like a general. Quickly the four gates were double-barred. The loopholes were manned, and two Indians sent up to the small look-out that projected above the north gate.

I sat on a small stool near the west window, which I opened the better to see what was taking place. I could see some thirty wigwams within the enclosure, all set in regular order, with paths leading from the space left in the centre of the encampment, to the four gates. Moxus was at one of the loopholes facing northward. He was a fearsome sight. He had discarded his shirt, and his naked body and face were painted with streaks of red ochre. In his scalp lock he had fastened a new osprey feather. His eyes flashed, and his nostrils quivered like those of an eager racehorse.

Perhaps ten minutes passed, then came a fusillade of musket shots from the northward. One of the warriors stationed in the look-out came down and reported to St. Castin that the enemy had followed a small gully, that takes a diagonal course from near the high land, to the bank of the river, and were using this natural trench as a breastwork.

I could hear them whooping, and from now on the intermittent discharge of their pieces. A few bullets thudded against the logs of the stockade. This was followed by the taunting yells of the defenders, which, added to the musketry of the besieged whenever an enemy exposed himself, filled my ears with an indescribable din.

Even the cabin reeked with powder smoke. Once a bullet entered a loophole, from which St. Castin had momentarily withdrawn to reload his musket, and buried itself in the wall on the opposite side of the stockade. He laughed and sent back a taunting shout. He was everywhere, moving like a wild animal from loophole to loophole, or crying to his men not to waste powder and lead, and, for he was now near my window, I heard him say grimly, "We may need it to-night."

I sensed what he meant. He was not afraid of the day, but of the dark, when the attackers might attempt to fire the Fort. But I was sure that, no matter how many the attackers, the Maliseets would fight to the last man, rather than be captured and tortured by their age-old enemies. And though the defenders of the Fort were fighting my own people and their Mohawk allies, I could not but feel a great admiration for them.

Following a fusillade from the attackers, I heard a crash, followed by a groan from the look-out tower. Arodowish ran up the ladder, and returned bearing the dead body of one of the defenders. He laid him on the ground beneath the window at which I sat. A musket ball had hit him in the throat. Without a word Arodowish returned to his loophole.

Thus the fight went on. The hours passed slowly, oh, so slowly, but towards nightfall the musketry of the enemy ceased. Food was now passed to the Maliseet warriors by two of the old men. It was hurriedly eaten and washed down with water, of which there was a plentiful supply in great copper and brass kettles. I was given a piece of corn bread and a bit of deer meat, and gladly did I eat both.

Arodowish came into the cabin for more powder and ball, and told me that the enemy were gathering brush to fire the Fort when dark had set in.

I went out of the cabin and scrambled up on the platform beside Moxus. He greeted me kindly. I told him of my quarrel that morning with the boy who had pushed me into the river, and how the squaws had chased me into the Fort and demanded of St. Castin that I be given up to them.

He looked very grave at this news, then said, "P'sazum, that blow you gave him was a mistake. After we beat off the Mohawks, the squaws will not be satisfied until they make you dance for them."

I said I was sorry to hear him say that. I was about to add that if the English took the Fort, I would be saved from their fury; but held my words. Perhaps he sensed what was in my mind, for he repeated, "We will beat off the Mohawks; then the squaws will return. But I will do what I can to protect you, P'sazum."

I thanked him with as much heartiness as I could muster. Darkness had now settled over the Flat, and looking from the loophole next to Moxus, I saw a trailing flame soaring towards the Fort. At first I thought it was a shooting star. But it was soon followed by another, and yet another. Moxus cried out, "Fire arrows!" Then they came thick and fast. Some alighted against the stockade, some on the wigwams, yet others on the cabin. The roof took fire. Water was rushed to it and the blaze extinguished. Now Moxus told me to go back to the cabin. "You be more safe there," he said. I obeyed, again taking up my position by the window. Howls and taunts filled the air. Under cover of the dark the Mohawks had crept nearer the Fort. During the day the attack had been entirely from the northward, but now it came from all sides: flaming arrows, musketry fire, which, answered from within, made an incessant din.

It must have been about ten o'clock that the Mohawks tore down one of the wigwams to the south of the Fort, set fire to it, and rushing forward, threw the blazing mass against the base of the stockade.

Anyone who has fired birchbark knows how quickly it becomes a roaring flame, giving off intense heat and black, acrid smoke.

Those of the defenders who could be spared from other points rushed to the danger spot. They carried great copper kettles filled with water, jumped up on the platform, and threw it over the stockade upon the burning mass. But the enemy was not idle. A steady musketry fire was kept up, which killed or wounded several of the garrison. St. Castin had ordered his warriors to charge their pieces with heavy duck shot, and these, spreading, found more than one target, for I could hear groans and cries of pain quite frequently.

Finally, the fire was put out, though not before it had weakened some of the logs of the stockade.

Now the attackers concentrated on the east side of the Fort. They rushed up the river bank, hurled great armfuls of brush and faggots against the stockade, ignited it with a sheet of flaming bark, and soon the whole was a roaring furnace. While the Maliseets were trying to quench this, other Mohawks rushed the rear of the stockade, carrying a great log which they used as a battering-ram. I could hear the heavy blows, the sound of axes, the discharge of muskets. Every one in the Fort, save those in the look-out tower, rushed to the points now threatened with destruction.

The attack I had witnessed on Fort Massachusetts was child's play compared to this. The Maliseets fought like wild beasts, urged on no less by their knowledge that if the Mohawks won the Fort they would all be tortured and butchered, as by the example of their leader. The flames from the burning brush made the whole area as bright as day. Two or three Mohawks rushed up with a scaling ladder. They flung it against the top of the stockade. In a moment a tall, naked Mohawk had rushed up it. He was shot by one of the warriors in the look-out. Two others followed him. They sprang inside. One was shot by Arodowish. The other, having discharged his musket, grasped the piece by the barrel. In his strong hands it became a formidable flail. I saw Arodowish go down under a terrific blow. Then St. Castin struck the fellow on the head with his tomahawk and stretched him lifeless. In the meantime other Mohawks had clambered up the ladder, dropped within the stockade, and closed with the defenders. So quickly they moved, I had difficulty in distinguishing Maliseets from Mohawks. But presently I witnessed that which caused me great sorrow. Moxus had been fighting like a very fiend. Now I saw him close with a tall, muscular Mohawk. Each had discarded his musket and, armed with tomahawk and knife, rained blows at the other. I saw the handle of Moxus' tomahawk break off close to the blade. He flung the handle straight at the other's face, then, shifting his knife to his right hand, he dashed at his adversary and seized him by the hand that held the descending axe. A few moments they staggered back and forth, then both went down, rolled over and over, now one, now the other on top. Presently I saw Moxus rise to his feet, give a yell of triumph, then topple over beside his prone antagonist.

I gave a groan of anguish, for he had been a staunch friend to me ever since he had captured me on the banks of the Hudson. Impulsively I sprang down from my stool, and flinging open the door, rushed out to give him what aid I could. Almost at the same moment the whole place was plunged in darkness.

The fire had been put out. Yet a little longer the fighting raged at the northern end of the stockade. Then I heard an English voice commanding the Mohawks to retreat. A few more shots, then the yells of the victorious Maliseets.

Some were for dashing out and following the enemy. But St. Castin ordered them to keep inside. The retreat, he cried, might be only a ruse.

But the Mohawks had had enough, and we did not hear any more from them.

Thus ended the famous attack on Medowktek. No doubt, in the years that followed, Maliseet mothers and fathers told of it to their children, and their children later to theirs, even as we recount the gallant exploits of our own national heroes.

Now the moon came up, and I saw a fearsome sight. Half a dozen Mohawks and as many Maliseets had fallen in the fight that had raged within the stockade; several of the latter had been wounded. Finally I found Moxus. He had killed his assailant, but had himself died from several knife thrusts. Tears dimmed my eyes as I gazed down upon his silent features. Then sadly I stumbled back to the cabin, and with heavy heart sat down on my stool.

No one bothered me. I saw Arodowish carried in, still unconscious from the blow he had received. St. Castin entered, looked him over, and decided he would be better for the letting of a little blood, the which St. Castin did for him, drawing off about half a pint. But it did not seem to do him any good. He lay in a stupor, seeming hardly to breathe.

I must say that, despite the fact that I liked not St. Castin for his treatment of me, I admired him greatly; and I have thought many times since, that if ever I needed someone to accompany me on a dangerous enterprise, I should ask for no better companion than this man, whose father was a Baron of France and his mother the daughter of a Penobscot chief.

He ordered a strict watch kept all night. and I do not believe that any man slept. When day dawned, no sign could be seen of the enemy. Scouts were sent out to the upper end of the Flat, where it was seen that they had embarked in the canoes they had secreted in the woods.

Five more of their dead were picked up; two near the gully northward, and three outside the stockade. But any wounded had been carried off by their comrades. The dead were promptly scalped. In all they had killed eleven warriors.

The Maliseet women and children now returned from the opposite hills. As soon as they had inspected their own dead, they set up a prolonged wailing that was most heart-rending.

The dead were prepared for burial by the squaws, who lamented that the priest was not present to administer the last rites of the Church.

Two days later I saw the dead interred in the burial ground a little beyond the chapel. Trenches had been dug in the sandy soil, and, the bodies having been wrapped in birchbark, and tied about with withes, they were solemnly laid in them, the feet to the river eastward, the heads to the west. Then the tomahawk, knife, and wampum beads belonging to each warrior in life were put beside him, with a little bag of powdered red ochre. To the tolling of the chapel bell the earth was filled in, then a little wooden cross placed at the head of each grave.

It was a sad occasion for me, for as I have said, Moxus had been a good friend. He had no wife living to mourn his passing; but his two young children were present, and his sister, and my heart ached for them.

That night, and for two nights following, fires were kept burning over the graves. The wives and other women—kindred of the dead warriors—sat in a circle, and beat their breasts with their hands, and kept up a wailing and sobbing that ended only with the coming of day.

It had been a strange ceremony; an admixture of Christian ritual and of an age-old primitive custom that, however much the difference in outward semblance, bespoke an abiding faith in the Life of the Spirit in another and better world.

CHAPTER 23

Abused by Squaws

Two days after the attempt to capture Medowktek, St. Castin and his Kennebeck Indian, Sactowino, departed by way of the famous portage to the Penobscot waters. What errand he had been on to the Governor of French Canada, I never learned; nor do I know that anyone in the village knew. I must admit I watched his departure with no little anxiety, for though I had dared to point his own pistol at him, and given him bold words, I had felt that he would not allow the squaws to harm me. Indeed, I now felt that with Moxus' passing, and Arodowish still in a coma, I had no friend in the village save it might be Chief Tomah's wife. For following the battle she had talked with me several times, given me food, and made sure that I had a blanket to cover me. The latter was now very necessary, for September brought cold, frosty nights. But the other squaws were ever ready with a scornful jibe or a push, and I greatly feared I would meet with other and more serious usage. I went with several of the men a mile into the woods and helped carry the poles and birchbark they peeled back to the village for new wigwams; and right glad I was to be of help. It took only a few days to complete these frail shelters; then the fort was vacated save by the wounded and a couple of squaws who ministered to them. A week after the battle, Arodowish, to my great joy, regained consciousness, but was still so very weak he could not stand. I asked to be allowed to see him but was repelled by the squaws.

I now helped gather the ears of corn, which had ripened; and this done, I went every day with the women-folk and boys to the hill to gather firewood. Since each wigwam had its camp-fire, there seemed no end to this labour, and I believe the squaws took delight in making me lug the heaviest pieces. If I faltered even a moment, I was the object of their jeers and laughter. When not engaged in this or other menial tasks, I was made to carry drinking-water from the spring, some four or five hundred yards distant. Two big copper kettles filled with water were enough to make even a much bigger lad than I stagger and pause for breath. But if the squaws thought I was longer than necessary, I had my ears or hair pulled, much to my hurt and anger.

Were it not that I lived in the hope of Tomah returning to his people, I am afraid I might have run into the woods to escape these abuses. But whichever way I had gone I had been captured again, either by my present masters or by other Indians. My only hope was the thought that I might possibly fall in with some French Acadian who would treat me kindly. Thinking thus, I longed for the priest's return to Medowktek. But evidently he considered his presence more necessary to the warriors on active service in southern Acadia than among those of his northern mission, for he came not. But the church was open, and any who desired to do so might go in at any time and say a prayer.

I have said little about the church. It was of squared logs on a stone foundation, with a small tower in which was the bell I have previously mentioned. The inside had a raised platform and brass altar rail, and there was a large image of the Christ, and of St. John the Baptist, in whose honour the church had been dedicated. There were many smaller images and gilded candlesticks, altar cloths, censers, and other holy vessels. And, which interested me much, there had been set up within the church a piece of slate stone, on which had been scratched in Latin the following: *To God, Most Excellent, Most High, in honour of Saint John Baptist the Maliseets erected this Church A.D. 1717, while Jean Loyard, a priest of the Society of Jesus, was Superintendent of this Mission.* Also scratched on the lower end of the slate was the name *P. Danielou.* This last, I learned, was the successor to Father Loyard.

When possible I often stole away from my tormentors, and entering this little sanctuary, sat down on one of the wooden benches and said a prayer. For I had been taught by my father, strict Presbyterian though he was, that God was everywhere, and that if one prayed with one's heart, He would hear in a Catholic church as well as in a Protestant church.

One day, in mid-October, I was all alone, as I thought, in this small chapel. I had bowed my head and prayed to God most fervently that he would soften the hearts of these people towards me. And then, as on many other occasions, I besought him to safely guide my friend Tomah through all dangers back to his own people.

I had just added, "And, oh God, I beseech thee, succour this thy child," when above me I heard the bell clanging. Startled, I jumped to my feet and turned in time to see the boy with whom I had quarrelled slipping out of the church door.

I was about to leave the church when the doorway was filled with a wild mob of Indians, men, women and children. One, the old man who had suggested that I had killed Tomah, was among the first to reach me. He jerked me this way and that, crying, "English dog! English dog!" and seizing my necklet of bear's teeth, gave it such a tug that the thong broke, and the teeth flew about the floor. Then I was wrenched from his grasp by three or four squaws, and dragged outside, where they cuffed me and pulled my hair, however much I cried out to them, "Wait—hear me!"

As they hustled me away I asked one squaw why they treated me so. To which she answered, "The bell, you made the bell ring, you, a heretic English."

Of course, the ringing of the bell was a welcome excuse for them to be revenged on me for daring to strike one of their own. And it would have availed me nothing had I told them that it was *A-bek-chee-loo* (which means the skunk) who had done it.

I merely cried out, "I did not ring the bell."

But the squaws only grinned at me, hurried me along to the space between the rear of the wigwams and the cornfield. Having armed themselves with hazel switches, they tore the clothes from my body, formed a circle about me and told me to dance, the which I did, while they struck at me with their switches.

If they thought to make me cry out, they were disappointed. I made no murmur, but endured their blows, their insults and howls, for some minutes. Then I dashed this way and that against them, hoping to break through the circle and throw myself into the river. But they drew closer together, kicked me, and knocked me sprawling backward. My flesh was raw; the blood ran down my shoulders and from my face and legs, and I thought I must faint. But I renewed my efforts to break through, deeming it beneath my pride to give them any further amusement by dancing. Finally, my breath was gone. I could fight no more. I staggered and fell to my knees, and the world seemed slipping away from me. Then someone came and threw a kettle of water over me. It revived me enough to look up at the cruel distorted faces of those who even yet mocked and gibed at my helplessness. Perhaps five minutes I knelt thus. Then a squaw came, and seizing me by the hair of my head, pulled me to my feet and began beating me again. But I backed away quickly, and then, head down, I dashed at her, striking her such a blow in the middle that she went over like a ninepin. Then the whole crew of them came at me. How long I fought I know not, but at last I could stand them off no longer, but stood there dumbly receiving their blows. Indeed, their blows seemed no longer to hurt me. It seemed that it was not my body that received their punishment, but that of some other captive, and I was observing him from a great height. And then, suddenly, there was a commotion among the men and the inner circle of women. They scattered sideways, this way and that, pushed by the hands of a giant who grew bigger and bigger—a giant with a scarred, wrathful face and a head shaved save for a scalp lock in which waved a long hawk's feather. He cried out with a loud voice, like the clanging of a bell. I saw him rush forward and, bending, pick up the body of the poor lad that was not me any more, and hold it against his breast. And his voice, that seemed to come from a great distance, now murmured:

"My poor little P'sazum; poor little P'sazum; he has been almost killed!"

Then I felt something cold on my face and brow, and with a sigh I came out of the mist, and looked up into the eyes of Tomah, the Maliseet Chief. And as sure as I lived to tell all this, I felt that I had died and gone to heaven. Then the woman, who was Tomah's squaw, came and laid her hand on his arm, and the others crowded around, crying awesomely, "*Tomah—Sachem Tomah.*"

He rose to his feet with me still in his arms. And his voice was filled with anger as he said, "My people, this was not well done. This boy is my son." Then he called his squaw, and without another word, carried me to his wigwam. And now I knew I had not died; but that in very truth Tomah had returned. But I was yet too weak save to murmur, "*Tomah—Tomah Sogomo—Kuluwazu Tomah.*"

He laid me on a bearskin rug covered with a blanket, had water brought, and himself washed my bruised and bleeding flesh. Then he rubbed a salve on it, made from the buds of a large warty poplar, known in this country as the Balm of Gilead, and dusted over the salve powdered cedar-bark. Then he put my clothing on me and bade me sleep, for no one would harm me more. And I slept, nor awakened until hot broth was brought me.

CHAPTER 24

The Story of Tomah

The following late afternoon I was taken to the big Council Lodge, and all the Maliseets of Medowktek, both men and women, gathered therein. A great feast had been prepared in honour of their Chief's return. Kettles of boiled salmon, beaver, moose flesh, and cakes of corn bread baked on hot stones were brought in. The men ate first, the squaws serving them.

I sat beside Tomah on a bear rug, clad in a new clean shirt and trousers of doeskin, and on my feet moccasins with beaded work and dyed porcupine quills. In my hair the Chief had put a hawk's feather, and about my neck was the necklet of bear's teeth that had been taken from me the previous day.

The Chief had garbed himself in new trousers of white buckskin. In his belt were his tomahawk and scalping knife. The upper part of his body was bare, and the flames from the lodge fire lighted up the salmon tattooed on his broad chest. Two silver bracelets flashed on his wrists; about his neck hung the medal presented to his father by the great Count Frontenac, and on his head was a close-fitting band of doeskin decorated with hawk's feathers. His face was unpainted. The crescent-shaped scar that stretched from the corner of his upper lip to below his right ear, far from being ugly, seemed to me to add dignity to his haughty countenance. The scar, he had told me earlier in the day, had been received in an affray with Iroquois, during his journey from the land of the Delawares.

After we had finished, the women filled their own bowls and ate. Then all the eating and cooking utensils were taken outside. A big pipe was now brought by Tomah's wife. The bowl was half as big as my fist and carved with curious animals. The stem was a foot long. The bowl of the pipe was filled with tobacco and presented to Tomah. Then his squaw stepped to the fire, lighted a cedar stick, and returning, held it over the bowl while the Chief pulled at the stem. When it was going nicely, he rose, lifted the pipe to the east, the west, the north and the south. Then, handing it to me, said, "Smoke, P'sazum." I drew in a breath and passed it back to him. He took a puff, and handed it to his neighbour on his right. Then it passed around the circle.

Now my friend rose to his full height, raised his hand, and silence fell upon the assembly. Then he spoke, slowly and clearly. And he told what I have already written of our first meeting, of my kindness to him aboard ship, our life on the plantation, our escape, and on down to the day I disappeared. And he said, his voice trembling with emotion, "And this boy, whom I named *Kuluwazu P'sazum*, I thought was gone forever from me, and my heart was sick. Then I went from these Lenapè. They gave me a gun, powder, and lead, and the Chief led me back to the ridge where he had left the boy on the rock while he followed the bear. I tried to pick up the trail of the Indians who had stolen him, but rain had come, and save for the ashes of a camp-fire and once the print of a moccasin a little farther on, I saw no sign of them. I travelled eastward. When I came to rivers I made a raft of poles and crossed over. Several times I saw Indians, but I hid from them and they knew not I was near them. But no man can go the distance I did and not meet enemies. I had crossed the Hudson River, and now turned more southward, hoping to reach the Connecticut and soon be among those who would be friendly. But one night, as I slept, I was set upon by a band of Senecas, and though I fought them I was overpowered and captured.

"They bound my hands and took me northward to one of their villages on the Mohawk River. The next day they bound me to a tree, and amused themselves dancing close to me, brandishing tomahawks and knives in front of my face to see if I would flinch. They laughed at me, and said that which I could not understand. For the speech of the Senecas is like the call of the blue jay crying for rain, and not like our own tongue. Then they untied me from the tree and two of their warriors took my feet and two others my head, and lifting me up they let my back strike the hard ground. But I gave no cry or moan, and this angered them, for they kept up the torture until I thought my back was broken. When they had finished, they stood me on my feet, but I fell flat and could not move. Then a warrior seized a war-club and came at me. I thought my hour was come, but the Chief said something to him and he threw down the club.

"I was taken to a wigwam. Food was brought me, and water, but I could not eat or drink at that time. Several days passed, and I ate and drank and grew stronger. But knowing they would not torture me further until I could stand, I made believe I was weaker than I was. That is, if they stood me on my feet, I fell to the ground, and lay there as if I had no power in my legs. They had unbound me, for my hands and wrists were swollen all about the rawhide, and the flies plagued me much. The chief came to look at me every day, and from the gestures he made, I gathered that he thought my back was broken. But all the time I was growing stronger and laughed to myself at the trick I was playing.

"Then, one night, while it was raining, and all the village asleep but the two warriors who guarded me, these two Senecas smoked their pipes and sat with their backs to me, talking among themselves. After a little I moved closer to them, and suddenly, reaching out my hand, I seized the tomahawk of one and drove it into his brain. Then I killed the other before he had a chance to give a whoop. And with his knife I took both their scalps. Then I stepped out into the night. Even the dogs were in out of the rain. I saw no one. I stole between the row of wigwams, then ran to the river, and finding a canoe and paddle I jumped in the canoe and paddled downstream all night until day came. Then I left the canoe and went into the woods. I saw no one. It was yet raining, and I was wet and cold. But I ran and walked, always eastward. When night came I slept but a few hours. Once I crawled into a great hollow log. Some time during that night I heard a noise and thought it was an Indian, but it was only *Mah-ti-gwess* (the rabbit) thumping his heels on the ground.

"Day after day I travelled. Then I came to the Kennebeck River and the country I now know well. I crossed the Kennebeck, and finally came to the Penobscot; then I made a raft and floated down it until I came to the Matawamkeag. Here I found allies of our own nation. They gave me a canoe, and I poled up the Matawamkeag along the old water route our forefathers used when the world was young. But, my people, when I made the last portage, and looked down on the village and saw that you were torturing someone, I little knew it was the boy who was my son. But, my people"—and here Tomah lifted his hand impressively—"from now we will try to make good the wrongs he has suffered in the village." He paused a moment, then added sternly, "Who does him any harm is my enemy!" Then, turning to me, he caught my hand and raised me to my feet.

A shout went up from the assembly, and each in turn came forward and took my hand and said, "Brother." And also the women. But Tomah's squaw said, "Son," and gently stroked my cheek with her hand.

Then Tomah took me by the hand and led me to his own wigwam. And I was at peace for the first time in many months.

CHAPTER 25

We spear Salmon

A few nights later, with Tomah and Arodowish, who was now quite well again, I went spearing salmon. For there was a heavy late run of these fish, both male and female, now on their way to the spawning grounds.

The Indian spear is a curious weapon, and ingenious in its construction. There are four chief parts to it: the eight-foot shaft of peeled spruce wood; the two jaws of rock maple; and the iron, or bone harpoon. The harpoon fits into the end of the shaft, two sides of which have been flattened. Then the two wooden jaws are laid against and securely bound to these flattened sides of the shaft, with narrow strips of either basket ash or elm bark. When finished, it takes the strength of a strong man, grasping one of the jaws with either hand, to spring it outward. Yet, when a fish is struck over the shoulders with a quick and direct blow, the jaws spring apart far enough to envelop both sides of the fish, and at the same time allow the harpoon to sink into the flesh. Any movement of the fish only serves to force it inexorably and securely upward within the jaws, so that the man who is spearing can lift it up and out of the water into his canoe.

Before going out, Tomah and Arodowish made more than a dozen birchbark flares. These are made in this wise: a strip of birchbark about twelve inches wide by eighteen inches long is folded back and forth on itself until it is finally a flattened bundle, the edge of the last fold being cut in narrow ribands, so that when set on fire it will burn brightly. The whole piece is now forced into a cleft made in a handle that is three or four feet long.

A moonless night is best for spearing salmon, or any fish, for that matter. There was no moon this night. I sat amidships. Arodowish poled the canoe. Tomah was in the bow. On the floor of the canoe was a small kettle in which he had made a little fire before setting out.

We poled upriver about two miles to where the river widens and flows swiftly over a rock-studded bar for perhaps a half mile. At the head of this bar, on the right, there enters the river a large brook, the water of which is very cold.

Now Tomah picked up one of his flares by the handle, and touched the riband edge to the little fire he had brought with him. It burst into flame. He held the spear handle in his left hand high above his head, and standing upright in the canoe, gazed down into the water as Arodowish poled the canoe this way and that way diagonally against the current. I was all eagerness and curiosity. I was seated on an old bearskin folded into a small bundle on the floor of the canoe. I grasped the gunwales with my hands, and craned my neck so I could look over the side without disturbing the balance of the craft. The light showed up the bottom for a space of several feet. I could see rocks, pieces of bark, a sunken log, eels, small fish. And there—we were approaching it now, a long grey fish that moved its broad tail just enough to keep it in a position a little to the left of, and slightly behind a good-sized boulder. "Go slow, easy," said Tomah to Arodowish, and I felt the canoe slow and finally come to a quivering standstill, as he held it there against the swift current.

Suddenly the salmon left its position. It was like a flash of lightning. It swung in a wide half-circle, came straight for the head of the canoe, then, with another flash, it swung to the left and disappeared. Then I felt the canoe ease towards the left, and hold. I saw Tomah's spear cleave the water; down—down, until only half the handle was above the surface. With a quick movement of his left hand Tomah doused his flare, then grasped the spear-shaft below the right hand. For a few moments, as the salmon's muscular body struggled within those confining jaws, I could feel the shaft beating a tattoo against the gunwale. Finally it ceased, and Tomah drew up the fish and deposited it in the bottom of the canoe.

"*Ka-loo-ut* (good)," was all Arodowish said. Tomah gave a low chuckle, then said to me, "You like that, P'sazum?"

"Yes," I answered, and, when Tomah lit another flare, and I was able to see the salmon, I exclaimed excitedly, "*Wul-e-nakw-so-Bulam*." (It is a nice salmon.) Then Arodowish said, "You make good Maliseet, P'sazum."

The salmon was very big, and would weigh no less than thirty pounds.

And that night I understood why Tomah had been nicknamed *Bulam* (the Salmon). For as the salmon is the swiftest of all fish, so was Tomah swift, and his eye as keen as that of the king of the water.

Half the night we speared, and when finally there were no more flares left, we slipped back home towards Medowktek, nor heard any sound save the ripple of the water, and once "*kahoo-agh!*" the cry of a great horned owl from far up the forested hillside, until, nearing the shore, an Indian dog raised his voice in raucous warning to his people.

The days that now followed were the happiest I had known since my abduction. I was allowed perfect freedom to do as I wished. No one, young or old, showed me anything but kindness. I had a canoe to use, and under Tomah's tuition I was soon able to stand up and pole or paddle it anywhere. The hillsides on both sides of the river contained many grouse, and, armed with Tomah's gun charged with small shot, I covered a wide extent of country in pursuit of them.

One day Tomah took me down to the lower end of the flat, where the Indian village stood long before the coming of the French. "Then my forefathers didn't know there were people anywhere in the world that were white," he said. "We thought everyone—north, east, south and west—was red. We believed that the great lord, *Glooscap*, made the world, as he made everything in it, all the animals and all the fish. And he made man in this way: He shot arrows at trees, the basket tree, which, as you know, P'sazum, is the ash. And where he shot the arrows Indians came out of the bark of the ash trees. He did everything for the Indians. But finally," said Tomah earnestly, "Glooscap went away. No one knows where he went. My father he say he went to the west. But no one knows, P'sazum. Some people say if you not afraid to travel, and not afraid, you can find the Great Sachem. They say he lives in great big wigwam. What he do? Oh, he make'm arrows, always make'm arrows. One side of big lodge is full of arrows. Now he start to fill other side. When lodge holds no more, he will come back and make big war. Then all bad people be killed, and new world begin. All better." Tomah ceased. He had been very much in earnest, and I have no doubt that, despite all his recent teaching from the white man, he still believed in his own divinity, the Great Glooscap.

"You never see stone arrows and knives Indians use?" he asked me.

"No, Tomah," I answered.

He went and cut a small sapling, which he sharpened at one end. Then he said, "I think maybe we find some just here." And he began to dig and scratch in the earth. And presently he turned out some broken pieces, then some whole ones, and he picked them up and dusting off the earth that clung to them, he put them in my hand.

They were beautifully shaped little things, like tiny spruce or fir trees, with a little indentation on each side near the base. Some were white, others black, yet others red.

And Tomah said, "They take arrow shaft, make little split on one end, and press arrow in. Then they tie it on with small rawhide string. *Ah-ha*," he added, "that's what my people used for kill deer and moose. *Ah-ha*, I suppose these same kind that Glooscap show them how to make." He paused, then added, "You keep them, P'sazum; take them with you to *Kamnokik* (England) to show people there what Indians used long time ago."

I thanked him, and several times in the days that followed I came to this place and dug. And I found quite a number of pieces—arrow points, and knives, and even big spear points, and brought them home. I understand a few of these have been picked up in Scotland and England, and some people have thought they were formed that way by nature; others that they fell down from the sky. And those who cling to this latter belief call them "thunder stones". But *I* know they are the same kind of stone weapons as made and used by the Indians of America. And they are the same as those formerly used by the Tartars, which race of people I found to be of the same colour as the Americans, and using much the same language.

When all the leaves had gone, and the nights became so cold that the water along the shore and in the still back-waters began freezing at night, several of the Indians of Medowktek departed on their winter hunt. They did not all go together, but in parties of four, or eight, or twelve; seldom more, and each in a different direction, or place, some far, some near.

Tomah and Arodowish and a fellow named Atwin went together, I with them. We spent the whole winter near a lake called *Nashwaak*, some sixty miles northeast of Medowktek. We went by canoe part of the way, then walked the remainder. We made camp near the lake, which was now frozen over with a thin skim of ice, by a little brook that flows into it. The camp was of poles, covered with birchbark that was overlapped so that no moisture would enter. A hole was left in the roof to let the smoke out, for my companions kept a fire going in a hole they dug in the ground. This fire hole was in depth about three feet, and in diameter across the top about the same.

Barely was the camp completed when Atwin shot and killed a moose. It was a very big one. After it was skinned, the meat was cut in quarters and hung up near the camp. Then the hide was scraped of hair and fat, and cut into long strips half an inch wide. These were suspended from the branch of a tree, a weight attached to the bottom, then left to stretch overnight. This was to be the webbing for the snowshoes which were to be made.

My friends now got ashwood for the frames. Having first cut a long piece the desired length, they whittled it with their knives to a thickness of three quarters of an inch, then steamed it over the copper kettle we had brought, bent it into the desired shape and fitted in the cross-bars. When done they were somewhat the shape of a tennis racquet. Now the webbing was filled in. It astonished me how quickly they did this. Of course, I watched every move they made; and I believe, after all the years that have passed, that I could make a fair show at making a pair of snowshoes.

Out of the hide covering the moose shanks they made me a pair of leggings and shoes combined, that came well above my knees. A little later they shot a bear. After skinning and roughly tanning the skin, they cut holes for my arms, and when this was laced about me, the hair inside, I was comfortable even on the coldest days.

Now they began constructing deadfalls around the lake, far down the outlet, and along brooks that entered the lake.

Thereafter we took beavers, otter, mink, martens and other small animals. These had to be skinned and the skins put on wooden stretchers made from cedar-wood, so that for the most part we were quite busy.

We saw no other hunters or trappers. We were alone in a vast wilderness known only to wandering Indians, and the wild beasts that lived there. Had it not been for my companions, I had lost track of the passage of time, but I found that they kept a fairly accurate account of the days and weeks by aid of the moon's phases. They knew, too, by unmistakable signs, when a change of weather was about to take place. For instance, if we awakened in the morning and found the trees covered with a thick white frost, they told me we would have a thaw, perhaps rain, or snow. And sure enough, within twenty-four hours, or less, we got the thaw and either rain or snow, as prophesied.

Sometimes I forgot that there were other people in the world or that a war was in progress. But on other occasions, especially when night closed in, and the trees cast their ghostly shadows on the snow, and the only sounds were those of some prowling night animal, or the hoot of an owl, my thoughts would often turn homeward. I pictured my stepmother—she who I felt sure had been responsible for my kidnapping and slavery—living on in my own home, going to church and receiving communion, and accepted by the people as an upright woman. And I wondered how God could let such things be, and if ever He would make it possible for me to return and claim my inheritance. Then I would imagine myself, clad in my bearskin coat and moosehide leggings, landing at the quay, and walking along the streets of Aberdeen to my guardian's house; the curious stares of the people who saw me; perhaps followed by a crowd of urchins to the very door. And thinking thus, I imagined the clothing I had left behind me: the bonny kilts and velvet jackets, the shoes with silver buckles, the great coat with horn buttons, and my tricorn hat—forgetting that none would fit me now.

We had been at this place about two months when we had a wild and prolonged blizzard that lasted three days and nights. So close together came the snowflakes that every object more than a few rods distant was blotted out. A howling nor'easter drove the snow with such force it stung the face like the lash of a whip. Occasionally an overburdened bough let fall its load of snow which, caught in the tempest, was swept away like smoke. All about us the hardwood trees swayed in the tumult; their bare limbs crashed together with sounds like those made by antlered moose or caribou, when the beasts meet in deadly combat.

Our wigwam was a white pyramid, from whose apex the poles protruded like a grotesque assortment of primitive spears. The coming of night seemed to me to add to our remoteness from all things human. To my imagination the wind wailing through the trees was like the crying of ghosts vainly trying to find rest and peace from the elements.

We had plenty of firewood—wood of the maple, and the birch, that gave off a great heat and burned for a long time. And we slept comfortably with our feet towards the fire-pit.

Often in the evenings the Indians told stories—stories of war and chase, and legends of their race reaching back into the remote past dealing with their conception of the origin of the world and its peoples, or the pranks of animals endowed with human-like attributes.

And they asked me about my own land of Kamnokik. And I did my best to tell them about its people, their customs, the churches, shipyards and shipping. When they asked me if there were as many people in Kamnokik as in Quebec, and I had said there were ten thousand times more in Kamnokik, Arodowish said I must be mistaken. There could not be so many.

I did not argue with them. The talk did us good. Hemmed in as we were by storm as wild and impenetrable by day as by night, these exchanges did much to pass what otherwise would have been particularly dull hours for me.

Finally the storm abated, and it became very cold, much colder than we had yet experienced. I remember the nights, and how big and close the stars looked; like lamps let down from the blue inverted dome of the sky. I remember the strange cannonade-like explosions from within the forest, and, turning questioning eyes on

Tomah, he told me it was the sound made by trees bursting open with the frost. And the next day he showed me one of them, and sure enough the bark of the tree had been split open, from above downward, and even into the heart of the tree, so that one could insert a knife blade two or three inches.

What amazed me was that these Indians knew the names of the stars. And their names were the same as those we know them by. Thus they say the North Star does not move, and the circumpolar stars never set. And they called the Great Bear *Moo-in*. And the Milky Way they call as we do. So that I have since thought that if we could only go back far enough we would find that all the human race evolved from the same cradle.

It seemed we had been ages away from Medowktek when finally spring came, and though there were still several feet of snow in the woods, and the lake still frozen over, all the little brooks were alive and laughing and making their way to join the big rivers. So on one toboggan we piled the furs we had caught, and moose meat on another, and putting on our snowshoes, we left the place and struck a course to where we had left the canoe the fall before. We found it safe, took it from beneath its covering of poles and bark, and loading it, got in and paddled down the stream. It was the Sikstahaw. Yes, spring was in the air—a sweet odour from birch and maple buds that heartened me and gave me new life.

Arriving at the Wulahstukw, we only paused long enough to eat, then set sail again. So swift the current, for the melting snows had raised it five or six feet higher than it was in the autumn, we reached Medowktek in a little over two hours. As we pulled in to shore beside the fort, we were greeted by dogs, children, men and women. An Indian seized hold of the canoe, and held it as we disembarked.

I stepped out on the bank and saw a black-robed man a few feet away. He had a pleasant face, and kindly, and it seemed as though I had seen him before. Then, as he came and took my hand, I knew. It was the priest of the Society of Jesus I had seen on the deck of the *Honfleur* as we parted from her almost four years before.

He addressed me kindly, and I was instantly won by his gracious manner. He said he would like to talk more to me later. Then he left me with a pat on the shoulder, to speak with Tomah. He seized the Chief by the hand and wrung it heartily and said, "Ah, Sachem Tomah, I never thought to see you again. I have heard about your captivity and escape. It is all miraculous. You must come tomorrow, and bring the English boy, and we will talk."

The following day we went to his cabin. He asked me many questions which I answered as best I could, and when I had ended, he said that he hoped I had not forgotten to give thanks to God for my many escapes from death. I assured him I had not, and recounted how I had entered his little chapel more than once to pray and receive comfort.

This pleased him greatly. He now asked me if there was aught he could do for me.

I said, "If I have any wish, it is to get back to my guardian in Scotland."

He replied, "This does not seem possible to me while the war is in progress. Unless—" he paused— "you are willing to journey to Quebec with some of the Maliseet warriors who will be going thither as soon as the woods are free of snow. But even there," he said, "it might be a long time before the authorities would be able to exchange you with the English for a French prisoner in their hands."

"Thank you, Father," I said. "I would rather stay at Medowktek than go to Quebec. For here," I added, "I have staunch friends, while at Quebec I would be among complete strangers."

He nodded assent to this, and said, "I think, my son, you have chosen wisely. In the meanwhile, if any avenue opens whereby I can send you to Boston or some other English port, rest assured I shall do so."

I thanked him and asked him how long he thought the war would last.

"God alone knows when peace will come to this stricken world," he said sadly. "But I hope, my son, it will not be long."

I thanked him for his kindness; and then, after he had given both Tomah and me his blessing, we took leave of him.

CHAPTER 26

Jeanne Chartier

The days and weeks passed. Once more the migrant birds returned, built nests and laid eggs, which in time hatched out tiny fledglings that kept the parents busy supplying their insatiable hunger. The ground was prepared; the corn sowed.

I was clad now in new garments made me by Tomah's wife: trousers of buckskin, a shirt of soft white doeskin, and moosehide moccasins ornamented with beads and porcupine quills.

Little happened to mar the quiet of the village. Occasionally a French trader came to barter for furs. Then came several warriors from the scene of strife in Acadia. They told of a fight at Grand Pré, in which a party of French, and Micmac, and Maliseet Indians, had marched on snowshoes more than fifty miles, come upon the English—who were billeted in ten houses—at night, killed many and forced the remainder to surrender.

I now witnessed a great feast and dance at Medowktek to commemorate this victory. The carcasses of two moose and many beavers were roasted, and feasting and dancing continued far into the morning hours. All the warriors were naked save for a breech clout, their bodies painted diverse colours. They danced to the monotonous thumping of a drum Governor Villebon had given the villagers many years before.

A short time later other news not so heartening to the Indians was brought by Canadian soldiers, accompanied by a few Hurons, on their way to Quebec. They told of a sea fight between English and French warships, the defeat of the latter, and the capture of a French marquis who was bound to Quebec to take over the governorship of Canada. But if the news was disheartening to the Indians, it was even more so to Father Germain. I overheard him talking to one of the French soldiers, whose language I now understood a little. "Alas! Alas!" he said. "I am afraid now that Louisburg will remain in English hands for many a day!"

But he was wrong. For, by the articles of peace signed at Aix-la-Chapelle in October the following year, England restored to France the island of Cape Breton and the fortress of Louisburg, which the people of New England had spent such a sum in blood and treasure to conquer.

And now the time is come to tell of the coming to Medowktek of Jeanne Chartier—she who even as a mere girl of twelve I loved, and who later became my wife.

On the second Saturday evening of June, two canoes came up the river poled by Indians. In one canoe were Raoul Chartier and his young daughter. The other canoe contained their baggage. This Raoul Chartier held a seigniory of several hundred acres below the Jemsec, and carried on a vast trade in peltry with the Indians.

I did not see them that night, but Tomah told me that both father and daughter had been given lodgings in the priest's house for the few days they would be at Medowktek. The Sieur Chartier was on his way to Quebec, where he was taking his daughter to enter her in the Nuns' Seminary there.

Sunday morning dawned beautiful and fair. I remember how peaceful everything was as the chapel bell rang out, calling the inhabitants of Medowktek to early mass.

With Tomah and his wife and children I walked to the chapel. For as I have said before, I felt that I could worship God in this sacred place as well as in any other.

I sat down on a wooden form beside Tomah and his wife and children, and, as they did, I bowed my head reverently and said a little prayer. Then, as I straightened and sat up, I saw Jeanne Chartier. She was with her father in the front row, and I could hardly restrain a gasp of astonishment at the pure beauty of her profile. Her skin was fair, her dark hair curling from beneath a little velvet cap, and falling to the white lace collar of her brown woollen bodice. The sun from the east window fell upon her and enhanced her loveliness. I could not remove my gaze, but just sat there in a trance. The sight of her swept my fancy back to my childhood in Scotland, and Scotch lasses demurely seated beside their parents in the old Kirk I had worshipped in so many times with my dear father. This morning, feasting my eyes on this charming French maiden, I was in a sense reborn, and I exulted in my rebirth.

The service was in the Maliseet tongue, for the good priest was well versed in it. It would have done you good to hear the Indians sing the chants. For assuredly, though I am familiar with several languages, the Maliseet is more like poetry than any other.

The service was all too short. When it was quite over, I walked back with Tomah to his wigwam, still in the dream evoked by the lovely maiden I had seen. Oh, yes, even then, at that my first sight of her, the candle of romance was lighted in my heart.

I saw her again the following day. Above the Indian fort, a short quarter of a mile, a small brook flows into the river. And at its mouth the trouts and other fish congregate in great number. Thither I had gone to catch some of them, not dreaming that she would be there. And as I walked along the pebbly beach towards the mouth of the brook, which was around a little neck of land that jutted out, my mind was filled with thoughts of her, as it had been most of my waking hours since I had seen her in the chapel.

As I rounded the neck of land I saw her, with two Indian boys, at the mouth of the brook. She was angling, using an alder pole one of them had cut for her.

My first thought was to withdraw and go back to the village, for the sight of her had filled me with a great shyness. Then, conquering my shyness, and with my heart beating more rapidly, I slowly approached them, and finally stopped a few yards' distance away. She had not heard me, but the Indian boys, her companions, trained to be quick of ear, turned, saw me, and then said something to her, for she gave me a glance over her shoulder, and then returned her eyes to the pool.

Though it all happened sixty years ago, I can recall the scene as though it were but yesterday: the river, rippling over the bar, the quiet, forest-clad hills, and the French girl, so intent on her angling, between her two Indian companions.

I sat down on the butt of a tree that had been left high on the beach by the spring flood, and watched them, or rather the girl. She did not seem to be having any luck; for though I could see fish breaking water, they refused to take the worm bait one of the boys had put on her hook.

And I thought how I could better the worm bait and catch trouts for her were it my privilege to do so. For on the hook that was tied to my linen line I had fastened a tiny feather of the wood duck, and to that had added another from the poll of a red-headed woodpecker. I had done it carefully and neatly as I had seen my father dress flies with which to lure the Dee sea trouts.

For perhaps fifteen minutes I watched her attempts to catch fish. Finally she pulled her line to shore, and I heard her say in Indian, "*Nha* (take it)," then, "*Mutjeg-n* (too bad)." And then in French something I did not understand.

But she looked so crestfallen, so disappointed at her ill-luck, that I, putting my shyness from me, rose from the log and went to where she stood, and said, in Maliseet, that if she would allow me, I would try to catch her a trout.

After her first moment of surprise, during which her hazel eyes looked straight into mine, she said, "*Wul-e-wun*," which is "thank you" in Maliseet.

So I lengthened my line and cast out in the pool where the fish were still breaking water, then began to draw the hook towards me. Suddenly there was a great splash and I was fast to a goodly trout that would weigh half a pound. I flung it over my head far up the beach, and in a trice the two Indian boys had seized upon it and brought it back to where the girl stood, her brown eyes dancing with delight. "*Ka-loo-ut—Ka-loo-ut*," she cried. "*Wul-e-wun*." (Good, thank you.) Then, "Would you please catch me another?" her eyes all eagerness.

I was thrilled beyond words, my shyness gone. I cast again, and again landed a fair trout. Then again, another. A dozen I caught and landed for her. And finally could land no more, for they stopped taking as quickly as they had begun.

One of the Indian boys cut a forked branch from a tree on the bank, and strung the trouts on it, then we walked back along the beach towards the village.

And as we went the girl talked. She said, "You are the English boy about whom Father Germain told us last night, are you not?"

"Yes," I answered, and told her my name. "But I have another," I added, "*Kuluwazu-P'sazum.*"

Her brows crinkled a moment in puzzlement. Then she smiled, showing her pretty white teeth. "Ah, I know now what that means." Then, pointing to the trouts dangling from the hand of the Indian boy, "To-day you have been my good star, is it not so?"

I felt my face crimson. Then I said lamely, "I but knew how to take them."

"It is all the same," she returned quickly. "Without you I would not be taking the trouts to my father." Then she paused, and said, "Of course, only two. It was two you caught for me. The others are yours."

"You may have all," I said, "I caught them all for you." Something, I know not what, but something more than my mere words, made her to understand that I would be hurt if she insisted any further, and with a low "*Wul-e-wun, P'sazum,*" she smiled, and followed the Indian lads to the priest's cabin.

Slowly, as in a dream, I walked to the wigwam of Tomah.

And that evening a messenger came from the priest's cabin and asked me to go there. I put on the deerskin trousers and jacket Tomah's wife had given me, washed my face and hands, and tied my long hair back with a string of rawhide; then, all in a tremble of excitement, went to the priest's cabin.

The good father came at my knock and led me into the main room, where, about a candle-lighted table, were Monsieur Raoul Chartier and Jeanne his daughter. They both rose. Jeanne smiled and dropped me a pretty curtsey. Then I was presented to M'sieu Chartier. He was a tall, dark-skinned, handsome man. He smiled at me and asked me in Maliseet where I had learned to catch fish with a dressed fly hook.

"In Kam-no-kik (England)," I answered. Then added, "I said Kam-no-kik, M'sieu. But it was in Scotland. There is no word in Maliseet for Scotland; but it is all the same."

He understood, for he nodded; and when I was seated on the stool the priest brought, he said, "I have heard of some of your strange adventures from Father Germain, and from my daughter. Will you be good enough to start at the beginning and tell all?"

"Yes," I answered. And there, in that little cabin of Father Germain's, with the candle-light casting its golden glow over the peeled spruce logs, and conscious that the eyes of Jeanne Chartier were on me, I began and told them what I have already told you.

When I had ended it was very late. And when I rose to go, M'sieu Chartier said it was the strangest tale he had ever heard. Then he added, "To-morrow we depart for Quebec. It is a long journey, and there will be several long portages before we reach our destination. Jeanne"—he smiled at his daughter—"will enter the seminary." He paused a moment as in deep thought, then said to the priest, "My father, if by any way you can get this poor lad to a ship going overseas, I would take it as a personal favour." He paused again, then added, "The war between our country and England will end some day. If not before—then after—we must see to it that he returns to his own land."

He held out his hand, took mine and pressed it warmly. Jeanne rose and dropped me a demure curtsey. The priest led me to the door, opened it, bade me goodnight.

A moment more, with a heart in which were commingled hope and sadness, I took myself to the wigwam of my foster-father.

The following morning I stood on the embankment and sorrowfully watched them depart. Jeanne sat in the canoe with her father, slightly ahead of him. The Indian thrust down his long spruce pole, gave a gentle push. The canoe moved gracefully against the current. The other canoe with its two Indians followed, the water purling from the upturned bows. The two passengers turned and waved a final farewell.

It seemed to me that the maiden's eyes were looking upward to where I stood, an odd, choking sensation in my throat. Then she had turned and looked straight ahead.

I stood a long while watching them—until the canoes became tiny specks on the blue water. Then I went slowly back to the village, with its bark wigwams, smouldering fire in front of each, and snarling dogs and half-naked children, and squaws, young and old, and filth with its myriad smells. I went into the wigwam and, throwing myself down on my bearskin rug, buried my face in my hands and wept bitter tears.

CHAPTER 27

I leave Medowktek

One afternoon, when the young blades of corn were half a foot high, a Kennebeck Indian came to Medowktek with messages for Father Germain from the missionary on the Penobscot.

That evening Father Germain sent for me. When I entered his little cabin and was seated, he said, "My son, I have good news for you. An English ship is at Casco loading pine masts to be taken to England. The Kennebeck Indian who brought me this news is returning to the Penobscot to-morrow, or the day following. If you desire it, you can accompany him back to that place, and I will send a letter to the priest there to forward you to Casco."

I felt myself all of a tremble. "Thank you, Father," I said. "You are very kind. I will go and tell Tomah."

So I ran and told Tomah the news. He spoke not for several moments, then he put both his hands on my shoulders and said, "Little P'sazum, I know this makes you happy, but the heart of Tomah is heavy. We have gone through many dangers together, and I have come to look on you as my own son. I had even hoped you would always stay with me. But I see that it is not to be. You will go. But Tomah will not trust you with the Kennebeck. I myself will take you by way of the rivers and lakes to Casco."

At this news I almost wept for gladness. Yet I said, "Tomah, may there not be danger for you? May not some English scout kill you?"

He shook his head. "I know the way to Casco. I alone will take you, P'sazum."

For some reason Tomah did not care to travel in the company of the Kennebeck, and quietly made arrangements to depart early the following day.

And so, after we had breakfast, and I had said my farewells to Father Germain and all the people in the village, I followed Tomah and Arodowish across the Flat to the upland and the ancient portage that leads to the Eel River waters, that same portage which, with but brief respite, many generations of Maliseet warriors had traversed to make war on the villages and homesteads of New England.

Arodowish carried over his head a light sixteen-foot birchbark canoe. Tomah carried the guns, and, in a pack basket on his shoulders, two blankets and the food we would need. I carried a pack basket Tomah's wife had given me. It was of ash splints, and I was very proud of it. I had it in a shirt the priest had given me, extra moccasins, a little birchbark basket, and another smaller one decorated with porcupine quills. In this I had carefully put my stone arrowheads, knives and spearheads, each one wrapped in a piece of doeskin. I had also something that gave me very great pleasure. It was a cap of white doeskin that Tomah's wife had made. Around the band it was decorated with small wigwams, coloured red and blue alternately. And in the band she had fastened two feathers, one from a hawk, the other from a partridge.

Reaching the height of the land, I turned and gazed back on the village. In front of the bark wigwams spirals of smoke lazily drifted into the blue. Northward was the palisaded fort with its look-out tower and flagstaff, above which fluttered the lilies of France. For a few moments my gaze rested on the tiny church, with its bell sent over leagues of sea, and transported by canoe up more leagues of tortuous current, to find at last a resting-place, and, awaking alien echoes in this inland forest, call to mass its red-skinned inhabitants. Then my eyes sought the noble river, lilting its age-old music over the gravelly bars, and lifted to the forested ridge beyond. Then I turned, an odd feeling at my heart, and followed in the wake of Arodowish and Tomah.

Five miles the portage led over a succession of ridges, between great trees of birch and maple, pine, hemlock, spruce, and many others. In two hours we came to the Eel River above the falls. Launching the canoe, we got in, and my companions poled upstream to the first Eel Lake, where on a point of land we camped for the night.

I was vastly interested in this journey. It was the same water route by which, almost half a century before my coming, the New England boy, John Giles, had been brought by his captors to spend six years of slavery at Medowktek.

In the morning we crossed the lake, landed, and went over a three mile carry to another lake. We paddled down this until it narrowed to a mere thread a hundred yards wide, that soon opened into a very long lake. The waves were quite high on this lake, and sometimes I wondered if our little craft could ride them. But she did, and opposite a long point that juts from the left-hand shore, we landed again, took the canoe out of the water and carried it first over a hill, then along the level until, after two miles, we came to a stream Tomah said was the Baskahegan.

We went down this several miles, until it enters the Matawamkeag; thence we followed the latter stream to the Penobscot. Then on to the principal village of the Penobscots, called Panawamakek, which was a palisaded fort like that of Medowktek.

Some of the women here were very curious, pressing about me, pointing at my hair, and wanting to know if I was *Pl-etch-emin* (French) or *Kamnokik* (English). Then one male Indian, who had visited Medowktek while I was there, said I was English.

Immediately a howl went up. They grasped my arms and tried to drag me away. But both Tomah and Arodowish got close to me and pushed them away.

I now understood one of the reasons that Tomah would not let me come with the Kennebeck.

When the priest who lived in this village had read Father Germain's letter, he turned to the people and told them that I was not to be harmed in any manner. He said that I was his guest, and that it would grieve him exceedingly if I was not treated with every courtesy. He then took my arm and led me to his cabin, where he kindly put me up for the night.

The next morning we left this place. Before going I said farewell to Arodowish, who was to remain with a relative until Tomah's return. He had been a good friend to me. He put his hand on my shoulder and said, "You good boy, P'sazum. Arodowish not happy to see you go. *Adio.*"

And that was the last I ever saw of Arodowish. Years later, when I revisited Medowktek, I learned that he had been ambushed and killed by Huron Indians and a few English rangers two months after I left, as he and other Maliseets were on their way to help their French and Micmac allies in Nova Scotia.

There is no need to describe in detail the remainder of our journey to Casco.

Coming to the Casco River, we went down it for several leagues, and at last, climbing a little hill, we saw the sea, the houses of Casco, and to my great joy, a large ship riding at anchor.

Ever since leaving Medowktek I had feared that she might have taken on her cargo of pine masting and departed. Now I felt my knees trembling.

When I had composed myself I said to Tomah, "I am all right now, Tomah. I need but to go to any of those houses and the inhabitants will receive me."

But he was yet loth to leave me. He said, "I will stay here, my son. Do you go and talk to your people. In the afternoon, come and tell me what they say." He pointed to a path. "Follow it, P'sazum. It will take you direct to the town. I will stay here."

Knowing that nothing I could say would change his purpose, I took the path he had indicated.

In ten minutes I reached the first row of houses. Stopping at one, I knocked at the door. A woman came. Seeing me, she gave a cry of surprise, with an admixture of fear. "Who—who are you?" she stammered.

I told her my name. "Is there a minister in this place?" I asked.

She nodded. Then, "Where did you come from, boy?"

I pointed to the forest. "I have been among the Indians," I said briefly.

"A captive?"

"Part of the time, Mistress."

"Poor lad," she said. "Are you hungry?"

"No, Mistress," I told her. "Will you kindly direct me to the minister's house?"

She came out and pointed to a house with a red roof. "Mr. Fenwick lives there," she said.

I thanked her and hurried off.

Nearing the house, I saw a tall, angular man hoeing in his garden to the rear of it. He paused, turning on me kindly eyes when I spoke to him.

"Good morning," he said, glancing at me curiously. "Yes, I am Mr. Fenwick, the minister. And your name, young man?"

I told him; then briefly my history, and my present desire to ship aboard the vessel in port.

"Poor lad," he said. "What an experience! Come into the house; you must need food. Come and meet my wife."

"I thank you," I said; "I am not hungry now. It is most important that I see the captain of the ship and find out if he will give me passage. Will you, Sir, go with me to him?"

"Certainly," he said, "but I assure you she will not be ready to sail for several days. I will get my coat, and then we will go and interview Captain Bates."

Going to the wharf, we found workmen and sailors making a great raft of pine logs to be towed out to the ship, put aboard, and taken overseas to be made into masts for the Royal Navy. Mr. Fenwick told one of the sailors he wanted to speak with Captain Bates.

In a few minutes the captain appeared. He was a short, thick-set man from Liverpool. Mr. Fenwick drew him to one side and talked with him for several minutes, at the end of which they both came to where I stood. "This is the lad, Captain Bates," said Mr. Fenwick.

Captain Bates shot out a heavy hand and gave my hand a powerful squeeze. "My lad," he said, "Mr. Fenwick has told me about you. I'll take you to Liverpool, and gladly. What is it you say—?"

"I was about to say, Sir, that I have no money, but if you will take me and let me work my passage I—"

He put up his hand. "Nay, lad, you've had enough hardship to warrant you a free crossing, as the captain's guest." He paused, clapped me on the shoulder, and added, "We hope to sail Monday next. Mr. Fenwick says he's keeping you at his house, or I'd ask you to take up your quarters with us."

I had much ado to thank him, for the lump in my throat.

As we were returning I said to Mr. Fenwick, "Sir, I have a confession to make to you. But if I tell you, will you promise me to keep it a strict secret?"

He stopped in his tracks, turned on me and said sternly, "A confession? Was it then a parcel of falsehoods you told me?"

"Oh, no, Sir," I said hastily. "It was every word truth, but I told you not all."

"Ah," he returned dryly, "I thought you had already told me more extraordinary happenings than I have heard in years. Well, go on, lad."

"You have been all kindness to me," I said, "and God will reward you. But if I tell you more, will you solemnly promise not to say or do anything that might bring harm to one I love as a father?"

He searched my face quickly, then said, "Of course not. Of course not, why should I?"

I gave a sigh of relief, then told him about Tomah, who awaited my word that all was well with me. "He has been both friend and father," I added, "and I would not have harm come to him for all my hopes of seeing home again."

He patted my shoulder kindly. "Fear not," he said. "Nor would I do aught to endanger his life. Come, David." And he led me into his house.

Mrs. Fenwick greeted me kindly. She was a small woman with quick, bird-like movements. She led me to a bench where there were basin and towel, and said I could wash. Then, as supper was ready, we sat down.

It was the first meal I had eaten in a house in many a long day. The white bread, butter, the cheese, the little cakes and coffee—how many times in my exile had I dreamed of them, when I had nothing but corn mush, moose steak, beaver flesh, or salmon, unsavoured save by the smoke from the open fires.

When we had quite finished, Mr. Fenwick packed a knapsack with food from the kitchen, and, taking me by the arm, we left the house. He walked with me to the foot of the hill, then handing me the knapsack, said, "Give this to your friend, David. I'll wait here until you return."

I thanked him and slowly entered the forest. I found Tomah sitting with his back to a great tree. He rose with the agility of a panther and came to me, an eager light in his black eyes. "Is the news *Ka-loo-ut* (good) or *Mutjego (bad)*?" he asked.

"*Ka-loo-ut*, Tomah," I cried joyously. Then I told him about the minister and the captain and the latter's offer to take me back home.

"*Agh*," he said, "good for you, P'sazum; not so good for Tomah. His days will be darkened without you."

I bowed my head. I had dreaded this moment of parting. Then I said, "I have promised I shall return, Tomah; yes, some time I will return. Then we will take salmon with the spear, and once more hunt the moose. I—I will bring you a new gun, Tomah, with your name on a brass plate set in the stock. I—" there was a lump in my throat, but I went on—"Oh, Tomah, I thank you for all your love and kindness to me. I shall never forget you—" I paused again.

He said, "And I not forget, P'sazum, I not forget how you take cords from Tomah's arms and legs on the ship. Tomah has good memory," and he put his hands on my shoulders.

Then I flung my arms about him, and he his about me. And he held me close, so close I could feel the great heart thudding against my cheek. The tears came to my eyes, and I wept. Yes, I wept, quietly, unrestrainedly, my face against his bare chest.

Finally I ceased, and looking up, I drew his face down and kissed him on each cheek. A smile came about his mouth and his black eyes glistened like reflected stars in a quiet lake. Then I drew away from him, and picking up the pack filled with food the minister had given me, I said to him, "Here is some food for your journey, Tomah."

"*Wul-e-wun*," he said simply.

I was the first to go. Sadly I began retracing my steps. Half-way down the hill where the trail bent, I turned and looked back. He was standing as I had left him, straight as an arrow. A shaft of sunlight strove through the tree foliage, fell on his noble face, on the hawk's feather in his scalp lock. Seeing me, he lifted his hand high above his head, palm outward. "*Adio*," he called. Then he let his hand fall to his side, and turning, he glided between the great trunks of the trees from my sight.

For a few moments I stood there, then slowly and sadly descended the hill.

CHAPTER 28

I Return

We were not wholly loaded until Wednesday noon. In the meanwhile three other vessels loaded with masting entered the harbour. They were convoyed by a British frigate of forty guns.

Having thanked Mr. Fenwick and his wife for their kindness to me, I now bade them farewell, and went on board with Captain Bates. A little later the vessels weighed anchor and we began our voyage.

It was a slow passage, marked by much foul weather. We saw no sign of any hostile vessel. On the way over I learned, for the first time, of the great rising of '45 in which Charles Stuart had sought to regain the throne; of how he was defeated at Culloden, and how the Duke of Cumberland had carried fire and sword throughout the Highlands. But not until I had returned to Aberdeen did I learn that "Bloody Cumberland", as he was known, had for a time made his headquarters in my beloved town.

Six weeks after leaving Casco we reached Liverpool. Captain Bates took me to his own home, where his wife received me with the greatest kindness and his children with curiosity. For I was yet clad in the garments of doeskin and the moccasins ornamented with beads and porcupine quills Tomah's wife had made for me. Moreover, my face was as tawny as any Indian's, and it seemed to me, on looking into a glass, that my hair was even redder than when I was kidnapped.

Captain Bates had told me that I was to stay at his home until he found a vessel that was ready to sail northward. I told him I had no money for a passage, and had considered walking. He said, "I will arrange the passage. It is too far to go by foot," at which I laughed and reminded him that I had travelled over half a continent, and a mere few hundred miles to Aberdeen would not hurt me.

"I admit that," he said. "But there are too many footpads on the road, David, who, given the chance, would sell you again into slavery, or to the Press Gang, for a few shillings; so, laddie, you bide here, and I'll secure you safe passage in a very short time."

The next day, Captain Bates having gone to his ship to supervise the unloading, I told his wife that I was going into the streets to look into the shop windows; for I had been so long from civilization that I was homesick for some of the sights.

I thoroughly washed my face, combed my hair back from my brow, and retied it at the nape of my neck with the bit of rawhide. Then, putting on my doeskin cap with its hawk and partridge feathers, I went out the front door and walked along the street. People turned and looked at me. Two maidens glanced at me, then giggled outright. I did not care; but I remember thinking them ill-bred, and contrasting their behaviour with the quiet decorum of the Indians, who would never think of laughing at one's raiment, be it little or much, gay or sombre.

I wandered down this street, and up that, interested in everything I saw. And finally, coming to a little shop, with a swinging sign on which was painted in faded letters "Timothy Cole, Books printed, and for Sale", I paused. In front of the dingy window were many books piled on a shelf. I had not seen a book of any description, other than Joel Venables' Bible, since my abduction four years before, and now I began fingering these, lifting the leather or paper covers, peering at the titles and the printed text. And, as I stood there, the door of the shop opened, and out came a little man. He had sparkling blue eyes, and spectacles pushed up on his brow. His face was thin and wrinkled, his hair mouse-coloured. He said to me, "Is there any particular—" He paused, his mouth open; he pulled down his glasses on his nose, gazed at me, then said, "Bless me, bless me—I beg your pardon—a thousand pardons. Is there any particular book you desire?"

I smiled at him. "No, thank you," I said, "but it is so long since I last saw a book, I just had to stop and look at these."

"Oh," he said; then, "If you have no objections, young man, would you tell me where you have been?"

"That is soon answered," I said. "I have been in America."

"Oh, America, bless me!" he said. "And would you mind telling me what you were doing in America?"

"Not at all," I answered. "I was a slave on a plantation—I escaped from it, was captured by Indians, lived with them over two years, and here I am," and I smiled at him.

He grasped me by the arm. "Come in—come in to my shop," he almost gasped, and opening a door with a bell that jangled, he pulled me in, all the while exclaiming, "What a story, extraordinary happenings, slavery, Indians—what a success—six-penny pamphlet—all hawkers in Liverpool clamouring to sell it—"

He pushed me into a chair, asked my name. I told him. He went on, "How about writing your narrative, having it printed, sold? All hawkers in Liverpool clamouring for it. You'd make a fortune."

"It is a good idea," said I. "But, Sir, I know not how to write a decent hand, or frame a right sentence. I—"

"It is not necessary," he said hastily. "All you have to do is tell your story to my partner, Dawkings by name. He'll put it in English that the Lord Chancellor couldn't better."

He paused, turned to a desk, drew a piece of paper in front of him and wrote for a few minutes. Then he looked up. "Here is the contract, Mr. David Cameron. Shall I read it to you—then you can sign here?"

"Thank you," I said, my canny Scots coming to the fore; "I'll read it," and I took the paper and read it.

Briefly, it was a contract giving him the sole right to publish the story of my kidnapping and life among the Indians of North America. He guaranteed to pay me one penny for every copy sold.

I thought it a very fair arrangement. He made another copy of the contract, which we both signed, he as printer and I as the author. This done, he led me to a door leading into another room, ushered me inside, and taking my arm, led me to where a man, as enormous as Mr. Timothy Cole was small, sat on a stool before a high desk, writing rapidly with a quill.

Hearing our approach, he turned, blinked at me, as though he were not sure he was dreaming, then gasped, "God bless my soul! God bless my soul! What's this you've brought me, Timothy?" He paused expectantly, his parted lips showing a missing front tooth.

Mr. Cole explained briefly. "Write down his story, Dawkings. Have a wood-cut made of him in this garb. Print five hundred copies. It will sell. I know a good seller."

I was asked by Mr. Dawkings to sit down. Mr. Cole departed to the other room.

I sat a long time watching Mr. Dawkings' broad back, and listening to the scratching of his quill as it raced over the sheets. It was a stuffy, booky, tobacco-smelling room. Odds and ends from every port in the world hung about the walls, or stood in corners.

Finally, Mr. Dawkings swung about, surveyed me quizzically, and said, "Well now, young sir, and what's this cock-and-bull story about kidnappings and slavery and Red Indians, and what not? Bless my soul! Timothy is forever ushering in some rare find that will send every hawker in the city to Cole and Dawkings' bookshop, pleading with us to let 'em have fifty or a hundred copies each. Oh, well, let's have it, young sir. Say it in short sentences; Job Dawkings will do the rest. Now—" and he pulled a clean sheet of paper in front of him and dipped his quill in the ink-pot.

I was rather nervous. He was such a great towering elephant of a man—so impersonal, as though he dwelt on a plane high above ordinary people.

I began, hesitatingly at first, then, as the injustice of my kidnapping was again forced upon me, I warmed to my story.

His pen scribbled away, nor said he a word until he had reached the bottom of the long sheet, when he paused, and exploded with, "God bless my soul! I'd say Timothy has drawn a winner this time. Proceed, young man. Just give me the main facts; no need for detail, genius of Dawkings will do the rest. Yes—"

Well, in two more visits my brief history was completed. An artist—where they got the fellow I know not—came and made a drawing of me, garbed in my doeskin trousers and fringed coat, my cap with its feathers and my beaded moccasins.

In a few days an edition of five hundred copies was printed. On the outside of the cover was a crude woodcut of a young man supposed to be myself. The title of the book was "Sold to the Plantations" and "Life among the Savages", by David Cameron. On the inside was the following: "Printed by J. D. for Timothy Cole, and to be sold at the Sign of the Glove, near the Fishmarket, Liverpool, 1747."

Almost immediately the book, a small pamphlet of sixty-two pages, was the talk of the town. Edition after edition was struck off, and as quickly called for and sold by hawkers. Within two weeks I was paid eighteen pounds, four shillings, two pence in royalties. Then, for Captain Bates had secured passage for me on a brig going to Aberdeen, I left my affairs in the good Captain's hands, and set sail.

In my pack basket I carried fifty copies of my pamphlet, and told Mr. Cole that if I desired more I would send for them at a sum we had agreed upon between us. You must not think that I made all these decisions myself. On the contrary, I had the advice of Captain Bates in everything, save one. He had advised me to purchase some new clothes, but I had a conceit to return to my native town garbed as I was. This I did. On the way I sold several copies of my book, not only to passengers, but to the crew members.

I arrived in Aberdeen the 28th day of September, 1747, three years and seven months from the day I was kidnapped. I was now almost sixteen years old. I was tall, strong, and in the best of health.

When I landed on the quay many stared at me and pointed, as though I were some strange creature from another planet. But I slipped the straps of my splint ash basket over my shoulders and sauntered along through the crowd, rather enjoying the sensation I was creating.

Oh, it was good to be on my own soil; and I was in a fine state of excitement as I swung along Ship Row, Exchequer Row, Huckster St. Reaching the Broad Gate, I came to the home of Dr. Malcolm, and mounting the steps I knocked at the door. It seemed ages before anyone came. Finally the door opened, and a servant I had not known in the old days peered out at me. Seeing me standing there, all tanned and long of hair and with my strange garb and basket, she looked startled but asked me my business.

"I want to see Dr. Malcolm, if he is at home," I said. "Or—or his wife," I added. Then quickly, for she seemed about to shut the door in my face, "Ye maun let me in, for I am a friend of the family."

At this I heard a door open inside and footsteps came down the hall. She stepped to one side then, and I saw him, his kindly face a little more seamed and his hair more grey. He said, "Well, young man, and what ill brings ye here the day?"

"Dr. Malcolm," I cried, "do you no' ken me?"

"Ken ye?" he cries. Then a light seemed to dawn on him. "It's no' David?" he cried haltingly, "no' David Cameron?"

"None other," I answered, though I had half forgotten my name.

Then he had me by the shoulders, his old eyes peering down into mine. "Yes," he said, "it's nane ither—it's Davy. Ah, this is a fine day! Come." He led me down the hall, opened the door of his wife's sewing-room, where she sat as I had so often seen her in the past. "Margaret—" he said, and I loved the Scotch speech of him, "Margaret, here's a braw lad come home at last."

She rose, came towards me with quick step. She was quicker than he, for she recognized me almost at once, and flung her arms about me, and cried a little as women will, and at length led me over to a chair by the great fire, and made me sit down, and ordered the servant to bring cakes and wine.

And, after I had refreshed myself, the good doctor lighted his pipe and said, "And now, David lad, let's hae it—the hale story."

Then I began and rehearsed as much of the story as was necessary to their proper understanding of what had passed after I had been kidnapped. It was late when I had finished. I was tired but happy. I had returned home again.

I was put in Ian's room. He was now serving in the Royal Navy. Nor did I awaken until the door opened and the servant brought me breakfast. I remember smiling to myself, after she left, as I visioned the faces of my Indian friends, could they see me propped up in the great four-poster eating my first meal of the day.

Barely had I finished when my guardian entered and sat down beside me. He told me that the morning following my disappearance my stepmother had come to him in great excitement, and asked him if I was at his house. When he had told her no, she had wrung her hands and cried out that I was missing, and she was afraid ill had befallen me.

"I was greatly distressed, David," pursued Dr. Malcolm, "and appealed to the Town Beadle to make a search. He promised to do so, and I know he did his part. There were some troops in the town and they joined in the search. Towards evening they found some of your clothing on the beach beyond the Links, and in one of the pockets a note in handwriting that both Mr. Grant and I reluctantly admitted was much like your own. The note, David, stated that you could not live without your dear father, and were going to join him.

"But despite this," pursued Dr. Malcolm, "neither of us believed that you had taken your own life. We made inquiries and learned that the *Bon Accord* had cleared for America with a consignment of children from the workhouse the night following your father's burial. We suspected that you had accompanied them. We wrote to Governor Clinton, of New York, asking him to try to trace you. Months later we received a reply saying that it was very doubtful if you could be traced. He was, however, having notices posted in several of the southern ports, advertising the importance of anyone having knowledge of the whereabouts of David Cameron communicating with the authorities.

"I was disappointed," said Dr. Malcolm, "but never did I give up my belief that you lived.

"Then, in little more than six months following your disappearance, your stepmother married Mr. Glegg, and they served papers on me and Mr. Grant, as executors of your father's estate, demanding that the Will be probated. But, David," and the good doctor gave a low chuckle, "we refused, as we did for three succeeding years. And then, a few months ago, a young sailor came to my door, gave me your letter written on the *Bon Accord*, and reading it, I knew that you lived, and by what name you had been sold into slavery. I wrote again to Governor Clinton, and told him you had been sold under the name of Dugald McNab. He wrote that he would give the matter his earnest attention, and

I would hear from him later. Yes, Janet?" to the servant who had entered the door.

"It's Mr. Grant, Sir," she said.

"Ah, good; show him up." And when she had gone, he said to me, "I sent him word that you had come home. This will be a happy day for him too, Davy."

CHAPTER 29

I am Arrested

It has been stated, as well as denied, that I personally sold in Aberdeen some of the pamphlets I had had printed in Liverpool. The fact is *I did* sell them. Angered at all I had endured, and convinced that several besides the Bailie were in the Ring that for years had carried on the nefarious traffic in human lives, I went into the streets garbed in my Indian costume, and in no time sold every pamphlet I possessed. Little did I know what the result would be.

The third afternoon, just after leaving Mr. Grant's office, I was stopped by the Town Beadle, who read a paper that charged me with having written and sold a book that contained false and libellous statements prejudicial to the good name of the Corporation of Aberdeen. Then the Beadle took my arm and led me to the Tolbooth. I protested, but it was of no avail, and I was locked up in the dreary place I had so dreaded as a child.

But I remained there only a few hours. Mr. Grant had heard of my arrest, gone to the Bailie, and offered surety for my release, until the day set for the trial. At first the Bailie refused, but later relented and accepted Mr. Grant's bond for my appearance at ten o'clock the following morning.

I attended court with Dr. Malcolm. There were quite a number of spectators, for it had got noised abroad that I had been arrested and what was my alleged crime. Moreover, my arrival home, in my odd garments, had created quite a sensation. Wherever I went I was stared or pointed at, and crowds of curious people followed me from shop to shop. Indeed, if I had fallen from Mars I could not have caused more curiosity and comments.

The charge having been read, dear Mr. Grant immediately arose and addressed the presiding Bailie.

"My Lord," he said, "I wish to take a preliminary objection to the jurisdiction of your lordship to preside over this action. It is the intention of the defence to produce evidence which will show your Lordship to be an interested party in this case."

There was a hush in the courtroom. Necks were craned in Mr. Grant's direction. The Bailie's face had gone red, then pale. He fumbled nervously with some papers. Then, with a renewed assumption of dignity, he demanded sharply, "What nature of evidence, Mr. Grant?"

I was looking at Mr. Grant. His eyes seemed to smile.

"Ah," he said blandly, "it is not according to law that the defence should be compelled to disclose its evidence until the evidence of the Crown is completed."

Again there was silence. Finally the Bailie spoke again. "Very well, Sir, when your evidence is produced, I will be able to judge if I am an interested party. In the meantime, I declare this court adjourned until this day week. But, Sir, in the interim, Master David Cameron is to be incarcerated in the Tolbooth."

Well, there was nothing for it. I was taken back to my loathsome quarters, where I spent a whole week, broken only by visits from my friends at certain official hours.

The interest and excitement evoked by my arrest, coupled with the court proceedings and Mr. Grant's challenging of the Bailie's jurisdiction in the case, had increased public curiosity a hundred-fold.

A Judge Ramsay presided over the Court on the day of my trial. Counsel for the Corporation of Aberdeen, which had laid the charge, was Mr. Fortescue; counsel for the Bailie a Mr. McPhail.

There is no need to go into the details. After the prosecuting Advocate had made his charge and produced his evidence (which was my pamphlet), that I had published a scurrilous and libellous book prejudicial to the good name of the Corporation of Aberdeen, and had rested his case, Mr. Grant rose slowly to his feet. Never shall I forget him. Though well past the three-score and five years' age, and small in stature, there was about him an air of quiet dignity and refinement and intellectual honesty that always impressed his hearers.

Quietly, but incisively, in a voice that penetrated every corner of the court-room, he began his defence. But he had been waiting for this opportunity for a long time, and his defence was soon an attack. He called upon the Bailie, and when he had been sworn, he began questioning him.

"Were you," he demanded suavely, "one of the principal shareholders in the ship *Bon Accord*?"

Mr. McPhail, the Bailie's counsel, sprang to his feet. "I object to this question, your Lordship,"—he appealed to the judge—"as having no bearing whatsoever on the case."

The Judge thought a moment. "Counsel's objection not sustained," he ruled.

Mr. Grant repeated his question.

"I was a shareholder," answered the Bailie.

"And," pursued Mr. Grant, "the *Bon Accord* was an armed merchant vessel, and carried letters of marque?"

"Yes," came the answer.

"And boys and girls from workhouses, or good homes, were put on board her and sold into the plantations in Virginia?"

Again the Bailie's counsel sprang up with an objection. Again he was ruled down by the court.

"The *Bon Accord* was an armed merchant vessel," said the Bailie.

"Yes, I know that. You have admitted it before. What I want you to admit is that you knew that the *Bon Accord* carried slaves into Virginia."

"I knew no such thing," said the Bailie stubbornly. "If there was any such traffic, it was done without my knowledge."

"Careful—careful, sir," said Mr. Grant gently. "It may be that you have forgotten. Allow me, sir, to refresh your memory:

"Did you, on the 28th of March, 1744, send a letter to Captain Barclay of the *Bon Accord*?"

"I have no recollection of sending a letter on that date," replied the Bailie, "though I often wrote him about important matters."

"Just a minute, sir," said Mr. Grant. He searched in his portfolio, and drawing out the letter taken by James McArthur from Captain

Barclay's despatch box, and brought to me in the hold of the *Bon Accord*, he turned to the judge and said:

"My Lord, as counsel for David Cameron, the accused, I wish to read this letter in his defence."

Once again Mr. McPhail sprang to his feet. He protested that the letter might be a forgery, and that in any case he objected to its contents being used in the defence. Once more his protest was not sustained by the Court.

Then slowly and distinctly Mr. Grant read the letter to the attentive court. When he had ended, he walked up to where the Judge sat and handed it to him. Then he went back to his place, and turning to the Bailie, said:

"Sir, you are nearly as old as I am. I will be kinder, more humane to you, than you were to my client, David Cameron. Pray sir, be seated."

Then Mr. Grant turned to the Judge. "My Lord," he said, "for some years it has been suspected that certain citizens of Aberdeen have been engaged in the traffic of human lives. But we could not, until recently, advance proof that would make for conviction. Today, my Lord, we have produced evidence that convicts at least one citizen of this Royal Burgh, and at the same time refutes the charge of the Corporation that in publishing the book that is described as libellous, my client was not within his rights." He paused a moment, then went on:

"My Lord, think of the hundreds, nay thousands, of boys, yes, and girls too, who have been shipped into the plantations. It takes little imagination to picture their hopeless grief in rat-infested holds, while the ship slowly made her way to the New World, where, my Lord, dwell a race of people whom we, to our shame be it said, call savages, but who, let this also be said, are not so inhuman that they sell into slavery their own blood kin. Nay, my Lord, that is left for us, the traducers of these people we call savages.

"We have put these children on board ship, and sold them like so much merchandise. My client was one of them. He was sold to an unprincipled planter in America; he worked from dawn to dark. He was whipped by angry overseers. The wonder, my Lord, is not that he lived to return to his native Burgh, but that he did not, as others have done, take his own life.

"My Lord, I have done. I ask, your Lordship, for my client's acquittal and release from durance, with compensation for his arrest and incarceration in the Tolbooth."

Well, I was acquitted and awarded by the Court five hundred pounds damages—a paltry sum for all I had undergone.

An important development following my trial was the instituting of a Royal Commission to investigate the whole business that had besmirched Aberdeen and several other seaport towns for almost a decade. The Commission made a most exhaustive report, which was published, with the result that the whole country was aroused and the traffic stopped.

And thus the little book printed by J. D. for Timothy Cole, at the Sign of the Glove, played its part in ending a traffic that even yet the people of England and Scotland remember with shame.

Do you not know me, Sachem Tomah?

CHAPTER 30

Medowktek Again

I did not see my stepmother nor Mr. Glegg. Of course, they knew of my return, and as soon as the Will was probated they both left Aberdeen for her old home in Cockermouth. She received her legacy, as the Will stipulated, until her death. Then her husband had the audacity to write reminding me that, as my tutor, he had ever held me in deep affection, and begging a small annuity to help him in his declining years. I sent him ten guineas, and suggested that he cease playing the hypocrite and make his peace with his Maker. I did not hear from him again.

But long before this I had returned to school, and on completion of my schooldays entered as a student in Marischal College. Perhaps my experience had unfitted me for the sedentary existence that the practice of law would have imposed on me. At any rate, in my second year, I gave up all thoughts of the law, and turned to shipping. I found my childhood chum a splendid partner, and the ships we had built, or acquired by purchase, did a brisk and profitable trade. Following the capture of Quebec, I told Ian I was going to North America to visit my Indian friend. He smiled, and giving me a poke in the ribs, said, "And to make inquiries about the wee French lassie?"

"Of course," I answered. "As you know, I have often wondered if she was caught like so many other Acadians and sent into exile." I paused, and he added, "Or remained in Quebec and married," and he smiled.

"Yes," I admitted.

"Ah, weel," he said, "gang awa, Davy, and find out. A bit vacation willna do ye any harm."

"Thank you, Ian," I said.

Well, I fitted out one of our new vessels, crammed her with merchandise for the New York and Boston trade, purchased a gun for Tomah, with his name on a brass plate set in the stock, and, in July of 1761, set sail for North America.

We had a quick voyage, landing at the mouth of the St. John or *Wul-ahs-tukw* River in one day less than five weeks. I was kindly received by the commandant of the fort, to whom I made known my desire to visit Medowktek.

At this he looked grave, and questioned my wisdom in going so far up the river. He added, "Although the war has been won, the Indians at Ek-pa-hawk and Medowktek still consider the country their own, and only last summer they turned back a party of surveyors who had gone up some eighty miles. Of course, Mr. Cameron, I have no authority to stop you, but—"

I thanked him for his anxiety for my welfare, but told him I had crossed the Atlantic for the purpose of going to Medowktek, and go I would.

At this he said that some Indians of that village had lately come to the fort with furs, and were even now camped a short distance away. He kindly took me to their wigwam. One of them, Pemyhawick, I knew. I told him who I was and asked him if Tomah yet lived. "*Ah-ha,*" he said, "Tomah well. You want to go to Medowktek, P'sazum?"

It pleased me that he remembered my name. "Yes," I said, "I want two canoemen; will you take me?"

He nodded. "*Ah-ha,*" he said, and talked to one of his companions, then said, "We go with you, me and Sacobie."

It was a matter of fifty leagues, and took several days of alternate paddling and poling. At one place we came to an English settlement, begun the year before, where we stopped and ate, and I talked with some of the people. Arriving in sight of Medowktek, the bowman stood up, cupped his mouth with both hands, and sent out a loud whoop that reached the ears of those in the distant village, for I could see many of them rushing down to the beach to await our coming.

How many times in former years returning warriors had thus heralded their coming with captives taken during forays against alien foes!

In a few minutes we reached the shore, and I had stepped out on the pebbly beach.

Immediately I was surrounded by two or three hundred men, women and children. Many of them I had known, some were strangers to me. I had expected the former to recognize me, forgetting that I was now a grown man, and but a lad when I left them. Suddenly I glanced up and saw the tall, noble figure of the Chief standing on the bank above, and making my way through the crowd, I ran up the incline and stood before him, my hand outstretched.

His dark eyes searched mine, dropped to the gun I carried, then back to my face.

"Do you not know me, Sachem Tomah?" I asked huskily.

"*Kadama* (no)," he said slowly. "Is it one of the white chiefs at the river's mouth?"

At this I smiled and took off my hat. His face lighted up. "P'sazum!" he cried in Maliseet; "*Kam-onok-sis!*" (He is little English.)

"I am he, my other father; come back as I gave you promise."

Now he had me by the hand, and the pressure he gave it told me he still loved me.

"See," I said, "I have brought you the gun as I promised," and pointed to the butt into which the gunsmith had inserted a brass plate, inscribed thus:

"To Tomah, the Maliseet Chief, the friend and second father of Kuluwazu P'sazum."

CHAPTER 31

Adio, Tomah

How I found Jeanne Chartier, for whom I caught trouts that now far-off day on the *Wul-ahs-tukw*, with others of her people, far in the interior of Acadia, whither they had fled following the expulsion of their kindred from Grand Pré—how I wooed her, and wed her, a few weeks following this my second coming to Medowktek, is a story that, if ever written, must be done at another time. This is already too long. Suffice it to say now that Tomah took us together down the river to the fort in his canoe.

My last memory of him, as the ship moved away from the wharf, is the sight of his tall figure, one hand grasping the barrel of his long rifle, the other raised high above his head in farewell. Then, across the widening water, I caught the last words I was ever to hear him speak. They come clear and tuneful, like the notes of the bell in the little chapel of his own Medowktek:

"Adio, Kuluwazu P'sazum."

Try it. Do they not sound like a bell?

THE END

EDITOR'S AFTERWORD

When I was a child, this was one of the books I read every year, right up there with L.M. Montgomery's *Anne of Green Gables* and Kipling's *The Jungle Book*. I thought it was wonderful. I still do.

The Sources of the story

One warm October day in 1932 George Frederick Clarke and a friend were digging for Maliseet First Nation artefacts at the mouth of the Shikethawk stream, where it enters the St. John River near Bristol, New Brunswick.

GFC stopped for a moment and said, "A good many people would think that this was mere slavery."

His friend replied: "Did you know there were white slaves in the mid-eighteenth century?" He went on to tell GFC that the centre of the traffic had been Aberdeen, in Scotland, where local dignitaries colluded with the traffickers, and press gangs kidnapped hundreds, perhaps thousands, of children to be sold as slaves in America.[2] One such boy, Peter Williamson, was about ten years old when he was kidnapped and enslaved on a Virginia plantation. After seven years he was freed, and started a farm, but was taken prisoner, first by Delaware Native Americans, then by the French. He eventually returned to Scotland and wrote a book about his adventures.[3]

GFC thought: What a splendid idea for a novel.

He read Williamson's book, and found a good deal of useful material. But it was by no means his only source of information

---

2   About 600 children were taken in the years 1740-1746 alone.

3   Williamson, Peter. *French and Indian Cruelty Exemplified in the Life And Various Vicissitudes of Fortune, of Peter Williamson.* York: J. Jackson, 1758.

and inspiration. He had already read the *Memoirs* of John Gyles, published in 1736[4]—one of the many "captivity narratives," as they are known, written by (or about) white colonists who had been kidnapped by North American indigenous peoples. Gyles was taken captive by Maliseets in 1689, near his home in southern Maine, when he was nine years old. He served as a slave at Meductic, on the St. John River, for six years; at some point he and his captors camped for a while at the mouth of the Meduxnekeag Creek, where the town of Woodstock, New Brunswick, began a century later— and where, a century after that, GFC spent his early childhood, in a house overlooking the Creek, only a stone's throw from that long-ago campsite. He always had a fellow feeling for the "friendless and lonely" young Gyles.[5]

The strongest literary influence on *David Cameron's Adventures* was Stevenson's *Kidnapped*,[6] which GFC read and loved as a child. *Kidnapped* was based on another true story of a boy taken to be sold into slavery. Stevenson's hero, like David Cameron, is kidnapped by agents of a wicked kinsman to be sold into slavery in America. But the slaving ship founders on the Scottish coast. There the plots of *Kidnapped* and *David Cameron's Adventures* diverge; yet the stories continue to have structural similarities. Each follows a young boy as he learns resourcefulness and self-reliance through capture, hardship, and the influence of a man who teaches him how to survive in the wild; both boys eventually win through to home, freedom and justice. It is one of the great basic plots, especially of books for young people.

---

4 Gyles, John. *Memoirs of Odd Adventures, Strange Deliverances, Etc. In the Captivity of John Gyles, Esq, Commander of the Garrison on St. George River, in the District of Maine. Written by Himself.* Boston, 1736.

5 Clarke, G. F. *Six Salmon Rivers—and Another.* Ed. Mary Bernard. Woodstock, New Brunswick: Chapel Street Editions, 1960 (4th ed. 2015). 97.

6 Stevenson, Robert Louis. *Kidnapped: Being Memoirs of the Adventures of David Balfour in the Year 1751.* London: Cassell, 1886.

   A less direct antecedent is Defoe's *Robinson Crusoe*, which GFC also read as a child.

A third source, or influence—and perhaps another reason why the Williamson story fired GFC's imagination—lay closer to home: in the story of his Jewish great grandfather, John Harris, who was born in London about 1790, kidnapped by a press-gang when he was thirteen, and forced to serve five years in the British navy—a form of servitude almost as harsh as plantation slavery. He escaped by jumping ship in Halifax, in 1810, made his way to New Brunswick, became a farmer, and married a Gentile. (He did not convert to Christianity, but his children were raised as Christians.)

John Harris died around 1860, but his descendants remembered and retold the dramatic story of his kidnapping and escape. GFC retold it too; John Harris was the only one of his great-grandparents whom he ever talked about.

Noel Polchies and Tomah

There is a signal difference between this novel and the captivity narratives. They portray indigenous peoples primarily as captors and often tormentors. *David Cameron's Adventures* depicts them far more sympathetically—and they are epitomised in Tomah.

Tomah was GFC's own addition, and a stroke of genius. He based the character of Tomah on memories of his own dearest friend, Noel Polchies. GFC loved and revered Noel for the twenty years he knew him (Noel died in 1927, in his late sixties) and made him a leading character in several books.[7] In each, Noel teaches a boy the woodcraft that Noel taught GFC and the respect for nature that Noel deepened in him.

The chieftain who dominates *David Cameron's Adventures* is named Tomah. He is younger than Noel Polchies when GFC knew him, but he is recognisably Noel Polchies: a good man, brave, stoical, unassumingly proud, loving and steadfast. Good people in books are usually dull. Tomah is anything but. From the moment he enters

---

7   The books in which Noel appears, as himself or as Tomah, are: *Chris in Canada*, *The Adventures of Jimmy-Why*, *Jimmy-Why and Noël Polchies* (these two now republished as *Jimmy-Why and Noël Polchies*), *David Cameron's Adventures*, *Return to Acadia* (now republished as *David Cameron's Return*), and the unpublished novel *Chris in the Wilderness*. There is also a biographical portrait of Noel in *Song of the Reel*, Chapter 11.

the book we read every page with delight, because of what we learn of him, and through him, as he and David travel through virgin forests with nothing to depend upon but Tomah's hatchet, knife and woodcraft. The love between the man and the boy is utterly believable, and quite touching. Every time I read the ending, where they part, tears come to my eyes.

GFC wrote a draft of the story in early 1936, but put the manuscript aside without even getting it typed. He had "lost heart and ambition,"[8] he said, after several book rejections in the early 1930s. For the next decade he wrote little.

Then early in 1948 he heard that the English film studio J Arthur Rank intended to film the life of Peter Williamson. "I have the *whole story*," he wrote to his daughter Dees in excitement, "much better than anyone else could do…for I know the Indians, their material culture, etc." He cabled Rank to say that his agent would send them his book.

Pneumonia interrupted him briefly: he had five inches of fluid in one lung. The doctor prescribed penicillin injections. GFC did them himself, in his hip, every three hours for a week. Whenever he felt a bit better, he sat up and revised the book. After fifteen minutes he would have to lie down and rest.

Rank turned it down; they said it was too much about the hero's life with the Indians. His agent sent the book to Twentieth-Century Fox, they too rejected it.[9] When she found a publisher, they wanted him to rename it. The original title was *Tomah the Maliseet Chief*. If that is anything to go by, GFC had not only added Noel to the plot—Noel as he might have been in the eighteenth century—Noel

---

8   Clarke, George Frederick. "Additional Information (for Bob Tweedie)." Unpublished memoir, TS & MS. Author's Collection. MG L 47. Unprocessed. Archives & Special Collections and George Frederick Clarke fonds, University of New Brunswick Libraries. Fredericton, New Brunswick, n.d. [1953]. 23 pp

9   In the early 1980s my friend Stephen Galloway who was working as an assistant to the director Martin Ritt, took an option on the film rights and tried to get producers interested. That, too, came to nothing.

renamed Tomah—but perhaps made him even more central than he is now. The book was briefly announced with the title *Unclasp a Secret Book*.[10] Luckily, that didn't stick. When it came out, in October, 1950, it was *David Cameron's Adventures*, a title that highlights the white boy, not the Maliseet chief. The 1936 manuscript has not survived, so there is no way of knowing whether Tomah was more prominent in it than in the published book. Perhaps not: it was, after all, Williamson's story that had set GFC's mind alight that day in 1932.

GFC took more than Tomah's character from life. The book is sprinkled with small details from his own life or the lives of people he knew. Here are a few. David's stepmother comes from Cockermouth, Cumberland, the birthplace of GFC's wife's mother. David wants "to do well and enter the Grammar School"—as did GFC, who was forced to leave school at fifteen. Tomah's grandmother tells him: "You not born to die in water." The grandmother of GFC's Maliseet friend Noel Moulton made the same prophecy about him.

The episode in Chapter 13 where David rescues a Delaware chief's small daughter from drowning also occurs in one of GFC's best short stories, "Chief of the Sixtahaw." The story, unpublished until 2015,[11] survives only in a carbon-copy typescript datable to the early or middle 1930s. At this remove it is impossible to work out which came first, the story or the incident in the novel.

GFC was fascinated by Maliseet crafts, and describes several in Chapter 13. He later published an article about First Nations' dyes,[12] and describes the game of *Al-stes-tug-in-uk* at some length in his last book, *Someone Before Us*.

---

10 "Dr G.F. Clarke's Novel Published." *The Carleton Sentinel* Feb. 3 1949: 1. Woodstock, New Brunswick. The passage in *Henry V* from which it was taken is still the book's epigraph, as it was in the first edition.

11 Clarke, G. F. *The Ghost of Nackawick Portage: The Collected Short Stories of George Frederick Clarke*. Ed. and comp. Mary Bernard. Woodstock, New Brunswick: Chapel Street Editions, 2015. 109–27

12 Clarke, George Frederick. "Dyes of the Maritime Indians." *Herbarist: A Publication of the Herb Society of America* No. 36 (Apr 1970): 12–15

Reception

GFC subscribed to a clipping service, but there are few reviews of *David Cameron's Adventures* among his surviving papers. It is possible that some perished in an attic fire that destroyed some of the papers after his death, but I think it more likely that the book was badly publicised and little reviewed. That may be partly because it was published by Blackie & Sons, in Scotland. He repeatedly wrote and cabled to Blackie, and to its Canadian distributors, the Ryerson Press in Toronto, urging them to get the book into Canadian bookstores. He had found that New Brunswick bookstores were eager to get copies, but Ryerson's kept saying they were out of stock. As he told Blackie's:

> Please let me be frank; I am much afraid that if you wholly depend upon the Ryerson Press to reorder books bearing your imprint, they will only do so in driblets, or under compulsion. In so far as pushing United Kingdom books, they are anything but agressive.[13]

The few reviews that I have found are favourable. *The Carleton Sentinel* said: "His descriptive powers flash brilliantly all through it. It is a book that a reader will drop everything else to finish."[14] *The Daily Gleaner*'s reviewer "picked up the book from curiosity, the author being a New Brunswick man, and then forgot everything but the story itself."[15]

The text, and the word "Indians"

I have worked from the first (and only previous) edition of *David Cameron's Adventures*, silently correcting a few typos and inconsistencies. I have also removed a few proper names of historical personages who are mentioned once, but play no part whatever in the story.

---

13   Clarke, George Frederick. Letter to Blackie & Sons, 20 October 1950. George Frederick Clarke Fonds, MG L 47. Unprocessed. Archives & Special Collections, University of New Brunswick Libraries. Fredericton, New Brunswick

14   "Dr G.F. Clarke's New Book Out." *The Carleton Sentinel* Sept. 29 1950. Woodstock, New Brunswick

15   December 1, 1950

GFC lived before the term "First Nations" was in common use. He called First Nations peoples Indians, and it was what they then called themselves. I have not changed his usage, or his spellings of the names of First Nations peoples.

The illustrations

The illustrations, including the cover, are from the first edition. They are by Will Nickless (1902-1977), a well-known English illustrator of children's books. I have restored the greyscale illustrations and edited the cover, darkening and shrinking the bears, which were pale brown and as big as polar bears. Eastern bears are considerably smaller, and they are usually black.

About myself

I am the daughter of GFC's elder daughter, Jane; GFC was my grandfather. In 2015 Chapel Street Editions published *The Last Romantic*, my story of his life.

About the George Frederick Clarke Project

Chapel Street Editions has undertaken a grand publishing project called the George Frederick Clarke Project, to publish all of GFC's books. I am editing the series. Eight books of the GFC Project are now in print:

> My biography of GFC: *The Last Romantic: The Life George Frederick Clarke, Master Storyteller of New Brunswick* (2015)

And the following books by GFC:

> *Six Salmon Rivers—and Another*, his first fishing memoir (2015)

> *The Ghost of Nackawick Portage: the Collected Short Stories of George Frederick Clarke*, the first collection of all his surviving short stories (2015)

> *The Song of the Reel*, his second fishing memoir (2016)

> *Jimmy-Why and Noël Polchies: their Adventures in the Great Woods*, his two books for young children, complete in one volume (2016)

Someone Before Us: Buried History in Central New Brunswick, his memoir of his archaeological finds and adventures (2016)

David Cameron's Adventures (2018)

David Cameron's Return (2018), the sequel to *David Cameron's Adventures*, originally published under the title *Return to Acadia*.

The next two books in the project are *Chris in Canada*, the story of an English boy who emigrates with his family to a farm on Howland Ridge, in New Brunswick, overlooking Taffa Lake; and *Chris in the Wilderness*, in which Chris and Noel Polchies go into the woods in winter. *Chris in the Wilderness* was never published, but it is one of GFC's best books.

Acknowledgment

As always, and for many very good reasons, I want to thank my publishers, Keith, Brendan and Ellen Helmuth, of Chapel Street Editions.

Mary Bernard
Cambridge, England,
January 2018

PUBLISHER'S AFTERWORD
Why Do We Read Historical Novels?

In a recent interview, the highly regarded graphic novelist Chris Ware was asked where his inspiration comes from. He replied, "It's all about memory. *Memory is all we have.*"

Indeed, when we think about it, this puts it in a nutshell. Every relationship, every step in puzzling out the situations that confront us day-by-day are composed of memories. Every piece of technology has been created through the accumulation and coordination of memory. Every detail of built environments and managed landscapes are constructed and maintained through memory.

There are two kinds of memory, personal and collective. Each of us maintains our sense of identity by keeping a steady focus on the memories of our accumulated experience and by continually running quick reviews of experiences that help guide us as our life unfolds. We don't even think about it. It's just the way our brains work.

But personal memory would be a weak reed on which to rely if it were not embedded in collective memory, the memory that builds up and is available in the stories, habits, and inventions of communities, cultures, and humanity as a whole. This is why we read historical novels, of which *David Cameron's Adventures* is a classic example; they make available to us a wider, deeper, more comprehensive store of memories than we can accumulate by personal experience.

Along with memory, humans have an amazing ability we call imagination, the ability to recall memory into thought and, thanks to language, compose traditions of stories that create the way we understand how our various cultural communities have come to be in the world. In the old days, before writing, before pen and ink, and before the printing press, oral story telling transmitted collective memory. Communities were alive with the stories of their ancestors. The skills of culture, both social and technical, were passed on in a flow of collective memory.

With the coming of the printing press and the making of books, a new mode of recording and transmitting collective memory became available. The imagination of storytellers could now be recorded and circulated far beyond local communities and their specific cultures. In the early 19th century, story telling took a turn in the imagination of a few writers and the historical novel emerged into world literature.

From the beginning, historical novels have often been characterized by adventure and romance along with a touch of the exotic. In 1801, in France, Chateaubriand surprized and delighted his readers with the publication of *Atala & Rene*. Not only were the two stories composing this book set in the wilderness of North America, they combined high adventure and strong emotion in a way that came to define the Romantic Movement in European literature, a movement that branched strongly into the writing of historical novels.

In 1814, in Scotland, Walter Scott began publishing the Waverly Novels. These historical novels, set in the 1700s, recreated the life and times of the Scottish Border Country and for a century were the most widely read novels in Europe. He continued to turn out historical novels going back through the centuries to 1097.

In North America, James Fenimore Cooper undertook a similar endeavour. The first of The Leatherstocking Tales, *The Deerslayer*, was published in 1841. Four more historical novels, chronicling the story of American frontier settlement and its displacement of Indigenous Peoples, were subsequently published and widely read. They are classics of American literature.

The historical novels of George Frederick Clarke are cut from the cloth of this great tradition. Although not published until the 1950s, they were clearly germinating in his writer's imagination for many decades. *David Cameron's Adventures* and *David Cameron's*

Return (originally titled *Return to Acadia*) are both historical novels with enduring appeal. For all Canadians, but especially for New Brunswickers and residents of the Bay of Fundy region and the Wolastoq (St. John River) watershed, these two novels are touchstones of a history that combines the stories of the the Wolastoqiyik (Maliseet), the Acadians, the English, and the Scots. We are indeed fortunate to have a writer from Woodstock, New Brunswick who, with a novelist's imagination, so immersed himself in this history that he could create the captivating story of David Cameron's adventures and of the emotional quest of his return to the wilderness of the upper Wolastoq valley.

Clarke's biographer, Mary Bernard, calls him "the last romantic."* His skill as a writer thrived on an approach to storytelling that helped define the Romantic Movement of the 19th century. By the time he wrote and published his David Cameron stories, many contemporary novelists were experimenting with new forms of narrative and had taken a turn toward the psychoanalytic in a way that was deliberately anti-romantic. This does not mean, however, that the literature of the Romantic Movement and the kind of story telling at which Clark excelled was to be superseded. Historical novels continue to be written and widely read. Adventure, romance, and exotic settings appeal to the imagination in a way that never grows old.

The historical novel has stood the test of time and, in recent years, has made a strong comeback with the work of such writers as Guy Vanderhaeghe, Gore Vidal, Hilary Mantel, E.L. Doctrow, and Toni Morrison, to name a few. With new editions of *David Cameron's Adventures* and its sequel, a new generation of readers who love historical novels will be able to enjoy George Frederick Clarke's contribution to this enduring tradition of literature.

> * *The Last Romantic: The Life of George Frederick Clarke, Master Storyteller of New Brunswick* by Mary Bernard: Chapel Street Editions, Woodstock, NB, 2015.

Keith Helmuth
Chapel Street Editions
Woodstock, New Brunswick